PUFFIN BOOKS

The Freedom Tree

James Watson was born in Darwin, Lancashire, and has worked for many years as a teacher. He now combines writing with full-time lecturing in communication and media studies. He is the author of nine novels and a collection of short stories for young people, all on the themes of history and human rights. His stories range in time and place from Renaissance Italy to the Civil War in 1930s Spain, from the anguished conflict in Angola to contemporary drama in Eastern Europe. His most recent work, *Justice of the Dagger*, centres on the struggle for independence of the people of East Timor, Indonesia.

James Watson has also written several plays for radio, as well as works on the subject of media studies. He is married, with three grown-up daughters and two granddaughters, and lives with his wife in Tunbridge Wells, Kent.

The Freedom Tree

James Watson

PUFFIN BOOKS

PUFFIN BOOKS

Published by the Penguin Group
Penguin Books Ltd, 27 Wrights Lane, London W8 5TZ, England
Penguin Putnam Inc., 375 Hudson Street, New York, New York 10014, USA
Penguin Books Australia Ltd, Ringwood, Victoria, Australia
Penguin Books Canada Ltd, 10 Alcorn Avenue, Toronto, Ontario, Canada M4V 3B2
Penguin Books (NZ) Ltd, Cnr Rosedale and Airborne Roads, Albany,
Auckland, New Zealand

Penguin Books Ltd, Registered Offices: Harmondsworth, Middlesex, England

First published by Victor Gollancz Ltd 1976
Published in Puffin Books 1998
1 3 5 7 9 10 8 6 4 2

Made and printed in England by Clays Ltd, St Ives plc

British Library Cataloguing in Publication Data
A CIP catalogue record for this book is available from the British Library

ISBN 0–141–30032–9

ACKNOWLEDGEMENTS

Few events in modern times have inspired so many books as the Spanish Civil War and I am indebted to many authors – historians, war veterans, diarists, newspaper correspondents – whose works have helped provide the historical basis for *The Freedom Tree*.

However, I wish to put on record the help of three survivors of the war who most kindly talked to me at length about their experiences – Nan Green, who was a nurse with the International Brigades and whose husband died in the Republican defence of the Ebro, and two ex-warriors of the International Brigades, Jim Brown and Peter Kerrigan, whose recollections of the fighting at Jarama and elsewhere were of immense value.

Also, acknowledgement is due to Maurice Levine of Cheshire for his vivid and evocative letters describing his service with the British Battalion.

England is silent under the same moon,
From the Clydeside to the gutted pits of Wales.
The innocent mask conceals that soon
Here, too, our freedom's swaying in the scales.
O understand before too late
Freedom was never held without a fight.

John Cornford

They gave us everything: their youth and
their maturity; their science and their
experience; their blood and their lives . . .

Dolores Ibarruri,
'La Pasionaria'

1936

In Britain, millions were out of work; millions more lived in the direst poverty. It was the age of the Great Depression, of dole queues, soup kitchens, widespread tuberculosis, of the heartless and dreaded Means Test – and of the Hunger Marches. The most famous of these was from Tyneside to London and was called the Jarrow Crusade.

When Jarrow's shipyard was bought out and then closed down by its competitors, virtually the entire work force of the town were without jobs for almost a decade. Ellen Wilkinson, Jarrow's Member of Parliament, described it as "the town that was murdered"

In Europe the shadows of military tyranny had lengthened. Hitler had achieved total power in Germany. He had destroyed parliamentary government, liquidated his opponents and started to build the infamous concentration camps. Italy's dictator, Mussolini, had violated international law and defied the League of Nations by attacking and seizing defenceless Abyssinia (1933–34).

Throughout the world freedom was under assault, nowhere more tragically that in the new Republic of Spain. There, the majority of the electorate had voted into office the Popular Front Government. Yet the old order – the landowners supported by the church – refused to accept the will of the people.

They plotted against the Government and, led by General Francisco Franco and other high-ranking army officers, rose up against it in July 1936.

The Spanish Civil War had begun.

CHAPTER ONE

Will Viljoen had never felt so cold. That was all his mind could encompass—the knife right into the bone. Never, until this spot over the grate and the airflow from a hotel kitchen. He crouched forward, pressing his fingers down on to the bars.

Food!

He forgot the cold and remembered he had never felt so hungry. Another record. In his head he saw new-baked bread, fried chicken, chips sizzling in deep fat. And I'll finish off with apple turnovers and custard.

He made himself into a human ball, pulling head and shoulders in to his knees, his ice-pick of a nose jammed inside his collar. Pancakes! He groaned.

Will was wondering how far away he was from dying. Yesterday he had spent the last of his savings on a bowl of soup and a stale sausage roll. This morning he had eaten what was left of a raw cabbage. He'd had a pain in his belly ever since.

If I keel over now, I'll be short on mourners. Not even a cat to say its prayers over me.

He listened. No cat and no prayers—but a sound.

All at once, he was alert. He was not dying. His eyes raced across the darkness. Out of the damp city shadows came a quick, darting form, tallish, gliding, at first blindly concentrating on a single target—the light beaming up from the basement steps a dozen paces away.

The figure was still now; still and staring, a youth like a rake. Slowly, he recorded Will's presence. He was neither startled nor curious.

"Warm, is it, mate?" The youth stepped closer. He held the railing, rubbing his hand along it.

Will nodded. He was glad of company—any company, and he made room for the newcomer. "Aye, and they're dishing out chicken and chips down there."

"Just what I was thinkin' of orderin'. Only in posh dumps like this they don't call 'em chips. Y'ask for French fried frites. What's your name?"

"Will Viljoen."

"Foreigner, are you?"

"You might say that. I'm from up North."

"Funny accents you people 'ave."

"It's all the black puddings we eat."

The skinny youth laughed. They liked each other. "Well I was born i' Wales, where I got me red 'air. But me passport's stamped London as I've been 'ere since I was three an' a bit. Griff's the name." He sniffed. "I'm for 'avin' some o' that, how about you? Grabbin' it, I mean."

Will Viljoen hesitated. He kept his eyes averted from Griff's eager face. He had managed without stealing so far. It was a fool's game, Da had always said. They only caught you and made things worse. Honest as the day was long, Will's Da had been.

As though reading Will's thoughts, Griff stretched out his hand. "It's either this or endin' up in t'cemetery, for they'll not catch me queuein' up for their piss-awful soup. Or praisin' Jesus at the Sally Army for a plate o' fatty 'orsemeat. Suit yourself, though."

Twenty-four hours before, Will would have heeded his Da's advice. But starving, he had decided, was an even bigger fool's game than stealing. He had tried asking. He had tried pleading, he had tried begging. It seemed people's hearts were shut against him. They were bad times for everyone.

Will was terrified, for he was breaking rules he respected. He was letting Da down; offending the dead. Yet his hand met Griff's. There was strength in it.

" 'owway, then!"

They tiptoed down the steps till they reached the kitchen door which was not only unlocked, but ajar. "Careless," Griff whispered. "Somebody ought to complain to t'manager." They entered a dark passage that turned right into a narrow corridor. A swing door led into the kitchen on the street side. "That your 'eart thumpin' or mine?"

Waiters entered from a far door at the end of the corridor. As soon as the sparkling lights of the restaurant were closed off behind them, they started to whistle or sing, and to call orders.

"Look at them leftovers," said Griff.

"Aye, enough to feed a brass band."

They waited in silence. Griff had been tugging at something in his coat. He brought out what Will at first guessed was a knife but which he then recognised as a giant-size screwdriver. Instantly, his hand was on Griff's arm.

"None of that, understand?"

Griff held the screwdriver by the blade. It made a formidable-looking club. "It saves too much explainin'."

"No!"

"Stop wettin' yourself. I don't actually plan to use it. I mean, they'll not just 'and over 'cause we've got pretty faces . . . an' grab this." He pushed a sack into Will's hand. "See you fill it."

They waited for the moment when all three waiters went into the restaurant together. "Right, no dawdlin'!"

Griff was lightning. His feet made no sound. He was through the kitchen door so fast Will was nearly trapped on the outside. He caught the door on the swing. He thrust his head into brilliant light.

"Bums against the wall, both of you!" Griff confronted a fat, swarthy cook, probably an Italian, and a youth of about Will's age, sunk to his elbows in washing-up. " 'is Majesty's sick of 'angin' round for 'is roast pheasant, so we've come to collect."

He held the screwdriver threateningly above his head. Its blade glistened with condensation in the steamy heat of the kitchen.

On Griff's instructions, Will made for the ovens. Pans of meat and vegetables stood on simmer plates.

"Use the ladle. Go on, Fatty, give it 'im." Griff seemed to

have sprung up in height in that confined space. He too was grabbing and stuffing.

Two steaks from the grill hit the bottom of Will's sack, followed by a shower of roast potatoes, leeks, mushrooms and whole onions nicely browned in their skins.

"It's shakin' 'ands wi' all them miners as makes 'is Majesty so peckish."

There was no time to run an eye down the wine-list or consider the apple turnovers. The first waiter had crashed through the door, with the second right on his heels. For Will the shock was all the worse for being expected. His reaction was slow. He was stunned. He had never been in a situation like this before.

Griff was running at the waiters.

"Here, what the——"

There was little chance for the leader even to raise his tray. Will felt sick. Griff didn't threaten. He acted.

The handle of the screwdriver came whipping downwards. It struck the waiter full on the forehead, while the weight of Griff's attack spun the injured man violently to the ground.

"Y'young bastard!" The second waiter was bigger. He had had time to think. He turned his tray into a weapon. He hurled it at Griff as he advanced.

The plates appeared to hang in the air, lazily revolving, then double their speed as they broke over Griff's upraised arms. Bodies collided.

Will attempted to slip towards the door. He was thrown back. He toppled into an open-fronted cupboard. Dishes, plates, cups and glasses spilled over him. Winded, he struggled to rise. He saw the portly cook break from his former terror. He saw him grasp a heavy pan. He was darkening the space above Will. The pan was coming, crashing. Will was breathless. Something had hit him in the ribs. He felt they had caved in.

He needed to breathe. He shot up one arm and the pan burst against his wrist. He yelled in pain. That was enough, more than enough. He hurled his sack into the cook's face. He saw nothing but the door. Yet he was held by the coat.

He used his elbows. He back-heeled. His coat tore and the result was to send him catapulting forward, over the first waiter who lay still as a side of beef between his colleagues and Griff, then out through the swing door.

As he plunged up the steps, Will heard his name called. He reached the pavement scarcely a second before Griff.

"Where's the sack?" Blood streamed from Griff's nose.

"Lost it."

"You—what!"

Will knew it was his turn to be beaten. He edged away, his eyes half on Griff's enraged face, half on the screwdriver which still quivered in Griff's hand.

"I ought to plaster you."

"He'd have killed me."

"How do you know *I* won't?"

Will hadn't enough strength to move. He merely lowered his head—though not his eyes—and made a weak motion with his hands as if to say, do what you will.

Instead of a blow from the screwdriver he received a cuff no worse than he might have got at school for reading the *Wizard* under the desk. And when his companion broke into a trot and headed for a dark and deserted alley, Will, the empty-handed first-time thief, followed.

There was a bond between them, created by a danger they had shared and survived. Yes, well, that was one way of putting it, mused Will as he padded and puffed from gutter to pavement, from one black crossroads to the next, feeling faint but mechanically going on to keep pace with the legs ahead of him. Another way was to remember that Griff's pockets were bulging with food.

Would he, though, be prepared to share it?

The city shrank away from them, its towering buildings reduced to jagged black walls in the distance. "This is 'yde Park, we'll be all right 'ere." Griff did not slow up as they

passed from hard stone pavement to soft, wet lawns and
under the trees. "I know a place we can 'ole up. Real dry."

Rain had begun to filter lightly down from masses of high,
dense cloud. It dampened and cooled Will's forehead and
he was grateful. It helped to ease his burning thirst.

"Follow me." Griff cocked a leg over low iron fencing. He
brushed through rhododendrons and emerged at the rear of
a gardener's hut. "If you can stomach t'smell of fertiliser,
you'll find this is 'ome sweet 'ome." With his screwdriver
Griff prised out a loose plank in the wall of the hut.

They squeezed inside. "What a pong!"

"It'll make your 'air grow." The hut was crammed with
sacks, the walls lined with spades and rakes. Griff produced
matches. He produced a candle. He produced light. "How
d'you like it?" He crossed the hut. He replaced the screwdriver where it belonged.

"You could've killed that waiter."

"What did he 'ave to come burstin' in for?"

"There was no need to hit him."

"It's done now." He put the candle on the bare, dusty
floor. He glanced up at Will. He pointed a long, bony finger.
"I've got to keep me eye on you, mate, till all this 'as blown
over. Understand?"

He spread out an empty sack before him and item by item
he placed his booty upon it—a quarter chicken, a chicken
leg, gobbets of stewed meat, round brown-topped bread
rolls and two finger-mauled slices of pastry covered with
icing.

" 'ere." He tossed the chicken leg towards Will. "An'
think yourself lucky."

Will dropped on to a half-empty sack. The chicken was
still warm. His fingers were bathed in grease. He had never
tasted anything so delicious. If he could have swallowed the
bone too, he would have done. He had to be content with
sucking it dry.

He looked up. There was nothing left on the sack but
the slices of pastry. "Y'can 'ave that piece if y'll promise

one thing, swear on it . . . That you'll not grass on me."

"Why should I want to do that? I was aiding and abetting."

"Aidin' an' what?"

"Abetting."

"You a bright spark, are you?"

"Me Da told me all about it—aiding and abetting a crime."

"A lawyer is 'e, your Dad?"

Will turned away. "He just read a lot." He watched the slow-moving shadows on the shed wall. These tools, this smell, reminded him of Da's precious allotment, overgrown now after all those years of loving care. "He's dead."

"An' your old lady?"

Will shook his head. "Long since."

"Then we're both poor little orphans lost i' the storm, eh? If 'e was in anythin' like the state you're in, Will, your Dad didn't die of overeatin'."

"He was killed. Fighting in Spain . . . for the Republic."

Griff picked up the second piece of pastry. He offered it to Will. "I can't understand it. Every Tom, Dick an' 'Arry's volunteerin' for Spain."

Will accepted the pastry gratefully. "There's not much to hang around these parts for, is there?"

"Don't say *you're* plannin' to volunteer?—you're crackers!"

Will responded hotly. "I came four hundred mile to volunteer, and then they wouldn't have me. Too young, they said. Come back next year."

Griff leaned over on to his elbow, feeling into the deep pocket of his worn but good-quality trench coat. "Want a fag? I've just two left. No? Very wise. Smokin' stunts your growth." He grinned. "An' for a kid your size y'need every inch you can get. How old are you?"

"Seventeen and three-quarters."

"Pull the other leg."

"All right, sixteen and a half."

"An' a daft sixteen an' a 'alf if you ask me. Wantin' to

go an' get your 'ead blown off just because your Dad——"

"It's not just because of my Da! I've thought about it, I've read about it—and it's what I want to do."

"Where're you from, exactly?"

"Jarrow."

"Jesus! Out of the fryin' pan into the fire—is that what you're after? A right glutton for punishment you are." Griff eased off when he saw his friend stare sadly, uncertainly into the white candle flame. "Sorry, mate, but what wi' the Jarrow March bein' in the news—'ere, why're you not wi' 'em seein' as you're a fighter for lost causes?"

Will shrugged. He hid a smile. "They wouldn't have me either. Too young. Hand-picked, the Marchers, all two hundred of them. They're due to arrive in London to-morrow."

"Good. We can give 'em a wave. 'ow did you get yourself down from Jarrow?"

"Said au revoir to me Auntie—and walked."

"Walked? Nobody walks four 'undred mile."

"Plus a few lifts—on lorries, tractors, a milk float, even on a parson's bicycle. Just outside Bedford, there was an express stuck at the points, so I rode to London in style, in a First Class lavatory."

"They may not 'ave much to eat i' Jarrow," said Griff, "but they breed 'em wi' quick wits." He leaned forward and nipped out the candlelight. "Waste not, want not, me old grannie used to say." For several moments they listened to the rain drumming on the shed roof. Eventually, in a kindly, sleepy voice, Griff asked, "What will you do now?"

"Grow a moustache, a beard, anything to persuade them to take me. My Mam was Spanish. Jarrow killed her. She died of TB when I was nine." He was suddenly angry like his father. "Hundreds and hundreds of innocent people are being murdered every day in Spain. Their towns are being bombed out of existence."

He was going to continue until he was checked by a loud, rumbling snore from Griff. He took a letter from the wallet pocket of his torn jacket. "This, Griff," he whispered towards sleeping ears, "is me Da's last letter from Spain. It's four wonderful pages and I know it by heart." He unfolded the letter as though it were a map of hidden treasure. It contained all his father's dreams, his beliefs, his love of his fellow men. It was a treasure beyond price.

On a warm August morning his Da had gone into action alongside his Spanish brother-in-law. They had been captured by the Fascists who had stood them against an olive tree and shot them.

"Don't you fret, Da—I'm coming!"

He dreamed of meat and potato pie with a thick crust on top and a jar of red cabbage all to himself. When he awoke, Will found the morning had been up long before him. But not Griff. He lay between the sacks of fertiliser like a sunken ship.

Ought I to shove off—quick? Will thought, but did not move. It cut against the grain just leaving without a word. Still, if that waiter's dead, I'm old enough to be hanged.

He listened intently. Beyond the drip-drip of rain from the trees overhanging the shed roof, he thought he could hear the beat of a bass drum. His heart was filled with excitement. Those were mouth organs too, in ragged unison and the tune was unmistakable: "There's a Long, Long Trail Awinding".

"They've made it!" He stumbled over the sacks. He shook Griff awake. "They've made it?"

"Christ almighty! I thought it was coppers!"

"They've made it!"

"Who've made it?"

"The lads from Jarrow. Listen! It's got to be them. Things couldn't have worked out better—they're on their way to Hyde Park, to this very spot!"

Griff stretched himself. He yawned. "All this way just for a lot o' speeches." For a moment they listened in silence to the soft thud of the drum. The mouth organs were taking a breather. Griff went on: "What'll they get for their weeks o' marchin'? I'll tell you. They'll be treated like all the rest who've come beggin' an' pleadin' for work—a cuppa cold tea at the 'ouse o' Commons, a pat on the 'ead an' nothin' but empty promises to take 'ome wi' em."

Will was at the rain-tracered window. Everything was grey, the light, the sky, the mist at the foot of the leafless trees. "Do you know, they came—strangers with cash—and took the shipyard apart, piece by piece. Stripped it to nothing while half the town stood in the dole queue. The lads have marched four hundred miles to seek simple justice —and I'm going to be out there cheering them on."

Griff accepted a hand up. "Right, I'm wi' you. Maybe one o' your mates'll stump us a bob for breakfast, eh?"

The approach of the Jarrow Marchers had put more immediate matters out of mind. If Griff and Will had not been talking so loudly they would have detected other voices outside; if they had not turned their backs on the window, they would have seen a park keeper press through the bushes, with two policemen behind him.

Griff used the screwdriver again to prise open his secret entrance. The unsuspecting friends crawled out on to wet earth.

"Okay, grab 'em!"

There was no point in struggling. Will's right arm was twisted up his back. The muscle burnt as though it had been touched by hot coals. Griff had been tripped then shouldered sideways, falling into rhododendrons.

"You'll be stepping along with us, boys."

"What for? We done nothin'!"

"Trespassing. Breaking and entering."

"Breakin' an' enterin' a bloody gardener's shed? What's up wi' you lot, 'ave all the real crooks gone to Sunday school?" Griff was dragged on to his feet and, for his insolence, bounced between the two policemen.

"We just went in for shelter," protested Will. "A human being's got a right to a roof over his head."

The policemen were brusque and unsympathetic. "If it's

speeches you want to make, laddie," said one, keeping Will's arm jammed close to breaking, "you should've joined the Reds on the Park this morning."

They were pushed through the bushes on to the pathway. It was bitterly cold. Hyde Park stretched into a grey twilight edged with the roofs of stately mansions.

Rain hung in the air, yet ahead of them there was movement and colour. Speakers' Corner was filling with people. They were streaming towards it from all directions, from Marble Arch and the Edgware Road, from side streets off Park Lane, from Piccadilly to the south; hundreds and hundreds of them.

Will could make out a speakers' platform draped with red cloth. Bright-coloured flags, banners and placards were raised and shaken in the fitful breeze.

The flags were mostly those of the Communists but several were of red, yellow and purple which Will recognised as the colours of the Spanish Republic.

The banners declared their messages in bold letters: SAVE SPAIN FROM FASCISM, said one; BRITAIN—SELL ARMS TO THE RIGHTFULLY ELECTED SPANISH GOVERNMENT urged another; REJECT FRANCO AND FASCISM demanded a third.

Will felt his anger grow as he was thrust round the fringes of the crowd. Here was where he ought to be, shouting his support for Spain and perhaps searching out someone who might make it possible for him to fight for her too. And his own kind—the Jarrow Marchers—didn't he need to hang on and give them a welcome?

As if in answer to his thoughts, he saw, dancing across a sea of heads, the biggest and best banner of them all:

THE JARROW CRUSADE

There were tears in his eyes. He could see no faces, but they were all present in his memory, the faces of his pals' elder brothers, their das, grandas and uncles. There too would be Mrs Wilkinson, the town's MP—a real fighter she was—and Mr Thompson, the mayor of Jarrow.

"Wait! Hang on just a second." Will slowed. He held back. He stood on tiptoe. A single glimpse of his friends would satisfy him, the men who wore out the pavements of Jarrow and Hebburn and Gateshead and Newcastle hunting for work and failing to find it: the best of men in the worst of times.

"Get along, sonny!"

It was too much for Will. These were his own people. If he could only get to speak to one or two, they would help him, put in a good word for him. He tried to explain but he was pushed roughly on.

Suddenly, like a goaded mule, he kicked out at the shins of the policeman. He wrenched his arm free and plunged away towards the centre of the crowd.

At last being "just a kid" proved its advantages: Will was able to slip as easily as quicksilver between tall backs, thrusting shoulders, under raised arms and swinging placards.

The crowd tightened. Will's passage closed before him and he was stuck. Men big and towering as Vikings jostled amicably round and above him.

Without warning, however, the mood of the crowd changed. The good humour and the smiles vanished. "Here come the Blackshirts!—Dirty Fascists!" cried a single voice that was immediately drowned by roars of fury. "Mosley's bullyboys!"

Will did not have far to look. Not ten yards away he saw a phalanx of men in military-style black uniforms. Imitating the precision and arrogance of their heroes—Hitler's Nazi stormtroopers—they had marched forward in goose-step. They carried banners bearing a white lightning flash on a black circle. They halted in an exact line and their voices joined in a chilling chorus: "Sieg Heil! Sieg Heil!"

From behind them came cries of support: "Up the Fascists!"

"Fascists for ever!"

The mass of the people had assembled to call upon the British Government to send arms, food and medical aid to the struggling Republic in Spain, attacked from within by the rebellion of army generals led by Franco. They were there to protest that Hitler's Germany and Mussolini's Italy were giving Franco every assistance while England and France stood by as though the cause of freedom and democracy meant nothing.

Similarly, the Jarrow Marchers had assembled to make their own appeal to the Government. They had been made welcome, for their cause was not altogether different from that of the Republic; yet now the Blackshirts turned concord into discord.

"Sieg Heil! Sieg Heil!" It was as if the Blackshirts were taunting the crowd. Then they raised the war-cry of their Fascist brothers in Spain:

"Arriba España! Arriba España! Long live Franco! Down with the Reds!"

The peaceful protests were over. Fascists and pro-Republicans met head-on, first pushing and elbowing, pelting each other with harsh words, then battling with fists and knees and poles and placards.

Police whistles pierced the growing thunder of voices. Will heard the thump of fists, the crack of knuckles against bone, the gasps of those struck hard. He also heard his name called. "We've got to get the 'ell out of 'ere, Will!" yelled Griff, free of his own policeman and two tall shoulders away.

But Will, having found himself in the front line, closed his ears to Griff's advice. He saw Blackshirts. Men of their belief had shot his Da. They were evil men; men who, Da had once said, had only one answer to those who disagreed with them—to destroy.

Will attacked as he had done so often in gang-wars on Jarrow Slake. This blow was for Da, this was for Mam's brother, this was for the bombs dropped on Madrid—bombs manufactured in German factories.

And this—was for Will Viljoen.

His knees snapped under the weight of a blow from a Blackshirt truncheon. His head was bursting. His skull was a hundred bells, out of time, wheeling and crashing. He tried to fight on, yet his head was pulling his body down. His arms dropped. Neither they nor his feet would obey him. He saw faces spinning against grey light, heaving shoulders betraying the vicious underswing of fists, elbows flung up in sharp, jerking angles.

He was slipping between thighs and knees, beneath fists, under the truncheons. He was almost flat on the cindery ground when a boot clouted him in the chest.

The grey light faded into black.

CHAPTER TWO

Will came to in the yellow glare of a police cell. " 'ow's the 'ead?" enquired Griff.

He winced. Another record: he'd never suffered a worse headache. The brilliant light did not help. He closed his eyes and felt as though he had just jumped off a kids' roundabout at fifty miles an hour.

His fingers tested the side of his head. A large plaster covered a swelling, throbbing bruise.

"Them ruddy Blackshirts trod all over you, Will. You'd 'ave been on a quick outin' to the Pearly Gates if it 'adn't been for this 'ere gent. Got punched up 'imself while 'e was at it."

A young man in his late twenties sat on the bunk opposite. "Sam Hannington's the name. And we're friends already, Will." He shook Will's hand. "They must have riveted a steel plate on to your head in Jarrow, the way you took that knock from the truncheon."

Sam had bright, handsome blue eyes. He was tall, narrowly-built but athletic. He was dressed like a mountaineer with thick woollen socks over baggy corduroys, tough-soled boots and a windjammer coloured dull green and yellow like military camouflage.

He also sported bruises on his forehead and both cheekbones. "From what your friend Griff tells me, you and I have one very important thing in common: we love Spain, and we can't wait to get out there."

Will levered himself on to his elbow. "Can you help me? You see, me Da——"

"Yes, I've got the whole story. I'm deeply sorry about your father. But that's another thing we've in common. My sister Molly is out there too. Heaven knows how she managed it—she's scarcely seventeen. She joined a Medical Aid unit in Barcelona. But would His Majesty's customs let yours cordially through? Not on your life! You'd think I was carrying diamonds stitched into my turnups. I've been refused a passport twenty-three times. I keep telling them, I'm an artist, I just want to go on a holiday to gay Paree, paint a few bridges and paddle my toes in the Seine. Oh no, they say. The Thames is good enough to paddle in. We know what you'll get up to—you'll go high-tailing off to fight for the Republic, and that'll never do. After all, the last thing in the world our dear Prime Minister wants is to upset Mr Hitler and his Fascist disciples. I tell you, every nit-picking obstacle's been stuck in my way—and in the way of hundreds of others as well." He beat the air with his fist. "But they'll have to put a bullet through my ticker to stop me!"

Sam paced fretfully up and down the cell. "Getting myself arrested like this threatens some carefully laid plans."

His anger faded and he relaxed. From his pocket he produced a huge bag of sweets. "Here, grab a few. They're barley sugars. Friends call me Candy Sam because of my weakness for liquorice allsorts, humbugs and anything else that rots the teeth."

He sat down again on his bunk. "It's possible I might be able to help you. That's if Lady Luck is feeling generous. Desperate circumstances often require desperate remedies. And my circumstances are desperate." He paused. "As yours seem to be, Griff informs me." He took a newspaper from his windjammer pocket. "Desperate enough to keep you both behind bars for a long time." He unfolded the paper and opened it.

"According to this, you two aren't in prison just for ringing old ladies' front doorbells."

"Show Will what it says, Sam."

Will was presented with an inside page. "Bottom corner, next to an advert recommending Bovril for beefy muscles. See it?"

Will's mouth became dry with fear as he read the headline: BRUTAL ATTACK ON LONDON WAITER—TWO YOUTHS SOUGHT.

"It were only an accident," insisted Griff. "Honest!"

"He ran on to your fist, did he?"

"We was starvin' to death."

"Well fortunately the poor devil's still alive, but with a fractured skull." Sam retrieved the newspaper from Will. "The police have obviously put one and one together. Tomorrow, they'll remand you in custody. You'll be charged with attempted murder."

Will turned to face the wall and closed his eyes on his pain. "We need a lot more than luck, we need a miracle."

Sam's hand reached out for his. "Do you really and truly want to fight in Spain, where it's odds on you'll be pushing up daisies within a month?"

Will nodded. "I promised."

"Your father wouldn't hold you to a promise like that."

"I promised myself and I'm going!"

Sam lay flat on his bunk. "Birds of a feather, you and my sister. All right—you're in business, we'll catch that boat together."

"But how?"

Smiling, Sam tapped his nose as if to indicate an unspoken secret. "You never know your luck."

"Y'mean——"

"No questions! Just say your prayers. Tomorrow, stick by me if you can—and be ready for some exercise."

When Will and Griff appeared in the Magistrates' Court next morning no charges were read out against them. The prosecution asked that the two youths be kept in prison till further enquiries had been made. "An' we don't 'ave to be good at readin' tea leaves to know what them enquiries is about," muttered Griff. "Huh, we should've asked for bail."

"Bail? What'd we use for money, tap washers?" Will felt sick. His head rang with pain and he was not seeing straight. "What happened to Candy Sam?"

His question was answered when they were escorted down corridors and stairs and out into a high-walled yard. Sam

Hannington was among several prisoners awaiting transport. He winked merrily at them and immediately Will felt more cheerful.

" 'e's better than a bacon an' egg breakfast, is that fellow," said Griff. "Look at 'im!"

Sam had waved his beret—a tartan stuck with a feather— at a police inspector who had entered the yard. "What sort of hotel is this, officer? No smoked haddock on the menu last night, and this morning not a fresh-picked mushroom for love or money. I demand to see the chef!"

The officer's response was not without sympathy or respect. "Stick to your paints and your easel, Mr Hannington, and you'll be free to order what dinner you like."

"But not on the boat-train to Paris, eh? This confounded country has no right to deny a passport to a law-abiding citizen."

"A law-abiding citizen you may be, Mr Hannington, but you are also a hot-headed young fool who has been classified as a security risk. All we want from you is a promise of good behaviour."

"No pasarán! Do you know what that means, officer?— they shall not pass. It's what the Spanish people are saying every day of their lives. No pasarán! To Franco, Hitler or you stodgy lot! So no promises!"

The inspector's goodwill ran out. "We'll have handcuffs on the rest of your little gang of brothers shortly, I assure you."

"Don't skin your rabbit before you catch it, officer."

A Black Maria turned into the yard and, handcuffed, the prisoners were ordered aboard. A police guard climbed in behind them. "Close as tar to a blanket, you two," Sam instructed Will and Griff. The rear doors were slammed shut and barred on the outside.

Will watched the passing streets through the steel-mesh windows. Half of his mind was crushed with worry, the other half strangely excited. The streets were grey and wet. The sky was grey and even the faces of the people seemed to be grey. The only colour in the world seemed to reside in Sam's tartan beret and in Griff's shock of red hair.

Tensely, restlessly, Sam divided his attention between his wrist-watch, the face of the police guard and the road behind the Black Maria. With the appearance of a heavy blunt-nosed truck from a side street, his tight lips parted. He gave a low whistle. He tapped his nose again. "I hope you both said your prayers."

The truck was following them, keeping a distance of about thirty yards yet closing up the gap whenever another vehicle attempted to overtake. The Black Maria slowed. The truck slowed. Candy Sam was on the edge of his seat rattling his handcuffs and whistling. The police guard watched him suspiciously, irritatedly.

"I guess you'll not know how Newcastle United got on on Saturday, will you, officer? For my young Tyneside friend here." Receiving no reply, Sam added: "I thought not. You'll have been breaking up too many honest protest meetings to care about the League tables."

The guard's fist shot to within inches of Sam's face. "If you want those shiny teeth still in your gums at the end of this journey, shut your big mouth."

The Black Maria forked left off the main road on to a narrow, gloomy street. The blunt-nosed truck was close behind. The police guard ought, by now, to have noticed the persistence of the truck, but his whole, furious attention was fixed upon the insolent smile of Sam Hannington.

"There's one of my favourite pawnshops along here, officer. It's got half my property in the front window."

"Shut it!"

"I'd love to—and get my euphonium back. Not to mention my electric footwarmer."

Will saw the three brass balls hanging above the pawnshop. Then, parked directly across the path of the Black Maria was a broken-down car, with two men thrusting their heads into its open bonnet. At the sight of the Black Maria, the men downed their tools. They turned. They advanced, wielding iron crowbars. The police driver banged his gears into reverse. He moved only a foot before he collided with the truck.

Sam had made his own move an instant before. Dragging his handcuffed fellow-prisoner with him, he had lunged at the police guard, hurling his entire weight across his neck and shoulders, forcing him on to the floor of the Black Maria. "Join me!" he bellowed at Griff and Will. Without requiring further persuasion, they fell upon the struggling, helpless guard.

There was a deafening crash of metal and glass. The driver had been attacked from both sides. The doors were torn open. The van rocked. There was a hum of voices. The driver fought hard but was overwhelmed and dragged into the road.

"Easy, everybody!" warned Candy Sam as the rear bar of the Black Maria was thrown up and the door unlocked. "No harm will come to you."

The raiders had donned strange, leering masks. One of them leapt aboard. "Okay, Sam?"

"Nicely timed. See to this one, will you? He's feeling a bit cross." Sam's handcuffs slipped off with a clatter. They were transferred to the wrists of the police guard, who was also gagged. "Release the rest—these two lads first . . . Have you got the cash?"

"As ordered."

Candy Sam passed a pound note to each prisoner. "For any inconvenience we caused you, gentlemen. If you've a short sentence to look forward to, we advise you to stay in the van. Alternatively, there's an underground station second right. Best of luck!"

"Away then, Sam!"

"These two are thumbing a lift."

"What!"

Sam was out of the Black Maria. To Will and Griff, he said, "Last chance for second thoughts."

The friends hesitated for only a second. "You bet!"

answered Griff. Will was down before him. They ran together behind Sam to the back of the truck. Sam swung open the doors. "In among the laundry. Jump!"

Will found himself pitched on to soft and smelly linen bags. Then followed two kicking but helpless policemen in the iron grip of their captors. Once again, grey was shut into black. The laundry truck accelerated away at twice the speed recommended by its manufacturers. Still wearing their masks, Sam's liberators had blindfolded the policemen as well as gagged and handcuffed them.

Will stared at his friend. Their thoughts were the same. "Out of the chip pan," he grinned, "into the fiery furnace!"

"Aye, if we was in trouble this mornin', what do y'call this? Kidnappin' coppers!"

In a quiet back street fifteen minutes later, the laundry truck was swapped for another, a dull grey vehicle belonging to a municipal water board. "In the best tradition of all self-respecting Chicago gangsters," observed Candy Sam as he got into the driver's seat. "Right, heads down, everybody, and no talking till we get out into the country."

The second truck moved faster. Will imagined London fading behind them. He should have felt afraid. Indeed it would not have been inappropriate if he had been shaking with terror. Instead, he was elated. He had taken warmly to Candy Sam. He was not glad they had broken the law but he was thrilled by what was happening to him now.

It was plain they were driving south: could Will be on his way to Spain at last?

After a half hour's desperate driving, the truck slowed and veered off on to what Will guessed was a cart track. "Time to wave bye-bye to the men in blue," called Sam. The truck stopped. The masked men lifted their cargo into the open.

For Will it was like stepping down into a place he had known all his life. They were among allotments just like his Da's: he saw hen-runs, slope-roofed cabins tarred against the weather, occasional greenhouses and everywhere corrugated tin fencing, rusted and leaning.

The only difference was that the whitewash artists wrote UP CHELSEA! on the shed walls rather than UP THE UNITED!

An empty hen hut awaited the policemen. "What've you got them for breakfast, Ike?"

"Chicken sandwiches and cucumber," replied one of the masked men, "and four bottles of light ale."

"Ready with the old magic potion, Ben?"

The smallest of the four masked men half-emptied a medicine bottle on to a piece of towelling. "That enough, Sam?" The smell of the chloroform reached Will several paces away.

Sam checked his watch. "Perfect timing. According to my fairy godmother these worthy upholders of the law will sleep like Rip Van Winkle till the stroke of midnight. Very well, lock them up. Howard, take the wheel, will you? I'll introduce our new friends."

He climbed into the back of the truck as it moved off. His men had removed their masks. "That was slickly done, lads. The job couldn't have been plotted more efficiently in a crime thriller." On every face there was a smile of pride and relief.

"Now shake hands with these two, comrades. Will here is from Jarrow. His father volunteered for Spain. He was killed—and so the boy wants to go too. There seems to be no denying him."

Will knew well enough what was troubling them in the brief silence that followed. "I'm not too young! I can be useful. I'm good with bandages, splints—and I know some Spanish."

"Steady, steady!" Sam put his hand soothingly on Will's shoulder. "It'll be your choice. I promised, didn't I? But first, meet the Six Bells Brigade, or rather the Six Bells and Bowling Green Brigade, after the pub we all met in."

One by one Sam pointed out his comrades. "Howard's up

front, the best map reader this side of the Land of Nod. Don't be put off by his lahdy-da accent. He can't help it, and I can assure you his father's money never went to his head." He gave a sly look and caused a laugh by adding, "In fact his father's money has been very usefully spent.

"This is Ike, the tough-guy among us, and the only one who's ever done any real fighting." He was thick-set, broad-faced and his bristly chin, Will thought, was a bit like Desperate Dan's in the *Dandy*.

"Ike's our sergeant major. If you decide to join us, he'll teach you how to fire and clean a rifle and, we hope, how to stay alive. Next, meet Roland. Take my word for it, behind that mighty beard and beneath those horn-rimmed specs is a face. You can see it sometimes when the sparrows aren't nesting in the thatch. Roland's our genius with anything mechanical, electrical, surgical or liturgical. A bit of a philosopher, too, if the truth be known.

"Finally, smallest but far from least, meet Ben—not to be confused with Ben Hur. Our Ben can not only serve a chloroform sandwich to our policemen friends, he is the finest omelette-maker within two thousand miles of the St Helen's Glassworks. He could make a feast out of a tea-towel."

Candy Sam raised his arm as though holding an invisible glass. "And to absent loved ones—my naughty runaway sister. Molly, who, while we were all sitting round talking about what we ought to do for Spain, actually got up and did something. May the gods bless and preserve her."

"Here, here!" chimed in the others.

At the thought of his sister, so far away, Sam was suddenly out of spirit. "I wonder how many brave men she's seen die today, how many wounded she's been unable to help because there've been no bandages, no medicines."

"If I know Molly," said Roland optimistically, "she'll not be feeling sorry for herself. And she'd cuss us for wasting sympathy when it's not asked for and not needed."

"A time for doing, eh, Roland?"

"Aye, and for dying if it comes to it."

A few more minutes and the truck turned off the smooth metalled road on to another bumpy track. Candy Sam rapped on the driver's cab. "Stop here, will you, Howard? Now you lads, this is as far as we can take any of you who's not booked his passage to Spain. The risks will be tremendous, the dangers impossible to exaggerate. As Roland said, it's not likely we'll return alive. And one more thing: volunteers such as us are as unwelcome in France as we are here in Britain. If we get caught it'll be a year in a stinking French jail."

Sam's gaze passed from Will, whose determination was unshifting—and showed on his face—to Griff whose mind was far from made up. Griff bit off the top of his thumbnail. "All I know about Spain is that they grow oranges an' kill bulls."

"No one is pressing you, Griff."

Another thumbnail was spat across the truck floor. Griff brightened. "All the same, I reckon I'll string along. Me Gran used to say travel broadens the mind, an' anythin' would be better than sewin' mail bags in Pentonville for the next ten year."

Sam banged on the cab again. "Full speed ahead, Howard." Half a mile or so later, the truck stopped. The doors opened on to rainy darkness. Will recognised farm outbuildings and ran with the others into the shelter of a large barn.

"First thing, Ben," said Candy Sam lighting a storm lantern, "is grub for these two starving jail-birds. And I'd not say no to a couple of rashers of fried bacon myself."

Inside the barn, surrounded by high-piled bales of sweet-smelling hay, was a third truck. Very odd looking, thought Will, as if it had been put together from spare parts—but the wrong ones. On the offside door was a winged horse stencilled in white paint.

"We've named her Pegasus," explained Sam bringing forward the lamp. "Roland suggested Puffing Billy. But with the Pyrenees to cross eventually we thought a pair of wings would come in handy. Mind you, she only takes any notice when we address her as plain, simple Peg. Take a look inside."

They were amazed. "Like the Ritz Hotel!" exclaimed Griff as the lamp illuminated the expertly fitted interior.

"A little thing our Roland knocked together. Like it?"

Peg contained fold-down bunks, a collapsible table, storage cupboards, a washbasin which unhooked from the wall—"An' even a portable bog!"

Troubled, Howard approached Candy Sam. "I hear you're going to take these two lads with us—surely that's unwise?"

"No one else has objected."

"That's not the point. They're just kids. They don't know what they're letting themselves in for."

"Do any of us—I mean really?"

"If my cousin Charles couldn't come, then——"

"Fiddlesticks, man! Your cousin Charles would've claimed he'd gone down with dysentery two days after his first glass of French water. We'd have had to put a bullet through his skull to stop him complaining.

"No more objections, Howard. The Republic needs every single heart and hand she can get if she's to survive. What's more, Will's mother taught him Spanish. That could be invaluable to us.

"From now on there'll be seven of us, so the Six Bells and Bowling Green Brigade will have to be renamed. Cheers to the Seven Bells Brigade!"

In darkness, they were on the road again. Ben's meal lay heavy and satisfying inside Will whose eyes were drooping towards sleep. Supper over, there had been work to do. The bales of hay, towering towards the roof of the barn, had been unstacked to reveal piles of wooden packing cases.

"Agricultural implements," announced Candy Sam. "To be supplied to the impoverished peasants of Andalusia."

Griff had laughed, disbelieving. "Them's guns!"

The boxes—whatever they contained—had been loaded on board Peg and then a false floor of interlocking planks laid over them.

They had been travelling for close on an hour when Sam, who was driving, called: "Hold tight for the next twenty minutes. I'm going to test the wings of this flying horse . . . Imagine you're on the Big Dipper at Blackpool and you'll be all right!"

Peg suddenly began to rear and jolt and rock wildly from side to side. The packing cases were shifting and banging beneath Will's feet. He fell first into Ike who steadied him, then into Ben who capsized with him on to the floor.

This was the Big Dipper and the Switchback rolled into one. Peg moaned and snorted, then plunged downwards at such a lurching tilt that the rest of the Seven Bells Brigade slithered against the rear of the driver's cab.

"All right in there?" called Sam cheerfully. "Come on, Howard, let's give 'em a song:

"'Twas a beautiful night and the stars shone bright
  And the moon o'er the Kelvin danced . . ."

And Peg danced. She hopped, she staggered; she did the high jump again, only there was no sandpit to catch her fall.

"When a student so pale sat on the bridge rail
  And down on the water he glanc'd . . ."

Will had disentangled himself from Ben but was sat on by Griff. "Sorry, mate. Forgot me parachute."

"With a tear in his eye, he heaved a deep sigh
  While over and over sang he . . ."

Sam was joined in the chorus by Howard:

"Moriar—Moriar—Moriar, O! Mel-po-me-ne,
  Moriar—Moriar—Moriar, O! Mel-po-me-ne."

Will did feel that Peg had taken wing—into another world, where mad gunrunners drove straight off the cliffs of Dover and sang strange songs as they fell towards the waves.

Yes, waves—for all at once Peg ceased to grumble. She was rock firm and steady, and faintly, though not far off, could be heard the soft murmur of the sea.

"Well done, old hoss!" cried Sam. "We made it. Okay, you lot? No bones broken?" He laughed. "A dented fetlock's a small price to pay for achieving the practically impossible. Hand round a tot of that rum, will you, Ike?"

They moved forward once more, over pebbles, over sand. "This'll do for the moment." Peg's engine cut out and the stillness was solid enough to grasp hold of. "Time?"

"Four-ten."

"Fingers crossed, everybody. Five minutes to wait." The sea rolled and hissed. Will's heart thumped. He was leaving England, leaving home; perhaps he would never return. He was afraid for the first time: would he manage, or would he want to turn and run like a rabbit when the testing time came?

Roland seemed to understand. "Chin up, son, we're all feeling a bit funny. It's our first time too."

Ike nodded in sympathy. "Take a swig of this." He handed Will the brandy bottle. "It gets rid of your goose pimples."

They waited, dry-lipped, shivery, huddled, and the wind winnowed in from the sea, carrying with it a light spray of rain. Candy Sam spoke through the small rear window of the cab. "A word in your ear, comrades. I'm quaking in my shoes too, so nobody'll be blamed for opting out to pick sea shells by the seashore."

No one answered.

Howard burst the silence. "There she is, Sam! Here, the binoculars."

"We'll wait for the signal."

"Long . . . Long . . . Short . . . Long. It's her! That's a relief!"

"Here goes, then." Sam switched Peg's headlights on and off. "Long . . . Long . . . Short . . . Long. How about that?— dead on time." Peg stirred into life. "Put the kettle on, Molly my love—we're on our way!"

They moved slowly forward. Will sensed the waves beneath Peg's wheels. He pictured the white foam given a faint glow by the rising dawn. He was cold. If he had not been very firm with them, his teeth would have started chattering.

"She doesn't seem to be getting any nearer, Sam."

"Maybe that's as far as the ship can reach." Candy Sam acted, decisive. "Out on your pins, everybody. Shoulders to the wheel."

The sea washed above Will's knees as he lowered himself from Peg's dry safety. They were on a wide, evenly sloping beach closed in by shadowy cliffs. Streaks of morning scarlet climbed up into loosening grey cloud.

A hundred yards away a dark mass hovered on the incoming tide. Sea mist obliterated all but its surface contour. The craft seemed to have risen from the waves rather than passed over them.

"She's still coming in, Sam," judged Ike. The craft was low in the water, solid, stubby in profile, with a funnel as well as masts. It approached to within thirty yards.

"Back in the cab, then, Howard, and not too much accelerator," instructed Sam.

The wind had freshened. It whipped curls of foam across the tide.

"On a count of three," shouted Sam, "heave for all you're worth." Either the rest of the Seven Bells Brigade didn't hear Sam clearly or they'd forgotten their numbers. They each heaved at different intervals. Peg rocked, jerked forward a foot and stuck.

"What are you?" howled Sam, "a bunch of innumerates— can't count! For the benefit of those who aren't mathematical geniuses, two comes after one and three comes after two."

"I guess we can remember that, Sam," grinned Roland

from behind sea-spattered spectacles. "But what time are we counting in—crochets, minims or semibreves?"

"Crochets or we'll be here till Christmas. Now! One . . . Two . . . Three—push!"

Peg trundled another yard.

"Good. That's six out of ten. Take a breath. Again—one . . . Two . . . Three!"

"We're sinking!" wailed Ben who had stepped into a hole in the sand and nearly disappeared.

"You should've eaten more carrots when you were a boy, Ben. Once more!" Forward. Sea deeper. Waves in a fury. "Un . . . Deux . . . Trois . . . Shovez vous!"

Perhaps all would have been well if Will had not remembered that he had never learnt to swim. He had heaved, stepped forward and found nothing to uphold him but watery space. His hands slipped from Peg's haunches. His knees were floating away somewhere. He choked on sea water, thrashed the waves with his arms and sank, spluttering and blinded, from view.

He struggled back on to his toes again, only to be knocked sideways by an uncharitable wave. Out of his grey deafness, Will heard Griff's voice, but he had no breath to reply. The tide was whirling him, dragging him downwards—would nobody help?

Will awoke from a sea sleep not in the next world but in a dark ship's cabin smelling of paraffin lamps and sausages. "Bangers and two fried eggs?" Candy Sam stood over him in dim, rocking lantern light.

"I thought I was——"

"Not quite. You floated aboard on Ike's broad back. Your plasters've washed off, but the wounds are dry. Have you an appetite?"

Out of the corner of his eye, Will could see the others at table. Griff was just mopping up his egg yolk with a wad of thickly buttered bread—and for the first time in the short history of Will Viljoen, he shook his head at the offer of food.

He felt terrible. "Yes, you *are* looking green. Try a stick of candy, it'll settle the old tum."

Will declined even candy. He slept and when he awoke again the porthole above him was a black circle in a black wall. The cabin was empty, the ship motionless. He was grateful for his dream, of when his Mam and Da were alive, and his little sister; when, together, they had made the best of the bad times.

He sat up. He fished out his Da's letter from Spain. It was soaked but the Indian ink wasn't even smudged. He peeled the pages apart and held them in front of the lantern to dry. His Da's words gave Will comfort and strength: "Volunteering for Spain was not the wise thing to do, or the sensible thing—but if a man lives by what he believes, it was the right thing."

Will went up on deck to see Peg being trundled along planks on to French soil. " 'ow's Sleepin' Beauty?" Griff raised his eyes from a corned-beef sandwich. "Want a bite?"

"Is it today or yesterday?" asked Will, having lost all track of time. Save for a dim ship's lantern, there was total blackness.

The captain of the secret ferry shook hands with Sam's men. "Bonne chance, messieurs! Long live the Republic!" The ship eased away from her moorings. "And remember, mes amis—everywhere in France, the gendarmes have orders to arrest those who travel to fight in Spain." He raised his arm in salute. "No pasarán!"

In reply and thanks, the Seven Bells Brigade shot their fists into the air. "No pasarán!"

CHAPTER THREE

Will gazed ahead of him along the beams of Peg's lights. The land was flat, the roads straight, the sky full of stars. On either side, rows of graceful poplars swooped towards, around and past them. He was glad of the chance to sit in the driver's cab with Sam and Howard, sharing their mood of wonder and excitement.

"France!" proclaimed Candy Sam. "My senses are tingling already. Once we've cooked Franco's goose, I'll be back among these green pastures, in body and spirit. I'll sit on the quay at Honfleur and draw and paint till my fingers are worn down to the gristle."

Will smelt the passing countryside, tinged still with a summery warmth that had long vanished from England. The lights of farmhouses twinkled from shady woods. Occasionally there were grander houses with high surrounding walls and wrought-iron gates.

"France!" Sam repeated, only in a less admiring way. "Along with the British, the Germans and the Italians, she signs the Treaty of Non-Intervention in Spain, but only the French and the cowardly British lion see fit to keep their side of the bargain. While Germany and Italy pour arms and men and aeroplanes into Spain to support Franco, volunteers like us aren't even allowed through to work in the hospitals. What a joke!"

"How did your Da get to Spain, Will?"

"He took a day-trip to Paris, then went by train to a place called Arles. They had to cross the Pyrenees on foot."

"Both sides of the Channel the authorities have got meaner since his time. I read in the paper that the French police uncovered a secret arms factory, making hand-grenades for shipment to the Republic. Now the police are stopping and searching everything on four wheels."

Without warning, Sam trod violently on the brakes. Peg's

tyres squealed their protest. She lurched sideways, rocking. He was forcing the truck rightwards into the trees.

"What the hell!" came a cry from inside Peg.

"Police!" shouted Sam, wrestling with the steering wheel as Peg lunged for one tree, missed it, then crashed past another. "A road block. Three cars, motor-cycles. They're armed."

A row of birch saplings halted Peg's further progress. In the back, Griff had got close to beating Ike at gin rummy but the cards were now scattered all over the floor; Roland was scrambling about for his glasses and Ben had nearly swallowed his pipe.

"Surely they're not looking for us, Sam?"

"Our own police could have tipped them off."

"What do we do—wait?"

"No. Darkness is our one chance. We must push on."

"Through a forest?"

"What do you think we brought old Howard along for? The original human bloodhound. Got your maps ready, Howard? It's your turn to be hero."

They got down from the cab. They stretched out Howard's maps on the ground. "Here, Will, shine the torch. Well, Howard, is there a way round?"

Will noticed how long Howard's hands were, and how white, his nails neatly filed.

"All these French woods have fire-breaks," he said. "They are at pretty frequent intervals so we should hit one whichever way we head."

"We head south, of course."

"No, Sam. It's got to be back north, two miles. See the village? We then swing north-west."

"Heavens, man, at this rate we'll be just in time for the ferry from Boulogne."

"That's the way it's got to be, I'm afraid. It's a long detour but we should still reach the Loire by dawn."

They had almost an hour of it—encounters with ruts a foot deep, nasty wrangles with trees whose roots rose from the dark earth like trip-wires. They were attacked by briar-hedges; they trampled over fields of vine and meadows of stubble until at last Peg reached a narrow but recognisable road.

They turned north, they veered west, they roared through sleeping villages that were scarcely black marks on Howard's map; and all the time Howard never hesitated. He appeared not only to be able to see in the dark, but to see at least two miles ahead of him.

Nerves settled, aching limbs took rest. "Sleeping again, Will?" grinned Sam as Will's head drooped towards his shoulder. "You must've been bitten by a tsetse fly. Don't worry, we've got a real four-poster bed waiting for you in this little château we're visiting by the Loire."

"When will we get to Spain?"

"In good time, lad. This morning's impatient soldier is this afternoon's corpse. We've a spot of training to do, rifle drill, where Ike does his bit. I mean, if you're following in your Da's footsteps, that's your choice, but it's my responsibility to see you stay alive."

He smiled. "And it's not every day a lad from Jarrow sleeps in the same bed as Pope John the Nineteenth . . ."

"Remember what I told you—tuck it hard into your shoulder."

Will lay on grass, with dew seeping into his trousers. Ike stood over him. "Are you ready to take aim?"

"No."

"What's the matter?"

"My collar bone." Will just did not seem able to find a comfortable place to fix the butt of the rifle.

"Ram it under the bone and 'old it there. Otherwise it'll kick you worse than a mule . . . That's the stuff, Griff, son. You're a natural by the looks of things."

Something from those dratted ferns was getting up Will's nose. He had been keen to try out a real rifle, but holding it, bearing its weight rather shakily, he suddenly felt ill at ease.

However, he pressed the clip of bullets successfully home. He cocked the firing pin.

"Take aim!"

It must be hay fever. He wanted to sneeze. He screwed up his nose. He squinted along the barrel and tried to align the sights.

"Steady, Jarrow," advised Candy Sam from behind him. "You're not conducting a brass band with the end of the rifle."

"Fire!"

Will hunched his body, closed his eyes, pulled the trigger —and sneezed, all at the same time. He opened his eyes to see (amid a roar of applause from the rest of the Seven Bells Brigade) a wood-pigeon halt its skyward flight and explode in a cascade of feathers.

"Good shootin'!" cried Ike. "And quick thinkin', eh, Sam?"

The shot inspired Candy Sam to poetry:

"See! from the brake the whirring pheasant springs,
    And mounts exulting on triumphant wings:
    Short is his joy; he feels the fiery wound,
    Flutters in blood, and panting beats the ground.

"Alexander Pope." He turned away, pacing towards the trees where he squatted down in the shade.

"You've rather upset him, I think, Will," said Howard. "He's very squeamish about that sort of thing, cruelty to birds or animals."

"I never meant to," protested Will. "I was aiming at the Green Man, at the target. Only I sneezed."

"You'll be aimin' at more than birds where we're goin'," reassured Ike. "Try again. Be patient."

Griff took his turn. He struck the Green Man low down. Another shot left a black hole in his face. Will felt angry with himself and depressed, for his own shots missed the target altogether. He could almost see Da shaking his head.

"Never mind, lad," Ike was saying. "It'll come with practice. When you see the whites of the Fascists' eyes, you'll shoot straight enough, mark my words. Rest your arms. Now for somethin' face to face. Get those sandbags swinging, will you, Ben?"

Will approached the brooding Candy Sam warily. He was seated against a pine, holding an autumn-goldened leaf as though it were the page of a book.

"Sorry about the bird, Sam."

"Forget it, Will. I shouldn't have quoted that poetry. The words affected me more than the poor old wood-pigeon. Know what I mean? Did they let you read much poetry at school?"

"Stuffed it down our throats. But I always preferred the songs me Da used to sing. Miners' songs like 'Geordie Black' and 'The Row Between the Cages'."

"Never heard of that one."

"It's about two pit cages, an old one and a new one. They have a scrap to see who's best. Da won a competition once, singing it. A basket of groceries. We ate more than the Prince of Wales that night."

"Meant a lot to you, your Da, didn't he?"

Will bowed his head.

"What was the one thing that clinched it for him, finally made him volunteer for Spain?"

Will thought for a long moment. "Not one thing. But two years back, do you remember, when the Moorish troops were sent in to butcher the miners who were on strike? That helped. And when Franco grabbed Morocco and shot down all those soldiers and civilians because they'd stayed loyal to the Government. Not one thing but one thing after another."

Ike was striding over towards them. "Come on, Will, try a bit of pig stickin'." He held out a rifle fixed with a bayonet. The Seven Bells Brigade formed a line facing sandbags suspended from the branches of trees thirty yards away.

"Right, the Moors is pourin' over the 'ill at you. Hundreds of 'em screamin' their 'eads off. It's ten to one against you, and you've not a bullet up the spout . . . Attack!"

Though Howard and Griff advanced with redoubtable speed and smote the enemy with vicious thrusts, the rest of the Seven Bells Brigade never reached their target.

Ben got his foot caught in a rabbit-hole, toppled sideways, and was very nearly despatched into the next world by Roland whose glasses flew into long grass.

"Get on with you—move!" yelled Ike when Will paused to help Ben to his feet and then joined Roland in the search for his glasses. "This isn't the three-legged race at the annual fête. It's war. Up! Try again. Accept no quarter, give no quarter. Those that fall, leave them for the stretcher-bearers."

Ike turned to Candy Sam. "My God, this lot wouldn't scare the skin off a rice pudding."

"They'll make out, Ike."

"Let's hope so, or this expedition's goin' to turn out a bloody shambles."

Candy Sam took over command. He marched to the sandbags. He gave each a push till it was swinging and spinning at the same time. "Listen, friends, and let the facts speak to your hearts. Put faces to these sandbags—it's the only way. Think of your enemy. Think of his deeds."

He indicated the swinging, spinning enemy. He spoke passionately, his usual good humour put aside. "A spot of history revision. In February the people of Spain, after centuries of tyranny, elect their first government. The rich land-owners start shivering in their shoes: what, distribute land to the peasants? Over our well-fed bodies, they say.

"Up pops the right arm of tyranny, the officer corps. Men like Mola, Queipo de Llano—and, of course, Franco, whom the Republic had not only failed to promote but had shipped to the Canary Islands out of harm's way. Not far enough, though. He raises the Insurgent banner among his Moroccan regiments. He executes three thousand soldiers and civilians who refuse to turn against the Republic."

Sam gave the sandbags another vicious swing. "Our enemies, lads. In Seville they slaughtered nine thousand men, women and children. They stacked their bodies in the streets and cemeteries. And for extra fun, they went round the poor quarters lobbing grenades through house windows."

Will closed his eyes. As Sam described them, he saw scenes of merciless cruelty, of Fascist machine-guns cutting down innocent and defenceless civilians, continuing into the night illuminated by searchlights; of hundreds made to dig their own graves before being murdered; of many buried alive.

"I know we're a pretty poor bunch to set against such professional butchers," concluded Sam, "so we'll need to do battle with the ferocity of ten men. Even then it'll not be enough, but we'll have paid our dues to what we believe in."

Ike's military training continued for several days. Will learnt how to carry the wounded under fire; he became adept with a stretcher; he learnt first-aid and for several hours a day he took driving lessons from Candy Sam till he could swing Peg around as though he was born to it.

As Sam had promised, Will had been provided with a four-poster bed all to himself. The château, amid forests a few miles south of the Loire, belonged to a gentle, silver-haired old man, partially blind, called Philippe. Sam said he was a count, a real aristocrat, but he did not conform to Will's idea of such folks.

For one thing, Philippe dressed more like a gardener than a lord, and there were undarned holes in his shabby jacket. He had one servant to cook for him and to help look after the ageing château: to till the vast, overgrown vegetable gardens, care for the orchards and husband the château's vast stretches of forest.

The air smelt of rising damp; the atmosphere was of decay. Yet Will knew he would be sorry to leave. "Why is Philippe taking such a risk and helping us?" he had asked Sam.

"Because of tragic memories," was the reply. "This old place is crammed full of them, and of dreams of what might have been. Philippe had two sons. The first was killed in the

Great War. Marcel, his second son, was my friend. A painter too.

"As you know, Molly and I lived with our uncle on a farm in Sussex. One brilliant summer's day a couple of years ago, when the wheatfields shone like gold, up our lane came Marcel, cycling and whistling, with his easel and his paints slung across his shoulder.

"He took one look at Molly and stayed a month, coming back several times afterwards. We expected him this summer —till the war broke out. He was among the first volunteers. Who knows, he might have fought alongside your Da in Spain. He was in the country for only four days. Philippe has no more sons."

Will lay awake in his four-poster watching the moonlight through an uncurtained window. He was thinking, the same silver light could be seen at this moment over Jarrow, sprinkled across the choppy Tyne. Tomorrow the dole queues would form up again. Men would faint in the cold for lack of food.

At least Jarrow was better off than Madrid, his mother's home, for though it had been robbed of its livelihood, death did not pour down from the night sky.

He could not sleep. He got up, opened the window and stared out. The moon gazed down at its own reflection in a lily pond. He was about to return to bed when he heard a footfall on the gravel below.

Though it could have been any of his friends taking a last turn around the gardens, Will knew instinctively and instantly that the noise was caused by a prowler. He leaned out just in time to catch sight of a shadow flitting towards the avenue of trees which curved away to the château entrance.

Will dragged on his boots. He skidded on to the carpetless stairs, then down into the hall. He saw the man again, a hundred yards away now, keeping to the grass verge.

The hall doors were not locked. Will paused on the ornate steps. From far off came a sawing chorus of grasshoppers. There was a sea-song in the pines.

He followed the man, ducking behind trees when he thought he might be glancing behind him. It was about a quarter of a mile to the main gates. These were made of wrought-iron, some fifteen feet high, chained shut. He was near enough to see the stone corncobs on the stout gateposts.

The intruder had stopped. He was signalling with a torch. Out of the pitch-black screen of trees came a reply—the wink of headlights. Police!

Will stood rock still between the trees. He saw the profiles of vehicles. Three cars, probably more. My God, there's going to be a raid! Still in line with the trees, he sprinted back to the château. He leapt the stairs. His boots echoed through the sleeping house. The loose banisters nearly broke away in his hands.

"Sam! Sam! The French police have caught up with us!"

No one cared to question Will's evidence. Within two minutes, the Seven Bells Brigade was dressed, armed, alert and awaiting orders from Candy Sam. By the main entrance stood Philippe as though prepared to fight off the whole French army should it dare to advance over his front doorstep.

"We'll have to slip out the back way," said Howard. "Through the birchwoods."

Candy Sam was not so sure. "That would give us ten minutes' start at the most. No, we need a diversion of some kind."

"We could tackle 'em head on," suggested Ike.

"I've another idea." Candy Sam crossed to Philippe. He took his arm. "Do you remember, Count, the practical jokes you were so famous for years ago? Marcel used to have us in stitches telling us about them—how you once auctioned off the Eiffel Tower at a conference of Yankee businessmen!"

Sam picked up the telephone from the table in a doorside alcove. "Here's your chance to go one better and at the same time assist the cause of the Republic."

The old man and the young man conferred, heads almost

touching. Count Philippe began to nod. His face was lit by
a boyish grin.

"Vive la Liberté!"

Philippe proceeded to make two telephone calls. Will
could understand nothing of what he said, but the note of
urgency, of excitement in the old man's voice, was clear
enough.

"What's happening?" asked Ben in a shaky whisper.

"We've just located a very serious outbreak of fire under
the Count's four-poster . . . And quite rightly, Philippe has
reported to the local constabulary that there are several sus-
picious-looking vehicles at the château gates."

"But that will——"

"Make things very crowded, yes."

They lined up to bid the Count farewell. They shook
hands. Then, in single file, they slipped through the kitchen
door into darkness.

Only Will seemed to have caught the Count's last words.
He paused for a brief second. The words glimmered like
clear lights in his brain:

"Above all things, protect the Freedom Tree."

The Freedom Tree, the Freedom Tree, the name echoed
to the sound of Will's footsteps. He tried to remember if his
Da had ever mentioned it to him; perhaps Mam had once
told him a story about it. He was in too much haste to
remember.

Out in the fresh air; backs bent below the prickly hedge
of the vegetable garden; breath sucked in and held.

Leafless trees in the orchard poked crinkly fingers into the
moonlight. Beyond were the outhouses where old Peg
waited with folded wings and a full tank of petrol.

"If they find them guns," growled Ike, "we'll be breakin'
rocks till Christ's second comin'."

"Mouths shut, everybody."

The outhouse doors were swung open. "Ike, up front with
Howard. The rest, on your bellies inside. It's still possible
things might go bang in the night."

"You'd best 'and out the rifles, then," said Griff.

"No, we're saving our bullets for Franco."

With trembling hands, Roland took out his handkerchief and began to polish his glasses. "Tension mounts, as the newspapers like to say."

They counted the seconds. The seconds dragged into minutes. Will could hear Sam's fingers drumming on Peg's steering wheel. "Hark at those grasshoppers. How do they make that awful racket, Roland?"

"Rubbing their back legs together."

"Thanks. That seems a pretty clever thing to do."

Time, the ticking of watches, the beating of hearts, each man listening to the other's breathing.

Then: "Here they come!"

The distant silence was swallowed by the clanging of a bell. "Highly efficient, these French fire brigades."

The roar from one direction was greeted by the roar from another. The local gendarmes were, it seemed, as quick off the mark as the fire brigade.

They met, amid a blaze of headlights and a screech of brakes, in front of the corncob gates. Men poured out on to the gravel. Voices were raised in query and protest. Orders were slapped down by counter-orders.

The night rang with claims of precedence: fires had first claim— "Non, non!" Police matters took precedence—and anyway, who the devil were these people blocking the road already? Strangers, plain-clothes men from the capital, were they? We'll see about that!

"Vive le Comte!" exclaimed Candy Sam. "Got your maps ready, Howard? We'll be needing them."

Peg spluttered into life. "Silent as the wind, old girl." She couldn't quite obey. Her roar was deafening, but the entangled voices by the gates were raised too high to hear her.

She rolled from the outhouse. She forged through the trees, leaving behind her a cloud of vapour.

"There goes the fire bell again. Those chaps'll come to blows if I'm not mistaken."

"What if they finds there's no fire, Sam?" called Griff.

"Won't Philippe get into trouble?" Roland wanted to know.

"It all depends."

They crossed a shallow, reed-filled river and passed over a cattle grid. The rear gate of the château was wide open.

"Depends on what, Sam?"

"Whether they catch the evidence!"

CHAPTER FOUR

Candy Sam ordered a stop for breakfast at three o'clock in the afternoon. They had driven out of darkness into a day of summer warmth. Although it was November, the ground seemed parched. A heat haze shimmered along the pine avenues, turning the roads into glistening rivers.

Howard had navigated Peg through twisting byways, through villages where the road was scarcely more than a mud track, even through farmyards, where chickens and ducks and geese were sent squawking in all directions.

Now they sat in the open beside a shallow, white-pebbled river, passing round a bottle of red wine. "By this time," estimated Sam, "the police will have mounted blockades at every regular crossing point into Spain." He stood up. "There's nothing for it but to go over the top." Faces were troubled, heads shook worriedly.

"Over the top o' what, Sam?" asked Griff, finishing his turn at the wine bottle.

"The Pyrenees. Europe's highest mountain range. Mountains and snowstorms could very well be Peg's speciality. Think you can find a way, Howard?"

"The Col de Puymorens, that's a possibility. Only at this time of year it could be under fifteen feet of snow."

"It's that or festering in a French prison, eating snails. Right, everybody, get yourselves into winter woollies. Reach them out, Ben."

Roland came round from the front of Peg where he had been checking the carburetter and the fuel pipe.

"Will she make it, Roland?"

"She'd scale Everest would this old hoss. But if we hit snow, keep up the revs. Stay in third gear as long as possible."

Will sat between Candy Sam and Howard feeling like a potato being roasted in its jacket. He wore corduroys, an inch-thick woollen sweater up to his neck, a windjammer on top of that and a woollen foraging cap pulled down over his ears.

"I'm meltin' like a pound o' lard," grumbled Griff in the back.

The road bid an abrupt goodbye to the level fields. The processions of green poplar were all at once below them. The fields were patchworks of green, brown and the golden stubble of harvested wheat.

Villages balanced precariously on steep slopes sprinkled with outcrops of white rock. There was a coolness in the air.

"Smell the breath of the mountains, Will?" asked Sam.

"How high are we going?"

"Put it this way, if you climbed to the peak of Ben Nevis, you'd be only two thirds there."

"And if there's snow?"

"We've spades or sacking. We'll be a public service." Candy Sam glanced in his mirror. "And—and we can count ourselves lucky that there's only one police car right behind us."

Howard shot round in dismay. "All those detours for nothing!"

"Rubbish, Howard. At least they're not between us and the mountain. Flat on your faces, everybody. We've a spot of trouble." Sam had accelerated. He moved into the centre of the narrow, winding road.

"Steady, mes enfants—no overtaking on hairpin bends, it's against the law."

"They'll fire, Sam, if we don't stop."

"Less blather, Howard, and keep a look out."

The sleek black police car had swung over to Peg's left; Sam swung Peg over to Peg's left. "Attention, monsieur! Pas pushez past moi s'il vous wish to avoidez un très unpleasant mal de tête!"

Will had nothing to hold on to. One second he was being shouldered upright by Sam, the next by Howard. Peg swung, braked, swung. The police car was full in the driver's mirror, then there was a gaping vision of the empty valley below.

Howard was for surrender. "Stop, Sam, or you'll kill us all."

"Here, have some barley sugar and calm down."

"You've got to stop!"

"These guns are going to Spain!"

When repeated flashes of headlights failed to check Peg's progress, the police car's horn began a continuous blare.

"But if we meet something coming down hill?"

"We close our eyes and say bon nuit!"

On a right-hand bend, Candy Sam leaned his head out of the window. "A bas le tyrannie!" he bellowed. "Aux armes, citoyens! Lieb Vaterland! And the Maple Leaf for ever!"

A bullet whistled into Peg's rump.

"Now that wasn't a particularly friendly gesture. Anybody hurt back there?"

"Okay in here, Sam. Just a crack of daylight."

Stung by the hot lead, Peg took a bend too quickly for comfort, pitching over on two wheels. Will stared below him. There was nothing but space. He pulled his head away from the view. At the same time, a second bullet burst through the cab.

It left a hole where Will had been sitting.

"A neat body swerve on the wing there, Will. If we ever come out of this alive, I'll get you a trial at St James's Park."

Peg's rear wheels skidded outwards. The edge of the road gave way. It crumbled. Fragments of rock and soil tippled into the void.

"Pull over, Sam!"

"That better?"

"Two inches better."

"Got to remember what Roland said—mustn't lose revs."

A third bullet struck Peg, glancing off her on the turn. A fourth missed but the sound of it stirred an echo in the gaunt cliff face above them.

"Here comes the snow." They braked, they climbed; round one hairpin bend after another, the steering wheel spinning, caught, spun again. "Thicker and thicker!"

Mountain and sky met in a haze of white. Afternoon had slipped into evening and evening into night almost in the closing of an eyelid.

"Oh my God," cried Howard, "look at those drifts!"

"Any minute now, we're going to have to get out and push."

"While those police are firing at us? We've had it, why don't you realise?"

Two more bullets bored their way into Peg's flanks.

"Reach me my pistol will you, lad?" Sam asked Will. "I think I've had enough of being mistaken for a clay pigeon."

Candy Sam waited for the road to straighten. With one hand he held the steering wheel, with the other, he took aim through the rear mirror. For the twentieth time the police car fought to pass between Peg and the snow-covered verge.

Bang!

"Got a headlight!"

Bang! A return shot. A mudguard holed, but not the precious tyres. Hands back on the wheel. Round the hairpin, skidding on the snow surface. So difficult to pull her on line again. To and fro, sliding.

"Come on, Peg!" Engine grinding, straining in third gear, begging to be changed down into second. Instead, Sam stood on the accelerator till it hit the floor, pumping it. "Sorry to bother you, Howard, but you'll have to do the shooting."

"Never! Not against the French."

"They're shooting at us, you crazy prune! We've no alternative."

"Yes we have. We can stop. Give ourselves up."

"Listen!" Candy Sam's voice rose shrill above the engine. "We go over the top, or we go over there!" He pointed to the precipice. "I mean it!"

Howard took the pistol. "It's all wrong. You're risking the lives of——"

"For Mother Hubbard's sake, get on with it!"

At first Howard could not get the window down. Then in came a blast of ice-laden wind.

"Go for the tyres."

"Hold her steady, then."

Snow billowed into the cab.

"Round we go. I'm making for the right verge, Howard, so he'll come at us on the left. Action stations!"

Howard had opened Peg's offside door. "Grab it, Will. Keep it from swinging." Will lay flat, arm outstretched, fist clamped round the handle. Howard's foot was on the running board.

"Shoot, man!"

"How can I when you're swaying about?"

"It's the ice—now shoot!"

Too late. The next bend was upon them. They skidded round it, advancing at a slant. "Again!"

"I can't. This blizzard!"

"The road to hell is paved with good intentions. Pull that trigger!"

Howard's first shot was lost in space. He was in the centre of the snowstorm. He was covered in white. But he took aim.

"Two seconds to turning!"

Bang!

"Hit her?"

"Don't know."

"Try again." Candy Sam looked in the mirror. "Yes! Radiator's leaking."

Howard's hand no longer shook. He waited. He ignored the blizzard. His next shot holed a tyre on the driver's side. "Done it!"

As swiftly as the cheering began, it ceased. Peg was suddenly up to her axles in snow. The truck slowed, veered—stopped.

"Oh no! Is it my imagination but——"

Will yelled out as though Sam were twenty yards away. "We're sliding backwards!"

"Not my imagination." Sam struggled to keep up the

forward revs, but Peg was on skates. She trundled straight for the motionless police car.

The three armed policemen leapt out a moment before impact. The leaking radiator was now a crushed radiator. The car bonnet sprang up, bent out of shape. Then the car slid towards the void. It heeled over into darkness.

As if well satisfied with her exploit, Peg halted within twelve feet of eternity. Her rear doors opened. Three rifles were trained on the advancing policemen.

"Messieurs, abandonnez vos armes, s'il vous plait." Sam came from round the cab, flashing his torch. Three revolvers were dropped into the snow. "Retrieve them, Griff lad. I'm sure we'll find a Spanish Republican who'll make better use of them than threatening the lives and limbs of innocent English tourists."

He strode towards the French policemen. Their heads and shoulders were fast being covered in snow. "Liberty, equality and fraternity—ever heard of those, messieurs? The French are supposed to have invented them. Shame on you!" He wagged his pistol dismissively. "Allez vous enfants de la Patrie! Le jour de glory will arrive up your posteriors if there's even a shadow of you left in five seconds."

The police understood not a word. But they understood Sam's meaning perfectly. They fled through the storm.

"Right, lads, just over the hill past that signpost sticking out of ten feet of snow, is a little town with bright lights, where we can expect a friendly Spanish welcome."

"Puigçerda," nodded Howard, who was, like the others, turning into a snowman.

"So grab the shovels and some sacking—and let's dig our way into Spain."

The feud between Will and Griff happened abruptly, unexpectedly. "No bad blood, no quarrelling!" Candy Sam had cried when, the following morning, Griff had elbowed Will away; and Will had raised his fists as though he had suffered the worst of insults.

Yet Griff had right on his side when he insisted it was his turn to ride up front with Sam and Howard. Will acknowledged this to himself. But he had dreamt of the moment when he would see Spain for the first time. He was proud. There was blood in him that belonged to Spain.

Yes, he admitted it, he wanted to ride in like a conquering hero. Now, for several hours on the journey from the mountains to Barcelona, he would have nothing but the side of the truck to stare at. The hills, the rivers, the valleys would be Griff's treat, not his.

It was only a small push, a jab in the chest, no force in it, but Will had been so enraged that Ike had to bundle him roughly into the back of Peg.

"Don't spoil a good breakfast, lad," he had said.

"Here, Will." Roland was sympathetic. "You can watch the view through the cab window. There'll be nothing but snow for a while."

Will did not take up the offer. He sat down where he was and battled with feelings he could scarcely understand. After all, everything had gone so well for Candy Sam's expedition: Peg had scaled the Pyrenees; the Seven Bells Brigade had been welcomed with lavish hospitality by Señor Hernandez, proprietor of a small hotel recommended by Count Philippe, and the steak the Spaniard served—on the house—was the best slice of meat Will had ever tasted.

Yet Señor Hernandez had only bad news to recount of the war. Supported by German and Italian aircraft and guns, Franco's rebel army held half of Spain; Government forces were being driven back on all fronts. Madrid, still holding out for the Republic, was bombed daily and there were reports of street battles between Government troops and the advance guard of Franco's Army of Africa.

Franco's control stretched in pincer formation around Spain's capital. It commanded the Straits of Gibraltar and southern cities such as Seville and Granada, then swept north to Corunna, north-east to Pamplona, isolating the Basque country from the rest of Republican Spain.

Even the central and north-western regions that had remained loyal to the Government were in imminent danger
of being surrounded as Franco consolidated his grip on
Saragossa and Teruel.

To add to the Government's difficulties, Franco commanded the sea. His battleships had bombarded those
southern ports which continued to fly the red, yellow and
purple flag of the Republic.

The latest and most disturbing news was of the formation
of a special German air command—the Condor Legion
under General Von Sperrle, comprising, so a radio report
had estimated, four bomber squadrons of twelve bombers
each.

With these German hammers—Junkers 52, Heinkels 51
and Messerschmidts 109—Franco would beat Madrid into
surrender. On 30th October, Señor Hernandez said, sixty
children had been among those who had been bombed to
death at Getalfe near the capital.

Will bore all this heavily in his mind. In face of such
despairing circumstances, he felt his own life threatening
to fall apart. Nothing was secure, and being relegated to
the darkness of Peg's interior increased his growing
dismay. Against all the laws of justice, the forces of evil
were prevailing. That was not how he had expected it to
be.

But the facts were clear as daylight: Goliath was triumph-
ing over David. Against thousands of trained German pilots,
against the most powerful weapons of war the world had
ever seen, what could international volunteers such as the
Seven Bells Brigade do except retreat and die?

The others shared Will's gloom and it took all Candy
Sam's irrepressible cheerfulness to put the spirit back into
his comrades.

"Be grateful for small mercies, my friends. The Russians
are sending arms for the Republic and Mexico is keeping her
promises of aid. One good Republican victory might turn
the tide. And you'll see—the International Brigades will

keep the Fascists out of Madrid. No pasarán! They shall not pass! Come on, you lot in there. Repeat after me."

A sky of deepest blue stretched between the Alps as Peg, spiralling ever downwards, left the snow behind. The landscape of smoky valleys and villages nestling under the hills betrayed no sign that here was a country at war with itself. There were no checkpoints, no men in uniform, no military vehicles. Even when Sam drove into Barcelona, capital of Catalonia and the largest Mediterranean city still under government control, the atmosphere was more like that of a fiesta than a time of war.

Hundreds of Republican and Catalan flags fluttered from roofs and windows, while along the Ramblas—elegant boulevards lined with trees—the entire population seemed to be out for a leisurely stroll in the autumn sun.

Only the long queues of women outside bread shops hinted at the true plight of the city. Beyond the western horizon, and just beyond earshot, the thunder of war rolled across the limestone hills of Aragon.

According to Señor Hernandez, the likeliest place to meet up with the British volunteer medical team and perhaps find Sam's sister Molly, was the Lenin Barracks. It was also where the Seven Bells Brigade might receive an official posting to the war front.

"Come on, Will," Sam called through the cab window. "Stretch your legs and let's see what's going on." Will had visions of a barracks bristling with action, of soldiers being marched in formation across the drill square. Instead, the only observable activity was a football match played between chalked goals.

The barracks had once been a stone-built palace of great nobility with what looked like a riding school attached. They were guarded by ill-clad sentries—without guns.

"Maybe we've come to the wrong place," suggested Will.

Sam shook his head. "I'm afraid this is how bad things have got for the Republic." For a minute, they watched the game. "Those'll be volunteers. Not one of them a day over eighteen, and plenty your age, Will."

They could find no one in authority, no officers, no sergeants, no one who had the slightest idea who was actually in charge. The only information they could gather was that the last batch of trainees had gone up to the front a few days earlier, escorted by brass bands and cheered on by thousands—who, it seemed, had now promptly forgotten them.

"Are we wise to be throwing in our lot with people like this?" Howard asked when Sam and Will returned.

"People like what, Howard?"

"Well . . . who've no——"

"Discipline?"

"Show me their commanders, then. I mean, the enemy could take the barracks with pea-shooters."

"The sooner we remember this isn't the damned Horse-guards' Parade, Howard, the better. Spaniards in these parts don't snap to attention as readily as the British. Orders have to be good orders before they'll obey them. But that doesn't mean they can't fight bravely when the time comes."

"I go along with that," nodded Roland. "But there's more to winning wars than just bravery."

"Look," said Ike, "now they're sending schoolboys to the front. Señor Hernandez didn't tell us things were this bad."

"Bad, señor?" The voice sprang from behind them. "Bad? They is not only bad, they is bloody hell fire calamity!" A tall, swarthy, warm-smiling Spaniard held out his hand. "Salud, comrades, and Rule Britannia!"

His teeth gleamed from under a floppy black moustache. He wore a zip-up waterproof jacket and a green forage cap. At his throat was a scarlet neckscarf.

"Federico the Basque man, at your conveniences." On a long cord across his shoulders, he carried a violin, about half the usual size, with a miniature bow tied on with string.

"Two years since ago, I make visit to your cow-ntry. Now I spick the Een-glish like the cannibal, eh?"

The day had all at once improved. Federico's crazy language turned serious matters on their head. He gathered the Seven Bells Brigade round him and took them into a bar for a drink.

"You no enquire extra at barracks. Cha-os it drive you round the bends quicker than you winkle the eye."

Will felt at home. These Spaniards—Federico, the barman who refilled the wine glasses before they were emptied, his merry wife who served huge omelettes, or tortillas as Federico called them—were as friendly and as welcoming as folks back home on Tyneside.

Federico had been wounded on the Aragon front. "But I listen you ask 'ow arrive this hombre from the Basque cow-ntry and the famous Bay of Biscay, where all the best Spaniards they live, to Catalonia where the wine taste like cat pees?"

He explained that like so many others he had been caught by the sudden outbreak of the war. Thousands of Spaniards, on business, visiting relatives, taking holidays, had woken up one morning in July to discover the roar of artillery and the snap of rifle fire had cut them off from their homes.

Though he had been shot in the thigh and found difficulty walking, Federico did a fair imitation of an Olympic high jumper when Candy Sam led him to Peg and told him of the arms she carried.

"Vivan los ingleses! Now we smoke up the vermin like Greek lighting . . . Where you unload these arms, eh?"

"Where there's most need."

"Then you come to Aragon. We got no guns, no bullets, no tinned 'elmets—nothing but cotton socks and chocolate to make good the bowels. You come!"

Sam hesitated. "We had planned to go south, to the HQ of the International Brigades at Albacete. Part of my own mission is to find my sister." He took out a postcard picture of Molly. "Have you ever seen her? She volunteered for Medical Aid. Her last letter was from Barcelona."

Federico handed back the photograph. "She much

beautiful. But I no such lucky. Still, is possible she at Lerida, or even already at front—if she brave and crazy.

"Stay, comrades—you fight 'ere. I mean, why you waste precious petrol? Albacete is miserable dump. It rain there worse than Manchester City." His giant hands closed round Sam's shoulder.

"Our need in Aragon is terrible bad. Stay, please very much. For a month! For a week! You know what gun I fire at front! I share German Mauser, made in 1896. Is true! I get it shoot twice the bleeding fortnight."

Sam knew his prime duty was to fight where the Republic needed him; that is what Molly would have told him to do. He glanced at the rest of the Seven Bells Brigade.

"With guns," urged Federico, "maybe we make big breakout. Win war before Christmas! Federico the Basque man—he beg you!"

CHAPTER FIVE

Will and Griff raced to be first in the driver's cab. Will proved nippier. They had not exchanged a word all day and now they recoiled from each other like the worst of enemies.

"Watch it, you two!" warned Sam. "The war's over who rules Spain, not who rides up front in Peg. Why're you behaving like spoilt kids all of a sudden?"

"Because 'e's gettin all the perks," complained Griff. "Teacher's pet."

Federico held the two apart as blows fanned the air. "Good—you is in fighting mood. I promise you much fight."

"All right, if we're playing games," said Sam, "then you'll take turn and turn about. Meantime, get these down you." He handed Will and Griff sticks of barley sugar. "And for God's sake don't let me have to give you both a leathering."

Once more Peg climbed hilly, winding and bumpy roads. The villages she passed through seemed to have been cast into a deep slumber; all doors were locked, the streets deserted.

The air became colder, trees grew sparser and the reddish soil of the coast changed to moorland. Colour drained from the landscape leaving only green and the grey-white of limestone. "It reminds me of Northumberland," said Will. "Up on Hadrian's Wall." He asked Federico why so many churches they passed were gutted by fire.

"In my cow-ntry, there is old saying: all Spain it run after the church, one half with candle, other half with big stick. Today is day of stick. This war, it much about the land— who possess the land. The church, it own millions of land. When Government say, land must go to people—boom! Priests, they take side of Franco." He paused. "Exception, that is, for good priests of Basque cow-ntry. They say hearts first, not the pocket, so we no cut their throats, eh?"

They reached Sietamo, a grey town among grey, wind-swept hills. Federico said it had been fought over, won and lost, several times. Then on, higher, into mist, heavy with drizzle, to Alcubierre, even more desolate that Sietamo; a grey fortress of stone.

"Like an El Greco painting," said Candy Sam.

"All España it like El Greco, my friend. Full of the melo-drama and the anguish."

They were in a street blasted by enemy shells. Federico asked Sam to pull up for a moment. "How do you say? Our tourist spot. But it not yet mention in guidebook."

He indicated a wall set back from the road. It was spat-tered with bullet holes. "One day, the Fascists, they shoot our boys. The next day our boys they shoot the Fascists. All Spaniards!

"Say the big cheerio to peace and comfort," warned Federico after another mile or two of mist and rain. " 'ere, it no more like Meester El Greco. Now we see paintings of Goya—monsters and peoples that is bewitched. 'ere Saturn 'e devour 'is children morning noose and night!"

The Seven Bells Brigade was given a clamorous welcome at the front. Vivan los ingleses!—Long live the English, went up the cry as Candy Sam's hoard of weapons and ammuni-tion was displayed. Not only were rifles and bullets distri-buted, and three Maxim machine-guns, but packets of Woodbine and precious boxes of matches.

In thanks, there was wine, bowls of over-salted soup, slaps on the back from eager but dirty-faced militiamen who looked more like mountain bandits than soldiers.

The older men took the new issue of rifles, passing their ancient carbines on to the younger recruits. There was much chatter in the language of the Catalans and yells of "Visca POUM!" and "Fascistas-maricones!"

The Spanish Will's mother had taught him was to become a valuable asset to the Seven Bells Brigade and he was de-lighted he was able to understand the questions the militia-men asked of the newcomers: were there any parcels and letters on the way? What about the promised issue of helmets?

Sam was pressed with requests as though he were Father Christmas and Peg his magic sleigh full of gifts. Had he, by any chance, brought field glasses?—only two pairs! Wire cutters, then?—no! Range finders, gun-oil, pull-throughs, a lantern or two?

At least he had brought electric torches—but only five for a whole army? In the face of so much need, it hardly seemed worth distributing the 150 hand-grenades stored in sawdust. Yet they were greeted with the biggest cheer of all.

Nobody, it seemed, had ever set eyes on a hand-grenade before.

"Where are the officers?" Howard wanted to know.

"No officers," replied Federico. "These is what you call the Anarchist regiments. They do not believe in officers, or stripes."

"Then who the devil gives the orders?"

Federico grinned widely. "The will of the peoples, it give the orders. The Catalans, they very lovable mens."

"This is no way to run a war."

Candy Sam took Howard's arm. "Let's give it a try, shall we?"

Celebrations over, Federico introduced the Seven Bells Brigade to what was to be " 'ome sweet 'ouse" for the indefinite future. The trench was like a gigantic eyelid below the brow of the hill. About fifty yards in diameter, it was fortified with a wall of sandbags inside of which was a limestone parapet. Below, the ground was a maze of dug-outs.

Another record, decided Will as he climbed into the trench. He'd never experienced a stink like this one.

"My God!" howled Griff. "This isn't mud—it's shit!"

They were up to their ankles in human excrement and, apart from the guard position along the parapet, there was nowhere else to stand.

"You expect the Savoy Hotel, comrades?" asked Federico, amused.

"The stench alone will kill us," protested Howard. "This is the fruit of ill-discipline."

"Shit, it make you grow tall. But if you no like, you 'ave alternative, my friend. Stand up, and the bullet it kill you. Any shakes, dead man he smell worse than shit."

"What's this you said about us getting ten pesetas a day?" Griff asked.

Before he could receive an answer, a gun went off, followed by a terrified scream. "Down!" The whole contingent dropped flat in the mud. Federico was running towards the parapet.

"It's just a lad!" called Ike.

"What happened?"

"Shot 'imself, with 'is first rifle!"

The youth had collapsed into the dug-out below the parapet. His cries of pain and fear panicked two other sixteen year olds. They dropped their rifles. They looked wildly, helplessly from side to side. They began to run.

Sam had moved up behind Federico. He got the first youth by the ankle before he could climb into the firing range of the enemy. Federico trapped the other as he tried to flee through the dug-outs. His voice was a lion's roar. His open hand sent the youth reeling into mud.

The shots, the cries, the disturbance, brought an immediate response from the Fascist trenches opposite. Echoing valley, darkening sky were raked with gunfire.

The wounded youth was curled up, knees to his chin, sobbing like a child who had been beaten for something he had not done. Federico and Sam lifted him from the mud. "Easy does it, keep him sitting up."

"You medical man, Sam?"

Roland had come forward to help. "He's bad. The First Aid box is still in Peg."

"I'll fetch it," volunteered Will.

"Serious is it?" called Ike above the gunfire, his own rifle warm from action.

"Blown a hole through his shoulder big as a golf ball."

Candy Sam fished in his windjammer pocket. "Suck this, lad. Best English barley sugar . . . He needs hospital right away, Fred."

Will had got half way over the hill behind which Peg was concealed before he realised, with a terrible shock, that the enemy was actually firing at *him*.

A bullet struck rock little more than a stride away from him. He'd not even zig-zagged as he and his pals had done fighting the Great War on Jarrow Slake, and as Ike had instructed him to do.

"This is for real," he muttered. "Why didn't somebody remind me?"

It was a great relief to find he would not have to make the return journey just yet. A slight lull in the firing was the signal for Candy Sam and Federico to carry the wounded boy out of the trenches—though not the way Will had chosen.

Sam was mad at him. "That was the world's stupidest thing to do!" They were crouched together behind a protective shoulder of limestone. "Did you want a machine-gun to cut you in two?" He pointed. "There's the safe way up. Use it in future!"

With the darkness came the cold. A wintry wind darted in cruel gusts along the parapets, sweeping dust and grit into the dug-outs. There would have been silence but for the trickle of limestone scree from above, and the hacking cough of a militiaman on guard behind the wall of sandbags.

Occasionally, a single, nervous shot cracked open the peace of the night.

Ben had managed to get a small fire burning. He heated tinned soup and stewing steak on a primus stove. He scraped and diced carrots with as much pride and care as if he had been top chef in a restaurant.

"Anythin' for afters, Ben?" enquired Griff. "Somethin' sweet, like?" And the Seven Bells Brigade was promptly served with apricots topped with tinned cream.

Candy Sam and Federico returned from driving the wounded boy for medical care in Alcubierre. "Some damned hospital! A draughty barn with a hole in the roof and a surgeon on the bottle."

"Any news of Molly?"

"One or two remember an English woman up here, at the beginning of the war. She was shot dead."

"Do you think——"

"I don't know what to think."

"But if she sent you a letter?"

"She forgot to date it."

Roland was reassuring. "They'd not let a lass her age near the front, Sam."

"Pretty well anything's possible in this excuse for an army," said Howard.

"No, no, it's more likely to have been some tourist who got caught in the cross-fire. They say there are English volunteers in trenches up the valley. We'll get more news from them, Sam."

Federico finished his dinner with a relishful belch. "Your cook, Sam, 'e worth 'is weight in gold coffee pods." His appetite satisfied, he raised his violin to his shoulder. He tuned it lovingly. "This evening, gentlemens, I play you songs of the Basque cow-ntry. Close your eyes and dream of the good days, eh?"

One after another, gay melodies floated out into the damp, almost freezing night. And for once, perhaps in appreciation, the enemy guns remained silent.

Despite the bitter cold and the uneven sharpness of the limestone "bed" beneath him, Will had dozed off. Yet he could not put away from him the vision of the boy who had shot himself, of his shoulder blasted into a red hole.

In the empty silence, Will seemed to hear again the lad's screams.

He awoke. His loneliness was like a huge weight pressing his body into the ground. He saw the figure of Ben on night watch. He too was scared. In fact, if there was a trembling hands competition, Ben would take the prize. He could hardly hold a cigarette steady in the flame of a match.

Will looked round him at his sleeping companions. There was no visible movement, yet he was sure he had heard something. Below him, a brushing sound, quick, nearer, scratching at limestone.

He pulled out the torch Candy Sam had lent him.

Rats! Like an army of their own in the filthy mud at the bottom of the trench, they squirmed and fought. They were plump as cats, slow on their feet and unafraid. The torch did not bother them.

Jarrow rats, Will recollected, were smaller, zippier. While not exactly regarding them as his favourite furry animals, he had grown used to their existence on the draughty stone-floored kitchen of his home, flopping on the stairs, sometimes gnawing at the pipes and skirting boards.

Rats had a bad reputation, simply, Will felt, because along with so many humans he knew, they never got enough to eat. "We'll have to hold a Love Thy Neighbourly Rat Day."

He put down some gristle from Ben's stew. One rat skittered over the stone ridge. It hesitated outside the circle of torchlight. Will pushed the gristle forward an inch. "Come on, Roger the Plodger." Its eyes flashed blackly as it crept into the circle. "Easy now, watch the old fingers."

The rat took the gristle. It did not retreat from the torch-light. Could a rat feel loneliness? "At a count of three, you'll turn into an aeroplane. Together we'll fly over General Franco's headquarters—and finish this war once and for all."

Clearly the rat, speaking only Spanish, failed to understand this command. Instead it advanced as far as Will's outstretched hand. It took the remainder of the gristle from the middle of his palm.

"Friends? You've my permission to come again. Remember the passwords: Up the United!"

Suddenly Griff, beside him, awoke. In terror, he leapt up.

His shout must have carried to the farthest ranks of the enemy and wakened every militiaman within two miles.

He had been examining and cleaning his pistol all evening. It was in his hand. He did not aim. He did not think. He fired straight into the torchlight, once, twice, till Will screamed for him to stop—though not before the rat had been blown into a blood-seeping hulk of fur.

"That could've been me!" howled Will. The torch was out.

"Rats!" was all Griff could answer.

There were other, louder, more devastating replies. The silent edifice of the night was shattered by machine-gun fire. Across the range of vision, the darkness was peppered with flashes of green light.

Will heard nothing, saw nothing. He had gone for Griff, for the pistol that had caused such needless destruction; that had broken faith.

The feud which had begun that morning broke into open warfare. Will butted Griff in the chest. He grasped his wrist, attempting to prise the pistol from his friend's fingers. Griff's hand was in his hair. He was held fast. Tears sprang to Will's eyes as his hair was wrenched to the roots.

They were falling. First against limestone, then into the mud and excrement in the trench bottom.

Voices: "What in hell's name——"

"You two, cut it! Cut it out!"

Griff lost the pistol but gained a fist. He rammed it into Will's face. Up came his knee and caught him in the stomach.

"Break it up, for Christ's sake!"

They rolled over, cold, mud-soaked, with Will repeating, "Why did you do it? Why did you do it? You'd no right, no right!"

Other hands were reaching for them from above. They punched and they kneed. There was blood, a pounding, but Will was on top.

"Enough, do you hear!"

The hands were crane hooks dragging him up, by his

arms, his ankles. He was lifted and cast forward like a sack of coal. Now he heard the firing. He saw figures at the sandbags. He saw Ben and Ike taking aim. He saw them fire.

And he felt a slap across the ear he had not experienced since his schooldays. "On your feet, both of you!" Candy Sam was blazing. "As if we'd not enough war on our hands, you two go and start another."

"There were rats!"

"He'd no right!" insisted Will.

"Pick up your rifles. Excuses later. The Fascists think they've been raided. What a fiasco!" Sam ran up the trench. "Keep by me, you two. Any more of this and I'll have to waste a couple of my own bullets."

Will's boots slipped on the rain-dampened limestone. His knee bore the impact of his fall. His nose had been bleeding, now it was his knee's turn. It stung and stuck on the inside of his trousers.

Above him, gun flashes; around him, militiamen cracking away into the darkness.

They might as well have been firing at the stars.

Candy Sam's men saved their ammunition. Federico had not moved. He remained snoring throughout the proceedings.

As abruptly as it had begun, the firing stopped. Something had been expressed, something got off the chest; points made. Further gunfire would ruin what was left of a good night's sleep.

"Futility draws its own truce." Candy Sam sank down below the wall of sandbags. He nodded towards the still sleeping Federico. "Eventually, I suppose, we'll be able to take things as calmly as Fred . . . How meaningless it all seems at this black time of the morning. Over there, the Fascists are as miserable and shivering as we are. And they're just Spanish lads like these."

Above them, the wind muttered through the loose fragments of limestone. It quarrelled restively with the branches of stunted oaks dotted about the hills.

Will and Griff were not permitted to retire peaceful to sleep. "It's jankers for you two," announced Candy Sam.

"Jankers?"

"The equivalent of fifty Hail Marys, five hundred lines or staying in on Saturday nights." They waited. "The three of us are off to collect firewood."

Griff's mouth dropped open. "In the dark?"

"I'll do fifty Hail Marys," opted Will.

"Firewood. If old Fred were awake, he'd tell you that next to food, firewood's more precious than the Bank of England."

"Can't we leave it till tomorrow?"

"You want to go out into no-man's land—in daylight?"

Will shuddered, less with cold than with shock. "Over the trench?" he asked weakly.

"We need a day's supply, and every twig's been gathered to our rear."

"But——"

"Fred says it's as safe as houses. So long as your feet don't talk too loudly and if we keep our heads down."

"Over the trench? I mean—out there?"

"Ready?"

"I'll volunteer to wake Fred."

"You're coming. And this won't be the last time, I assure you. Leave your rifles. All you need is your pistol and knife. On a count of three—away!"

In that silence, as they climbed the limestone parapet and dropped into no-man's land, Will cursed the wasted moments of his life when he could have studied the ways of the Red Indian: how he slipped across the ground noiselessly, knees of rubber, feet at a certain angle.

But then the Red Indians wore soft mocassins, while this poor involuntary volunteer had to make do with steel-shod boots designed to make the biggest possible noise over crackly limestone.

"When you hear a shot," Sam had instructed, "drop flat on your faces. It's a thousand to one against being hit."

Every footstep, for Will, was agony because he could hear it. And if he could hear it, so could the watchful enemy. He might as well have had bells tied to his feet.

The ground dipped steeply and crookedly. Will tried to keep his legs bent as Davy Crocket might have advised. Yet even if he softened his own step, he could still hear Griff behind him.

Boulders were the chief hazard and Will Crocket tripped straight over one. He fell among firewood.

"Roots!"

"Drag them up, then."

He was grateful to halt this progress towards the enemy lines. He hacked at the rough limb of stunted oak. "This'll never burn in a month of Sundays." The tree took five minutes' sawing. It quivered and fought for its survival until Will began to feel sorry for it. Yet he moved on. He saw Griff twisting a shrub from its roots and, ahead, Candy Sam severing everything in his way that would burn.

They were almost at the bottom of the valley between the opposing armies. The darkness seemed to be more complete there than it had been fifty yards nearer the sky. When Candy Sam stopped, Will and Griff stopped.

All at once: "Down!"

Flat. Another knee damaged. Will had got the prickly oak right under him.

"Somebody approaching."

The pulses of Will's body beat as clearly to him as the distant crunch of boots on stone. He looked. He forced his eyes wide open and still could discern nothing against the ebony hillside.

"Night patrol. A dozen, I guess."

Coming this way.

There were so many soft but clinking footfalls that it was not hard to imagine a whole army on the advance. The empty darkness had become a crowded street to a blind man.

The hill swooped high above them. It bulged into a ridge

over their heads and thus the enemy patrol appeared almost to be descending from the clouds.

"Faces down. Still as mutton."

It was sensible—white of the eyes and all that; but Will would have preferred to witness his doom.

He obeyed orders. He buried his face in his sleeve, into which he had also withdrawn his white, tell-tale hands.

The marching, scuttering, slithering feet were near enough to take a penalty. Dislodged pebbles rolled downwards in a stream. One touched Will's foot. He was so numb, so still, that he had the feeling he was already dead: killed by shock.

They were coming straight on, ten yards away. Less. He drew in a breath. He held it and somehow his pulses beat all the louder. Though he did not see the patrol, Will knew its presence, its outline, its solidity and he could practically count, one by one, the bayoneted rifles piercing the dark.

He needed more breath. He exhaled into his sleeve. He sucked in the damp black air. He waited. He tensed himself for the entry of the bayonet. It was probably how Da was captured. A shadow, over him, alongside him. Past him. He let out his breath and his heart thundered with joy—crazy, fragile, but perfect.

The patrol had missed them.

He wished this could have been a film, one of those serials in fifteen parts. Part Fifteen: cut back to camp, mission completed, and opening Christmas parcels.

No luck. The next episode found Will Viljoen exactly where he had been lying at the last never-to-be-missed cliff-hanging moment, on his belly, bruised by stones, pricked by the stunted oak.

"Good lads!" Sam had crawled back to join Will and Griff. "Know where we are?" he whispered.

"Southend Pier," muttered Griff. "An' t'tide's comin' in, so let's be off."

"Wait. We're right under a machine-gun nest." Sam

pointed upwards to where the hilltop vanished in mist. "Tempting, isn't it?"

"Temptin' bloody what?"

"What do you think?—in for a penny, in for a pound."

"That's what I said when I got meself into this mess."

"We've only pistols," urged Will, the thunder of joy totally faded.

"I've grenades."

Will's mind ticked forward in time: how would they manage the return journey? What about the foot patrol out there in no-man's land?

Candy Sam had started to unlace his boots. "It's too risky for you lads. Here, take the boots and my firewood. That could very well be old Philippe's Freedom Tree, Will, it's so stunted.

"At the double, now, back to the trench. I'll give you sixty seconds to be on your way."

They scrambled a few yards. They turned to watch him go. "Who the 'ell does 'e think 'e is? We gets the jankers carryin' wood, an' 'e gets the fun lobbin' grenades."

Will nodded in agreement. It would have been a chance to do his Da proud, and one in the eye for Franco, but he slung Sam's boots over his shoulder. "Come on."

They hesitated. They glanced at each other. "Which way?"

In the dark, north, south, east and west wore the same featureless mask. The stars were overclouded, and anyway neither Will nor Griff could read the stars.

The thought of crawling into a trench and finding not Federico and the Seven Bells Brigade but a scowling enemy, made Will stop. "We need to take our bearings."

Instinctively, they crouched down and at the very same moment the hill halfway up the sky burst into flame. An explosion raised the lid of darkness.

"He managed it!"

Smaller explosions burst on the heels of the first.

" 'e's not just an arty-farty artist after all."

There was one second of silence before the entire battlefront unleased its armoury. Somehow the blackness made things worse. Distances closed in. Between a machine-gun barrel and the victim was sightlessness—no matter that in daylight you couldn't see the bullets either.

Head down, smelling the bitter winter earth, hands clamped over ears. A bullet smashed stone close by. Another ricocheted off rocks to left or right.

Will raised his eyes as the intensity of the gunfire wavered —and got the very worst shock of his life. His gaze fell on another face.

The enemy soldier lay belly down, pointing in the direction of his own trenches as Will and Griff were pointing at theirs. He was as terrified as Will—and as young: wan faced, pop-eyed, immovable as though his limbs had been driven into the ground with wooden stakes.

If he was armed, there was no sign of it. At the sight of two of the enemy, he rolled sideways like a rabbit springing from the hand about to descend upon its neck.

Will said "Please!" It was all he could think of: please— don't do anything, don't shoot, don't run. But Griff cut words. This was the closest bang, the closest bullet and it drowned Will's anguished "No, Griff!"

Too late. The bullet was straight. The enemy turned half in a circle. His hand was raised as if to some invisible support, some arm held out to him in the last flash of his living mind.

His pop-eyed face fell back before the rest of him.

"There was no need!"

" 'im or us."

"He'd no gun."

"Beggar that!"

Will was across the body. "If he's only wounded——"

"Forget 'im. 'e's dead."

The young Spaniard lay as only the dead lie. Yet Will would not let him go. Feebly, he bent over him, willing breath back into him.

"Sorry, sorry . . ."

He no longer heard the flying bullets. He did not care whether they struck him. The pop eyes were in his head. He could see nothing but them.

One life. Sixteen years of caring and loving and feeding, of laughing and crying and running and talking—turned, in a single moment, to cold flesh.

Will cocked his head. He lifted himself. Great waves of nausea drove upwards through him. He was sick in his throat, sick down his nostrils.

When the nausea departed it was replaced by anger and disgust. His mind had never prepared itself for this. It had imagined other, nobler pictures—all shattered.

In these seconds, Will's hatred was not for the Fascists but for Griff. The look in his companion's eyes—which again and again reverted to the dead Spaniard—was of pride. He was glad of what he had done.

They lay flat and the guns split the heavens.

"What's that?"

A shadow flitted between rocks above them. Once more, Griff levelled his pistol. There were rapid footsteps on the limestone scree.

"Wait, Griff!" hissed Will. "It might be——"

Griff fired.

Candy Sam dived forward on to the ground. "Mind where you aim that thing, lad!" The bullet had missed him by a fraction. His face steamed with sweat. He gulped for breath.

"Managed it! Saw me first, though. Close thing . . . Bullet through my sleeve . . . Boots? Ta . . . Have to send to Woollies for a new pair of feet."

He peered forward. "Who's this?"

"I shot 'im."

"How're you feeling?"

"Good."

"Brave lad."

Will held his peace.

"Saved Will's life, did you?"

"You could say that."

Will gathered up the firewood they had collected. He felt no fear, for he felt nothing. He was changed. Something—perhaps everything—of his past self lay with the young Spaniard.

He took out his pistol. He handed it to Sam once they had climbed to safety in the Republican lines. "Give it somebody else, please. I want none of it."

CHAPTER SIX

"Are we to be stuck in this rat hole till they sell our bones for compost?" Ike's words echoed the thoughts of the Seven Bells Brigade. Days had stumbled heavy-footed into weeks. "We don't advance, we don't retreat. All we do is shy at one another to remind us there's somebody out there."

"Just the same, there've been plenty of casualties," Howard said.

"Aye, but only because the lads were bored out of their heads and got careless," observed Roland. "Sometimes I think catching a bullet'd be the smart thing to do, what with the freezing nights and these ruddy lice sucking away our life's blood."

Two sides of equal strength and equal weakness, the combatants on the Aragon front waited for orders; they waited for reinforcements, for developments beyond their control. True, there was action: alerts occurred several times a day. A trigger pulled by accident would set the whole battlefield ablaze.

The most important thing in the world had become firewood. The winter cold was bitter and crushing. It was the worst enemy and fighting it was worth the risk of bullets. The hunt for stunted oak and rosemary—both sparse and reluctant to catch alight—was relentless.

Will was not asked to bear a rifle or a pistol again. His weapons were the scout knife and the stretcher. He became a loner. The menace of bullets no longer worried him. The prospect of death was less horrifying than a night without the warmth of a fire.

Soon his excursions into no-man's land were carried out in broad daylight. He ignored the bullets that winged over him. Somehow, he learnt, bullets never seem to get close to the ground; at least not at this distance from the enemy lines.

Such ventures gave him not so much courage as cold nerve—useful later when, after a small but disastrous attack by the Republicans on the Fascist positions, casualties had to be brought in. Will and Griff, on speaking terms again after their differences, ducked machine-gun fire three times to drag badly wounded youths to safety.

Will lived from hour to hour. It occurred to him as he sat hunched over firelight during the endless winter nights, that he had almost forgotten about the war, forgotten why he had been so determined to fight in Spain. "Somebody back in Jarrow would know more of what's going on here than I do," he confessed to Candy Sam.

It was a strange feeling to read an English newspaper that had appeared in a bundle of mail sent out from Barcelona. STALEMATE IN ARRAGON, the paper declared; FRANCO MOVES TO CUT MADRID'S LIFELINE TO SEA.

"That's where we ought to be," cried Sam, hurling the paper down. "South, where the real fighting is; where we can be of use—where every man's desperately needed. We fiddle and rot while Rome burns!"

"We could do a vanishin' trick," suggested Ike. Instead, Candy Sam put in an urgent request to Barcelona for a transfer. There was no reply.

Christmas—celebrated with an extra plateful of bully beef stew (to which Ben added a pinch of curry) and bottles of Spanish champagne—came and went. The cold deepened. Snow powdered the land. The mud hardened though never froze completely.

For Will, the companionship of the Seven Bells Brigade became as engrossing and as valuable to him as a library of books. Their knowledge of life, their experience of it, became his. They were to be the best schooling he ever had.

He would sit beside Sam for hours watching him sketch scenes of the trenches, portraits of his comrades and of the dour mountain landscape. Howard taught him how to read and draw maps. Ike fascinated him with card tricks and tales of his travels in the Far East.

Roland had found a burnt-out and abandoned motor van on the road behind the Republican positions. He dragged the engine into the trench and proceeded to dismantle and then rebuild it, polishing every part as though it were a work of art. From Roland, Will learnt his car mechanics, from Ben's little library of cook books, he learnt to tell the difference between a Lobster Chowder and a Lobster Thermidor—and from Federico he learnt of the Freedom Tree.

Federico had been describing his native Basque country to Will. "When peace it come, I bring you to my 'ome. The Garden of Eden is nothing in comparing." He had talked affectionately of Guernica, his home town a few miles inland from the Atlantic.

He promised Will walks in the cool green hills, visits to ancient churches and palaces, journeys into a history older than that of any other state in Europe.

"But will you be able to show me the Freedom Tree?" Will had expected the usual puzzled expression and shake of the head. To his amazement he had been treated to a wild hug.

"You 'as 'eard of our tree! Magnifico!"

"Then it's real—there actually is such a tree?"

"Real? I tell you, Will, it more famoso in Spain than Leaning Tower of Pizza. Since thousand years ago, my 'ome is place where the kings of the Basque cow-ntry they make promise to people—to keep the liberty. Under the Oak of Guernica, they sitted, each year. Under the mighty branches they swear—no tyranny!"

"Somebody we met in France told us we must protect the Freedom Tree."

"Protect?" Federico slapped his thigh. "From who, amigo—the greenfly? There is no Spaniard alive-o who dare touch the Oak of Guernica. No!" The very thought upset Federico.

Then he smiled. "I show you, eh? And you come meet my family, my seester who 'ave the twins, and my dog, Vasco

Da Gama—you will like 'im. Then I come nosey around
Jarrow—big bargain?"

"Big bargain!"

Gradually, Will began to discover fear again. The more he
knew of his friends, the more attached to them he became,
and the more he feared for their lives.

He learnt that they had come to Spain for other reasons
than just to fight for a good cause. Howard had quarrelled
bitterly with his father. Roland, like Will's Da, had been out
of work, a burden on his family. Ben's wife had left him and
taken his beloved little boy with her. She had gone without a
word and Ben had never been able to trace them.

Ike was the wanderer. He had fought in the Great War.
He had tried a score of occupations in a dozen different
countries, failing at them all. Only in the heat of battle did
he realise his true potential. Griff had been in as many
children's homes as Ike had had jobs and the two of them
had become fast friends. Together, they organised an inter-
trench Gin Rummy tournament and won the prize of two
slabs of chocolate and a bottle of Moroccan hair tonic, which
Griff gave to the balding Roland.

Candy Sam sketched Will. "You've a genuine aquiline
nose, did you realise?"

"Snotty, do you mean? It's because Griff's borrowed my
silk handkerchief."

"No—curved like an eagle's beak. A good face for an
artist. Plenty of strength in it, but gentleness too. And a
touch of Spanish for good measure. Molly's face combines
strength and gentleness with . . . an uncanny radiance."

As he sketched, Sam talked lovingly of his sister, of how she
had been a tomboy, disliking girls' clothes. "She preferred
birds' nesting to dolls. She could climb rocks like a mountain
goat. Fred's not the only one with a Garden of Eden to show
you, Will. If we ever get out of Spain alive, I'll show you our
Sussex—Molly's and mine:

"The great hills of the South Country
They stand along the sea:
And it's there walking in the high woods
That I could wish to be,
And the men who were boys when I was a boy
Walking along with me.

"That's the poem I love the best, by Hilaire Belloc. The hills and woods of Sussex. I could paint happily among them for the rest of my life."

"What happened to your Mam and Da?"

"They travelled a lot. They drowned when a steamer they were sailing on sank in the Indian Ocean. But Molly and I grew up the happiest of orphans. We'd camp out on the Downs for days. We stitched up blankets to make sleeping bags. We caught fish and grilled them over wood fires. Ever heard of the Long Man of Wilmington? I'll take you to see him one day. He's from pre-history, laid out in chalk against the green grass of the hill and he's like a giant sentinel overlooking the land. For Molly and me the Long Man was a little bit like Fred's Freedom Tree. It came to stand for everything that was good and beautiful and worth preserving."

Was there anything in particular, Will asked, that had made Molly suddenly volunteer for service with the Republic? Candy Sam gave a shrug. He paused from his sketching.

"She could see, as perhaps we all could, that if Fascist tyranny wins in Spain, its forces will spread like the plague throughout the world. If Franco triumphs, the people of Spain will be enslaved. There were so many things that came together, to persuade her: the execution of prisoners, the bombings, the way the Church blessed the firing squads. Yet there was one act, of senseless brutality, which might have made up her mind. The Fascists in Granada went to the house of one of Spain's greatest poets, Federico Garcia Lorca. They took him from his desk. They didn't try him;

they didn't listen to him. His wonderful words meant nothing to them. They took him out into his orchard and they shot him . . . The day the news was reported in the English papers, Molly packed a hold-all and went."

Eventually, when the Seven Bells Brigade had despaired of ever seeing more of Spain than the limestone hills opposite them, reinforcements arrived from Barcelona and with them a crinkled, coffee-stained document for Candy Sam.

"We're free!"

"Fred too?"

"All of us! So that makes it official—we're the Eight Bells Brigade from now on. They thank us for our services and wish us well. This document should get us through checkpoints to the south."

"Then it's goin' to be some real fightin'," said Ike, grinning with delight.

Sharing the general spirit of excitement and relief, Griff actually invited Will to be first to sit up front in Peg. "I'll 'ave a celebration game o' cards wi' Ike."

What a pleasure it was to be aboard old Peg once more, with the smell of her leather seats, the squeak of her springs and the wind whistling freshly through the cab—away from the flying bullets, the grim trenches and the winter-hardened ground.

"I'm not leaving Barcelona till I've had a hot bath," resolved Howard, "and killed every last one of these lice."

"A cold beer for me," said Roland, "and a long, lingering look at some pretty women."

"One hour!" declared Candy Sam. "If what that newspaper said is true, Malaga is about to fall to the Italians. That's like the enemy taking Southampton in its effort to cut off London from the south coast. We'll top up with petrol and provisions—then away."

For a moment on the rough, corkscrew road, Candy Sam braked. He turned off Peg's engine. "Hear that, everybody? Something I'd almost forgotten existed—the song of birds!

Treasure it, for there'll be no birds singing where we're going."

After Barcelona, the road wound through pinewoods towards the sea. They cruised past Tarragona's white sandy beaches and green headlands. They crossed the great plain of the Ebro, alongside irrigation canals and fields of rice and rye grass.

Beyond the river, greens gave way to golden browns and reds. "Real Spain!" exclaimed Candy Sam. "With apologies, that is, to the Basque Cow-ntry." White-washed farmhouses gleamed among groves of olive and vine. "Watch out for your first orange trees, Will."

The land flattened to the level of the sea whose glitter was answered by the domes of distant village churches clad with tiles of shining blue, purple or maroon.

"Swim, lads?"

Sam pulled up a pebble's throw from the white-edged Mediterranean. "We deserve this after all those nosy checkpoints."

The Eight Bells Brigade dashed, cheering and singing, over the shingle and cast themselves into the sea fully clothed.

"It's warmer than Clacton at midsummer," cried Ike, on his back, kicking up spray. "Come on, Ben, stop workin' out them menus. You're only up to your nobbly knees. You'll never drown your lice that way."

"I reckon Ben's considering how he can serve up lice as a dessert," said Howard.

"There aren't any sharks in these waters, are there, Fred?" asked Roland.

"Fear not," called Federico, rolling like a porpoise. "All the sharks is Republicans."

Candy Sam laughed. "It's a pity the battleships are all Fascist."

Above the swish of the waves rose another sound. " 'ear that?" Griff abandoned his bath in the shallows. "That's a plane, i'n't it?"

The sky behind the coastal hills was blue and clear, except for a small dark scar. "Comin' this way!"

Wings sprouted from the scar. Sunlight glinted on metal. "Recognise it, Fred? One of ours?"

The plane climbed. It wheeled along the shore. It banked and headed straight for the Eight Bells Brigade.

"We could try giving her a friendly wave." Nobody—not even Candy Sam himself—took his advice. Every head crashed down into water. The plane cast a gigantic shadow over the sea.

"Is bad!" shouted Federico. "Italiano!"

A wave had washed over Will's face. He swallowed salt water and began to splutter.

The plane turned, its sea shadow diminished, narrowed. Its engine throbbed in the changing air-flow, preparatory to the full-throated roar of attack.

"Here he comes!"

Down pitched the wings. The headland swung up violently behind the plane's tail. Will could actually see the pilot's helmet and goggles.

Really, this was nothing new. Will had played the strafing game often enough back home as a boy (until next door's dog had chewed up his model fighter plane); how satisfying, then, had been the zooming descent from the clouds, the perfectly-timed thumb on the canon.

It was his turn to be one of the lead soldiers about to be scattered over the kitchen table.

The first salvo of bullets drove a straight line of explosions across the pebbles. "No messing, lads," commanded Sam, as the plane climbed away and upwards, circling for another attack. "Shelter behind Peg!"

While the others made Peg their shield, Ike wrenched at the rear doors. "Hellfire!" They had never stuck before, but they stuck now. He tore at the handles.

"Duck!"

Candy Sam's men threw themselves against Peg's wheels or rammed their backs against the truck's tough wooden walls.

"Bloody Italiano!" yelled Federico. "Shameful damn-blast you!"

This time the machine-gun fire was so loud Will clamped his palms over his ears. It struck different surfaces, playing a deathly drum-roll on the metalled road, on steel, on wood-work, on glass. Peg rocked with the blows.

One tyre burst with a sad hiss and the wheel sank on to its rim. Candy Sam and Ike got the doors open. They entered Peg like divers taking off from the high board.

"It's going—no. Round three!"

" 'e 'aving the big fun, eh? Much better than Ludo."

Rifles came pitching from the truck. "We could do with those Maxims now . . . and to think they'll be 'oldin' up the washin' line over in Aragon."

The Italian pilot was clearly set on gathering scalps. Here was an easy mission against the Reds—which was what all Republicans were called by the Fascists, whatever their political opinions; an open target, undefended.

He swooped again. Once more gunfire bisected the rays of evening sun. Will felt poor old Peg's agony. The wind-screen shattered. The skylight shattered. A headlamp exploded.

"We'll be safer in that ditch. With so much petrol on board, Peg could blow us back to Barcelona." Candy Sam led the way. "Spread out. Heads down till he's passed, then fire at the pilot—it's our only chance."

The plane crossed the deepening sun. Will could see Ben trembling against the grass. He saw Griff, legs outstretched to steady himself, taking careful aim. "I'm goin' for the petrol tank. If we brings 'im down, I bags 'is goggles."

In came the plane. Its wings shone. Bullets streamed out like tracers of gold. Light, sound, motion, shadow beat to-gether over Will's head.

He saw the tilt of Sam's rifle. He saw its shadow lie over a sprinkling of yellow flowers. He saw Federico close one eye, press his moustache to the grey steel, his shoulder hunching into the rifle butt.

This time there was a shuddering bang.

"Bombs!"

"That or a grenade."

The missile holed the road directly behind Peg, showering her with stones and tar.

"We've got to get out of here!" wailed Howard, without moving.

"We thumb 'im the lift, eh?" suggested Federico.

"See that!" Sam turned on his back. "Petrol vapour. Griff, lad, I think you did it!"

The Italian pilot had not noticed the injury to his plane. He was returning to the attack. Will slid down the grass slope. He and Ben were touching. Instinctively, he put out his hand as he might have done to his Da. Ben clutched it. "There, lad—it'll pass." To both of them, it was a comfort, a consolation.

Will's heart beat against stone and grass. He heard the screaming roar. He stuck his face into a patch of cracked brown mud. He waited.

The shadow of the plane darkened the landscape.

"Diving lower. Aim and fire!"

Will recorded the shots and the answering machine-gun fire. He heard something whistling through the air. Another shadow was over him.

"Ben!"

He felt a weight over his back, not heavy, not a bad weight. Then suddenly there was a more devastating weight beneath him, around him. He was carried up. He sensed the earth go away from him.

"I'm hit!"

Earth, fallen, far off. "Will! Oh Christ! And Ben . . ."

He felt wetness, a pouring. Arms and legs were all at once no part of him. In his head—a soaring, damp, slipping down, tumbling-over head—there was a pain, a screaming bird trapped in a belfry, beating its wings till bells burst the ears.

"Ben must've seen it comin'!"

"But both of them!"

"First aid, Griff, fast! Easy now, lift him off . . . Ben? All right?"

Ike: "Afraid 'e's past first aid."

He? I? Will Viljoen. Put me together, Da. Where are my hands? Am I in one piece?

Candy Sam: "So long as the lad's all right——"

"Plane's gone, Sam."

"When we've wiped the blood off, we'll know."

Griff: "Let me do it. Will, can you 'ear your old mate? It's Griff." He bent down. " 'is ticker's goin'. Ben saved 'im. Shielded 'im."

Will lay unconscious in the ditch, stained with blood— with Ben's blood. And Ben too lay in the ditch, his contribution to the cause of free Spain at an end.

The Eight Bells Brigade had once more become seven. They buried Ben overlooking the sea and Roland, his eyes red with grief, fashioned for his comrade a driftwood cross.

"Fear no more the heat o' the sun," Sam recited gravely, twisting his tartan beret between his fingers,

> "Nor the furious winter's rages;
> Thou thy world task hast done,
> Home art gone, and ta'en thy wages . . ."

"Will?"

Blue light penetrated his closed lids. He felt another hand than Sam's rest over his knuckles, smaller, soft-touching. He fought for sight. His head ached. His whole body ached.

"Try not to move." A girl's voice, husky, reminding him of his beautiful second cousin Mary from Hexham. He did try to move and the voice became firmer. "Doctor's orders!"

Will arrived at total consciousness. He opened his eyes and life greeted him.

"This is Molly, Will."

She was even more beautiful than his second cousin Mary from Hexham. She was Sam all over again, with his smile, his spark of merriment—but transformed to a vision.

Her eyes were the dark blue of cornflower. She wore a

grey dress and a white nurse's cap with a red cross on it. Will
noticed splashes of dried blood on the apron tied round her
waist.

"Where are we? What's happened to Ben?"

"No questions till you're safe in the dressing station—
please!" He was carried out of Peg by Sam and Ike, with
Griff holding on to his feet as though his boots might fall off
into the mud. He glimpsed hill country, copses of trees
sinking into twilight and the entrance gates to farm buildings
and a courtyard.

"We're making use of an old wine cellar dug into the hillside," Molly explained. "With artillery shells likely to fall from
the skies any minute, it's about the safest place in Spain."

Beyond the voices, Will recognised the drone of heavy
trucks and then, nipping his heart with fear, the boom of
guns. He was taken into a round-roofed, brick-lined cavern.
Hospital beds had been placed between rows of huge, glistening wine vats.

"It's on hire from Ali Baba and his Forty Thieves. Once
upon a time the only red liquid that flowed here was delicious wine." Will was laid down gently on a bed near the
cavern's entrance.

"A good sign, this, Molly," said Candy Sam, "a dressing
station with no patients."

"You should have been here earlier. We'd a hundred in
during the day. Walking casualties mainly. Our job's to
patch and despatch. By truck to hospital in Chinchon or
Colminar."

"How come they let a woman up 'ere so near the front?"
Ike asked.

"They didn't, not officially. But in Valencia where the
Government's set up its temporary headquarters, the right
hand's no idea what the left hand's doing. I just decided I'd
be more use bandaging the wounded on the spot than letting
them bleed to death or be shaken to death over miles of cart
tracks and bad roads. I hitched a lift—I mean, everything's
in such confusion since Malaga fell. There's no organisation,

hardly any supplies. The only thing we're not short of is dirt."

"You've a doctor here?"

"One—a Spaniard, very good. And Charlie, our orderly. He was a medical student from Milwaukee in the States. After his first year they advised him to switch to electrical engineering." Molly laughed. "Charlie's bandages invariably fall off, but he's a dab-hand with anything mechanical. He's invented a contraption that'll pump blood from a donor straight into a wounded man."

Will tried to lever himself up. He remembered so little and he was suddenly convulsed with alarm when he could see neither Ben nor Howard among the faces around him. "Where are they, where are they?" he cried, his voice dry and shaky.

Candy Sam gripped his wrist. "Steady. You're suffering from concussion and shock. Ben is dead. You must accept that. Before the next twenty-four hours is up, there may be others among us lining up for little wooden crosses."

"But Howard—and Fred!"

"Howard is taking a stroll to the front, drawing maps of the battlefield. He'll be back soon. Fred's just stretching his legs."

"Which front, which battlefield?" Will felt as though he had been asleep for a century. It was time to catch up on things.

"Lie still—you must rest a while."

"He's from Jarrow, Molly. They breed them tough in those parts."

"And stubborn too." She smiled. "If I have any trouble with you, young man, we'll take these tins of creosote from the legs of your bed and let the rats creep all over you in the night."

Will sensed his apprehension die away. "So that's what they're for! I reckoned they were to stop the beds deserting." Nurse and patient laughed, and from that instant they were friends.

"We're at a place called Jarama," explained Sam.

"Only they pronounce it Harama," added Roland. "As Harrow is to Jarrow."

Sam said that Madrid was about twenty miles to the north. "A mile or two away from this spot, the most vital battle of the war is being fought along the River Jarama. If the Republican army fails to hold its positions, Franco will sweep eastwards and cut off the Madrid–Valencia road. Should that happen, we might as well pull down the flag and run like hell."

According to Molly, the Fascists had brought up massive reinforcements. The much-feared Army of Africa—the Moroccans—had made extensive gains in the valley of the Jarama. They were backed up by six batteries of 155 mm guns and 88 mm guns of the German Condor Legion.

She lit an oil lamp. Its bright yellow glow illuminated her face, tired, drawn and all at once immensely sad. "What can the poor Spanish Government do against troops equipped with the latest weapons from Hitler's war factories? We have no artillery. Tanks are promised but never arrive—even the rifles the men have been issued with jam and very often refuse to fire."

"What about the aid Russia promised?"

"A drop in the ocean." She sighed. "By first light tomorrow, we expect the British Battalion of the International Brigade to arrive from Albacete. They'll be sent against Franco's proud Moroccans, who fight like wild tigers. As Charlie says, it'll be lambs to the slaughter . . . Ah, here comes our Man from Milwaukee now!"

Federico strode in from the twilit courtyard with his arm round the shoulder of a bony young man with fair hair and a straggly beard. "This is being Charlie, comrades, one gen-u-wine Yankee Diddle Brandy from the land of the biffburger."

"Hi! British are you? Then where the devil's the rest of your battalion?"

"They aren't the battalion at all, Charlie," said Molly. "They're my search party."

Charlie shook Candy Sam's hand warmly. "Quite a famous painter, I hear."

"That's history."

"You bet it is! I came over to Spain to see the pictures in the Prado—and look where I've landed up." He told the Seven Bells Brigade that they had arrived at the worst possible time. Jarama, he believed, was going to be the bloodiest battle of the war. Boadilla, Lopera, Las Rozas—they would be regarded as mere skirmishes in comparison. "Franco will grab the Madrid–Valencia road if he's to sacrifice half the sons of Spain in the process."

Charlie was the messenger of bad news. The Republicans had been thrown back from the river. "Our boys were ordered to hold the Pindoque bridge. French volunteers— André Marty Battalion. They didn't reckon on the Moroccans creeping up in the dark and slitting the guards' throats. Right behind them came the Fascist armoured cavalry."

"Didn't the Government troops have dynamite to blow up the bridge?"

"Good question. Yes, there was dynamite. The sappers did their best, but what can you do with untrained amateurs —tally clerks from Lyons, baggage men from Paris? They blew up the bridge all right, only it fell straight into place again. The latest news is that there's been a second crossing up at the Arganda bridge. It never rains but it pours!

"Listen, fellas, if you've a mind to get into that old bus out there and pretend you've never heard of this place, we'd not give a damn. By this time tomorrow—I warn you— whoever sticks around and fights will be cold mutton and potatoes under the olive trees."

"Are you always as cheerful as this, Charlie?" asked Roland, polishing his glasses unconcernedly.

The American's mood changed. "Okay, I admit it—it's laughing so much that keeps me going. Forget this son-of-a-bitch said anything but God's in his heaven and all's right

with the world. Put it down to lack of sleep. I'd swap the
Empire State Building for a hot shower . . . But as long as
Little Blue Eyes here—that's what the soldiers call her—as
long as she keeps steaming on, this Yankee Diddle Brandy'll
match her yawn for yawn. Sam, they'll put a statue up to
your sister one day. Florence Nightingale—nothing!"

He paused, tired. "It's what she deserves, anyway."

Will insisted on getting up and accompanying the others
when they went over to the main farm building to have supper. Though the distant gunfire rumbled fitfully throughout
the night, everything remained strangely peaceful.

Faced with the probability of his own death in a few hours,
Will cherished each passing moment. There had been little
time in Spain to be happy, yet now he knew happiness—
greater, indeed, than any he had known since childhood.

With his comrades and friends he ate, drank wine—and
forgot his headache completely. He watched brother and
sister, reunited at last, catching up on lost months. He
watched Howard, in perfect contentment, studying his maps,
Roland puffing at his pipe, lighting it and relighting it, Ike
and Griff bent over their thousandth game of cards.

He listened to Federico conjuring magic tunes from his
violin and Charlie from Milwaukee explaining the intrica-
cies of the game of baseball to anyone who would listen.

It was too late to conclude that these friends meant more
to him than any country or any cause, for promises had been
made. Yet he could not help himself regretting the pity of it,
the waste on the field of battle of such good men.

For a golden hour, Will chatted to Molly. He seemed to
have known her all his life. She surprised him by how much
she knew of his home town. "Wasn't it a villain called Sir
James Lythgoe who shut down Palmer's shipyard and put
the town out of work? And when an American called Salt
wanted to build a steelworks, big business and the banks
stopped him getting permission? You know, Will, when your
Da came to Spain, he was fighting for Jarrow too. Because
until the Republic was born, the peasants were treated worse

than Roman slaves. Now they've been given their own land to work on. If we lose this war, it will be taken from them again."

Molly showed Will round the farmhouse. It was a gracious, well-appointed building. Hung over the walls were framed black-and-white and coloured cartoons.

"The house belonged to a famous illustrator called Bogaria. They're the funniest of cartoons—there's even one in the lav. Most of them attack the Spanish church." She broke off for a second. "Did you know that priests bless the Fascist execution squads, Will, and that the bishops give the Nazi salute?"

There was one room Will had to see. "It's a kind of memorial chapel to a bullfighter who died in the ring." They went up a wide staircase and through the silent darkness to the torero's room. It was furnished with a simple iron bedstead and a dressing table. The walls were decorated with tasselled swords, banderillas and bullfight posters celebrating the great Sanchez.

Will sensed the reverence of the place and it reminded him powerfully and movingly of old St Paul's in Jarrow where the Don spilt its waters into the Tyne, and where the spirit of the Venerable Bede seemed to hang in the musty air.

"Have you ever heard of the poet Lorca?" Molly asked.

"He was the one who was taken out and shot in his own back garden, wasn't he?"

"Among the olive groves near Granada. This Sanchez was his friend. He wrote a beautiful poem in Sanchez' honour, which could have been Lorca's own epitaph:

"But now he sleeps for ever.
Now the moss and the grass
open with sure fingers
the flower of his skull.

"Oh, Will, how beautiful and sad those lines are, and how beautiful and sad Spain is!" She led him to a balcony overlooking the courtyard. The heavens burned white with stars.

There was a fragrance in the air and a hollow stillness like that in a vast cathedral. "I've seen so many boys die, Will, so many brave boys." Instinctively, Will slipped his hand into his windjammer jacket. "I wonder, would you be interested in reading my Da's last letter? There's a bit in it—well, that I'd like to share."

Molly's fingers touched his sleeve. "I'd rather you read it out to me."

He unfolded the letter. He swallowed. "Just a few lines, then?"

" 'On this particular day we were marching over rough country from one battle to the next when I got separated from the rest of the lads. It had never happened to me before, but I found myself completely alone. The hills were silent. Not a bird sang—and all at once I came upon a field full of dead people. It was uncanny!

" 'They were peasants—poor farmers, fifteen of them, maybe more. They lay flat on their bellies with their faces hard against the dry, yellow earth. Had they been shot? Had they fallen dead from starvation?—it was difficult to say. They were stretched out there with no story to tell, and no one to weep at their passing.

" 'All they had been allowed to know was that there was war, that death comes quickly, and to the poor it comes as swiftly as light.

" 'I wondered: had they understood what cause they had died for? I stood there for ages, with the wind howling through my brain and the olive branches lurching—and suddenly I knew for certain why I was fighting in Spain.

" 'These, Will, were good men who had done no harm; good men who had never been given a chance.

" 'These were my dead brothers!' "

Molly's face relaxed into a faint smile as Will closed the letter and replaced it in his pocket. She raised her hand. Her fingers clenched into the Republican salute:

"No pasarán!"

"They shall not pass!" answered Will gravely.

CHAPTER SEVEN

In the early hours of the next morning Will was wakened by Griff carrying a mug of steaming coffee. " 'ere, get this down you—things is 'appenin'."

Will looked about him. The previously empty dressing station in the wine cellar under the hill was packed with soldiers.

The British Battalion had arrived at Jamara.

"They look whacked, the lot of 'em," said Griff, "as if they'd just tramped forty mile wi' all that clobber on their backs."

The men lay on the ground or propped along the walls, some fast asleep, others dozing fitfully, a few smoking precious cigarettes and gazing into space. They wore shabby brown corduroy jackets that buttoned up to the neck, and wide, flapping trousers.

Beside each man lay a tightly rolled cotton blanket and groundsheet.

"Them's French 'elmets they've bin issued wi', 1914–18 variety. T'rifles is Russian . . . You should 'ear Charlie rantin' on about the old rifles, Steyrs or somethin'. Jammin' up every second shot. Bloody useless!"

Molly Hannington entered from the courtyard. "Feeling strong enough to lend a hand, Will?" Morning was gathering up the farmhouse shadows. "Charlie's rabbit stew is on the boil. Slip over and ask Captain Wintringham if we can serve it to the boys. They were too dog-tired to eat it earlier on."

Will and Griff crossed the courtyard under fine, spreading trees and passed an old stone well. They spotted the rest of the Seven Bells Brigade on the first floor balcony of the farmhouse in earnest conversation with a slim, bald-headed man wearing steel-framed spectacles.

"That's Wintringham. Gaffer o' all this lot."

They went upstairs. "Another member of our outing,

Captain Wintringham," introduced Sam. "Stretcher-bearer and second-reserve ambulance driver—Will Viljoen."

"So this is the young man you were talking about." Wintringham grasped Will's hand. "Understand this, though I might permit a second member of your family to join the struggle for justice in Spain, one death is more than enough. You are too young to lay down your life in this or any other cause. See that they both remain well behind the lines, Mr Hannington."

"I'm for fighting, sir!" pleaded Griff. "If there's a rifle spare."

Captain Wintringham shook his head. "My duty would be to pack both of you off to England. Considering that is impossible, your task will be to help Charlie here with the wounded."

He turned to the men of the Seven Bells Brigade. "As for you, gentlemen, it's highly irregular for you to pop up out of nowhere like this. But let's admit it—everything about this war is highly irregular, and at least you've been blooded on the Aragon front."

He said they were to be attached to Number Three Company under Bill Briskey. "He used to be a bus driver before he volunteered. He's tough but friendly. You'll like him. I'll say to you what I've told the rest of the men. The Fascist General Orgaz is thought to have 40,000 men under his command. We alone will stand between them and the Madrid–Valencia road to our rear. At all costs we must protect that road, and that means holding on to our positions. Put this day in your diaries, gentlemen—12th February, 1937. One way or another, history will be made. Good luck! And remember—No pasarán!"

Will and Griff dished out Charlie's rabbit stew to the men. They paused and they chatted. "There's one o' everythin'," commented Griff. "Butchers, bakers, miners, blokes from college . . ."

"Anybody from Jarrow?" wondered Will. He met Scots, Welsh, Lancastrians, Yorkshire Tykes, Brummies. There were those who had given up good jobs; there were those whom the Slump had robbed of work. They were brothers. Yes, thought Will, in their way they had come to protect the Freedom Tree.

The bitter moment arrived when he had to say goodbye to Candy Sam and to Ike, Howard, Roland and Federico. Sam distributed barley sugars all round. He was pale. He linked his arm in Molly's and he spoke cheerfully.

"This is no time for fine speeches. But I want to say this— I consider I've been blessed with the loveliest and kindest-hearted sister in the world, and the best friends a man ever had. And I thank whoever's up there for granting me such good fortune."

He embraced each of the Seven Bells Brigade. "Will, care for Molly while I'm away. And take my sketchbook. It might even be worth a stick of Brighton rock one day." He tapped his rifle. "The first bullet's going to be for Ben. Right, as Will's Geordie pals would say—Howway, lads!"

They went up the green ridge crowned with olives. They smiled. They waved. They passed over the hill. Molly covered her dejection with busy activity while Charlie brought out a rolled-up stretcher for Will and Griff.

"Now get it clear in your heads, both of you. Your job's to spot the wounded. Make sure they don't wander off in the wrong direction."

"What about them as is too bad to walk?"

"If their comrades don't drag them to safety, then they wait till nightfall."

"They could bleed to death."

"Most of them do. Okay? Then let's go and watch some action." Charlie led them from the stately farmhouse gates along the route taken by the British Battalion. The ground sloped gently upwards to a protective ridge, flanked to right and left by low hills thick with olives.

Will pressed Candy Sam's binoculars close to his eyes and brought the battlefield of Jarama into focus. A smell of wild thyme wafted in from the gorse-covered hills. From beyond vision he heard the crackle of riflefire, thin and spasmodic.

Then, all at once, the sky lost its silence and became the Big Top of a circus. The air was crowded with acrobats—small fighter planes wheeling out of the blue, their faraway wings and fuselages glinting in the clear sunlight.

Their machine-guns sent echoes along the valleys.

"Ruddy Germans!" cursed Griff.

"Funny thing," replied Charlie, "but there are practically as many Jerries and sons of Spaghettiland fighting for the Republic as for Franco . . . The Thaelmanns, the Garibaldis, ashamed of their own governments. A swell bunch of lads."

The battle in the sky was so unreal for Will that he might as well have been watching a newsreel at the pictures. The planes looked so pretty, so harmless.

"See him!" Charlie had pointed swiftly at a uniformed man riding pillion on a motor cycle. "That's George Nathan checking on the trench positions. He's brigade commander; a brilliant man, cool as a cucumber under fire—one of the few real heroes in this damned war.

"There he goes, daring the bullets to hit him! What was that saying about mad dogs and Englishmen?"

They watched the four companies of the British Battalion advance to their positions. Number One circled the hill to the north, Number Three, reinforced by the Seven Bells Brigade, skirted southwards. Number Four—the machine-gun company, Charlie said, under Harry Fry—pursued a direct route between the hills, followed some way behind by Number Two Company.

"Can you make out the sunken road, Will?—stretching across the view."

He couldn't quite, but his time was up and it was Griff's turn with the binoculars. "Sunken? What 'appened to it?"

"Something typically Spanish, a road worn down below ground level through centuries of rumbling old ox-carts and rain. Four feet deep. An ideal natural trench. If the lads hold that, then the Fascists won't get to the Madrid–Valencia highway."

Beyond the safety of the sunken road there would be little protection from enemy attack. "Strategic point number two is that hill in the middle distance, the one with the white farmhouse—Casa Blanca Hill. It commands the ground running up from the river. Both sides'll be under orders to grab that hill fast and before the day's out I reckon somebody'll have christened it Suicide Hill. There are plenty of those in Spain."

Griff lowered the binoculars. "They're diggin' in . . . Why can't they use shovels instead o' bayonets an' 'elmets?"

"Because, pal, there's not a shovel between here and the Straits of Gibraltar." The American began to chuckle. "This war's not thrown up many jokes, but here's one . . . At Las Rozas the British were under attack and wanted to dig trenches. So they shouted for shovels. The Frenchies thought they wanted chevaux—and ran about all day looking for horses!"

The cold sun climbed higher in the February sky. The unreal battle ended and the real battle began. The thunder of it rolled up the hills that concealed the once-peaceful flow of the River Jarama.

Abruptly, deafeningly, the air was rent by the massive boom of Fascist artillery. Will clamped his hands over his ears. He imagined an earthquake would sound like this, and indeed the earth trembled beneath him.

"Get a look at those 88 mm shells falling. Presents from 'Appy Adolph. Our poor devils have nothing to touch them." Charlie grabbed the binoculars. "Am I dreaming or is the machine-gun company not firing?"

There was movement in Harry Fry's Number Two Company, but no sign that a trigger had been pulled.

"I'll tell you why!" Charlie leapt on to his feet then pounded back on to his chest again. "Either those Colts have all jammed or some idiot's sent them the wrong ammunition."

There was little need of the binoculars to see the first pin-prick figures of the Fascist infantry, moving cautiously up the valley.

"Moroccans—Army of Africa, enough to scare the pants off the bravest opposition. The best fighters in this war. And the dirtiest: two hundred rounds of ammo each and a curved knife to slit your throat."

"Guns arrivin'," observed Griff.

"Well that's something. Those'll be Maxims. Yes, Harry Fry's boys are about to sign for them. The Maxims are as old as your grannie, but at least they fire."

Will recognised Captain Wintringham in the sunken road. He took back the binoculars. Smoke was spreading across the battlefront but he managed to bring Candy Sam into focus. He was lodged perilously beyond the sunken road on an exposed slope with only the gnarled trunks of olives between him and the Fascist small-arms fire.

There too, close by, was Fred, his violin still strung over his shoulder. Ike, Howard and Roland lay sprawled behind olive roots or ridges of uneven ground.

"That's the order to advance—God protect you, lads! Come on, you two, give the British Battalion a cheer!"

Will opened his mouth. "I can't."

"What's happened? Has your voice shrunk into your boots? Thought so. You're suffering from honest, old-fashioned terror. Me too!"

Charlie's eyes reverted to the battle. "They're going to meet the Moroccans head on. Blast that ruddy smoke! Away they go. Number One Company. Now Sam and Bill Briskey's merry boys. But where the diablo is Number Four Company? Surely not buzzed off for a crap!"

He tried the binoculars again. "No sign of them. That's terrible! The flank'll be left wide open."

The colossal fire power of the Fascists concentrated on Casa Blanca Hill. The British Number Three Company's positions were enveloped in trails of billowing smoke and dust.

They had advanced, but their progress slowed. It stopped. Men fell. They had met a solid wall of bullets. Charlie's voice became a wail of anguish. "They'll get crucified! There's no cover—nothing!"

There was a brief thinning of the smoke clouds. Some men were flat against the olives, some were crawling forward despite the murderous barrage, sights fixed upon the white-washed farmhouse. Others fought the hard earth with their bayonets, attempting to carve out shallow fox-holes to shelter them from the machine-gun fire that raked the bumpy surface of the ground.

Some lay motionless where death had struck them down.

"Their only chance is to count the rounds. While the machine-gunners are changing belts—you make a dash for it."

To the north, another battle raged, beyond the enemy-held heights of Pingarrón.

"What did I tell you? The Colts aren't firing! Nor are those bloody futile shossers! We're sending innocents to the slaughter."

The advance of the British Battalion on Casa Blanca Hill was at an end. Gunfire poured down on them from all directions. "There come the first wounded. See them? Staggering for the sunken road. We're going to be busy!"

Charlie dragged forward the rolled-up stretcher. "What were Captain Wintringham's orders? Not to go beyond this point. Well I guess he never thought things would get as bad as this so early in the day."

He glanced at Will and then Griff. "Which one of you is going to be the first to disobey orders?"

Will and Griff raised their hands simultaneously. "Good, now first we attempt to break the Olympic four hundred metres record." Heads down, the three of them wove a light-ning path across the open ground. Though the Condor shells were falling half a mile away, the green slopes shuddered.

Will had grown used to flying bullets on the Aragon front. These, somehow, were different. They were not idle pot-shots fired out of boredom. They were aimed to kill. And they did kill.

"The quicker we're in, the quicker we're out. Will, go for the walking wounded. Give them a hand, get them to Molly.

Griff, grab hold of the end of this stretcher when I tell you."

Suddenly: "Grass!" A shell screamed through the air above them. Will hit earth. Mixed in with the dry stench of explosives was the whiff of thyme. He looked up. He saw men dying, riddled by ground-level bursts of machine-gun fire.

In front of him, stumbling and dazed, rose a casualty, his arm, his shoulder, his neck, drenched in blood. He fell. He crawled, bearing his suffering in numb silence.

"Easy now, I've got you." Will lifted the wounded man back on his knees. "Lean against me."

"Is it far?"

"Over the ridge. You'll be all right."

"My rifle—it wouldn't fire. Got it jammed somehow. So sorry." He was close to fainting. Will stuck a shoulder underneath him. He levered him up. "I left my rifle . . . Left it against a tree. Damn silly. Will I get into trouble?"

Will half carried him, half dragged him. The man's arm had almost been severed from his body, yet he seemed to be more concerned about the way he had let everybody down.

"My pal, got one in the head. I couldn't shift him. Couldn't do anything."

So began Will's marathon. The hours staggered agonisingly away as he heaved and carted one casualty after another to the safety of Molly Hannington's dressing station in Ali Baba's cave. Each time he arrived, the number of wounded seemed to have doubled. There was not a foot of space to step between them.

The Spanish doctor and Molly went from body to body, bandaging, binding, stitching, applying splints, swathing heads in reams of white, giving water, giving comfort—and all the while making room for more.

When Charlie was delayed, helping Molly in the dressing station, Will went out again with Griff. This time they got as far as the sunken road. It was under heavy fire.

The news made Will sick with dismay: Casa Blanca Hill had almost fallen to the enemy. Number Three Company had been massacred. Briskey was dead. Half the Company were dead.

A familiar face came swaying out of the smoke.

"Roland!"

Will was held back from climbing up from the sunken road. Others went forward. Roland was lifted out of line of the Fascist fire. He was as pale as snow. His glasses were shattered. He had been hit in the hand and the knee—but most seriously in the stomach.

"I keep telling them, it's a wasp sting. Dab some vinegar on, dab some vinegar on!" His flesh was opened up as if for an operation. Desperation was their strength. They ran with him. Roland's weight on the stretcher was nothing compared to the urgency that drove Will and Griff to get their friend to a doctor's care before it was too late.

"Poor Ike. He'd have walked himself. But no feet. And his best pack of cards all over the grass. Sorry, Griff, lad." He groaned. He was delirious. He tried to look at his mangled stomach.

"Don't worry, Will. I'll give your love to your Da when we meet."

"You'll be all right, Roland! All right!"

"How long did I last? . . . Eh? Three hours? . . . and never potted one of the bastards!"

They rushed him to Molly. They could hardly see her for the wounded. The farmhouse courtyard was strewn with them, waiting, heads bowed, calling for a drink, for a smoke or hauntingly for their loved ones at home.

"Please, Molly! Roland—he's bad!"

"Dr Diaz!" Molly and the Spanish doctor began to work on Roland together.

"Here you two!" Charlie pushed forward. "Take care you don't spill any of your own blood, because I may be needing some of it later on." He looked proud. "My transfusion machine's working a treat. Sure as the Lord made little green apples, it'll win me a Nobel prize!"

Will saw Griff pick up a rifle. "No, Griff!"

"I'm 'avin' a lend—Christ, why not? At this rate there'll be nobody left to stick a round up the spout."

"We need two of us! I can't carry a stretcher on my own."

Molly came between them. "Please, Griff, go on bringing in the wounded. There are too many fighting and dying already."

Griff swung round. Then he stopped. He considered the matter. Hesitation was something new for him. He gave Molly a curt nod. He leaned the rifle against the wall.

He grabbed a stretcher, its blood-marks drying in the sun. "Come on then, Jarrow, let's pick up the pieces."

Their advance on Casa Blanca Hill halted, the British Battalion were now being driven yard by yard back the way they had come. Will and Griff stopped within thirty yards of the sunken road. It was too dangerous to go on. Bullets seemed to be coming out of the ground.

The skies were clear yet they hailed down bullets. Fifty blast furnaces together could not equal this roar of destruction. "Charlie was right. Suicide Hill is what they'll call it."

"It's like a rubbish tip." Griff pointed towards the sloping ground ahead of them. It was strewn with abandoned rifles, blankets, helmets; books, even; and with the dead and dying.

The cry had gone up from the line: "Moroccans!" There seemed to be thousands of them. They raced up the valley towards the shattered Republican positions.

"Charlie says them darkies 'ave a bad 'abit o' choppin' their prisoners' 'eads off an' stickin' 'em up on poles."

"He also said that's what makes men fight all the harder against them."

The Moroccans were fleet-footed as goats, visible then invisible as they ducked for shelter in shallow folds of the ground. Each wore a brown headcloth and a blanket like a poncho slipped over his shoulders. This swayed about him as he moved, strangely and menacingly.

Some fell. Yet the great horde of them surged on, chanting and screaming. If they had the sure-footedness of goats on those slippery hill slopes, the Moroccans also possessed the swiftness of rabbits in dropping to cover, only to pop up a moment later, shooting as they ran.

Even if they had remained in solid order, the British Battalion would have been outnumbered; but it was already devastated, its force reduced to less than a third.

Despite this threat of being completely overrun, the Battalion did not budge.

"They've got to retreat! They've got to!"

But the command from Brigade headquarters was absolute: no retreat.

"Them Maxims is still bangin' away . . . Jesus, what we'd've done wi' decent weapons!" The Moroccans swarmed like flies; and they could have been destroyed like flies, but Harry Fry's machine-gun company were already running short of ammunition. "It's a bleedin' tragedy!"

No more words. Will and Griff ignored the bullets. They crawled to the sunken road which had become the Battalion's last line of defence. They completed one journey back to the dressing station, then another.

Will came to know what had sustained Molly hour after hour: the need of the men, their total faith placed in her—that was her strength. He too experienced the child-like trust of the wounded. The more badly they were hit, the more grateful they appeared for words of comfort and reassurance.

"Don't worry, they'll ship you back home after this. You've done your bit!" Such promises brought smiles of contentment to the lips of the dying.

They were returning to the front when Molly called them. "Can one of you give some blood? At least you'll be able to lie down and rest awhile."

Will looked at Griff. Griff looked at Will. "Just one of us?"

"You'll not feel anything. And you'll be paid with an egg and a tin of milk."

"Come on, make up your minds!" called Charlie. "My contraption's chugging away in the house."

Griff coughed. He was nervous. "Brains before beauty, Will . . . Look, if you're needin' a drop o' the stuff after this, you can 'ave a spoonful o' mine to top up the bottle."

There was not a spot of colour in the wounded man's face as Will lay down beside him, with Charlie's contraption between them. His eyes and cheeks were sunken, lips white. Molly rolled up Will's sleeve. Her fingers were cool and soft.

"Just a prick of the needle. Ready, Charlie?"

"Okay."

The blood seeped easily from Will's arm, warmly into the rubber tube. He ignored the throb of Charlie's machine. He looked up at Molly. "Will Roland be all right?"

"Touch and go, if he gets to Chinchon without being shaken to death . . . Any news of Sam?"

"Sorry, nothing." Will turned his head. Suddenly he felt himself in the presence of a miracle. Slowly yet dramatically the wounded man was coming to life again.

The colour was flooding back into his cheeks, to his lips, and though there were tears pricking at Will's eyes, he felt like whooping with joy.

In his exhaustion Will dropped off to sleep. He was wakened after half an hour by Charlie with a pint pot of sweet tea.

"I'd better get going."

"Take it easy. Gather your strength, Jarama won't be lost because one stretcher bearer insisted on his tea break."

"Are we going to lose, Charlie?"

"Lose?" Charlie laughed without smiling. "The battle or the war? Today or next week? Half those British lads who came trooping through here this morning are dead. But they deserve a bucket of medals. They've held on. And those goddamned Moroccans won't look back on this as a holiday either."

They went out into the darkening courtyard. The roar of battle was undiminished. Most of the wounded had been transferred to hospital or moved into Ali Baba's cave among the wine vats. Molly was treating those whose injuries were not serious enough to prevent them returning to the battle— and those who refused to go to hospital whatever their injuries.

One gruff, big-boned Englishman had "escaped" back to the lines despite being wounded three times. On the third occasion, a bullet had scooped the workings clean out of his wrist-watch.

Griff had been taking food to the men. "There's 'ardly anybody left to eat it. Still, things is quietenin' a bit—and them Moroccans've caught a right basinful." He squatted down. "Lord, what I'd give for a bacon sandwich!"

"We've more trips to make," replied Charlie. "As soon as it's dark, we must get to those olive trees below Casa Blanca Hill. There'll be plenty of wounded keeping their fingers crossed we've not forgotten them. But this I promise— there'll be baked beans and bangers for you when this lot's over."

They had scarcely left the shelter of the farmhouse when a shrill, arresting yell came from the gloom. "Help! Please, somebody!"

"It's Sam!"

He was staggering up the ridge. Over his shoulder, he carried Howard, head bouncing like a hen with its neck broken. They were both covered in blood.

"He's bad!"

"We've got him. Are *you* all right?"

"See to Howard, see to Howard!"

They rushed back to the dressing station, Griff and Charlie bearing Howard limp on a stretcher, Will steadying Candy Sam along the crooked, stony path. Oil lamps had been lit in Ali Baba's cave. A fleeting smile told of Molly's relief that her brother was alive.

"Treat him, Molly, treat him for God's sake!"

The bed was already soaked with another man's blood as Howard was laid on it. Red soaked into red. Still clutched in his hand was the map of the war front he had sketched the night before.

"Sam, what about your wounds? Charlie, check him over."

"It's nothing. Grazes." He raised his arm, then his foot, bandaged with shirtsleeves. "Howard got it in the chest."

Molly ceased her examination. She had been holding Howard's wrist. She placed it gently by his side, removing the crumpled map from his hand.

"He's dead, Sam."

All eyes rested on Candy Sam's face. He was speechless. His lips opened. He had known, but he had refused to believe the worst. He came forward. He stooped over his friend.

"I persuaded him to come . . . I persuaded them all!" His voice was faint with shock. "Do you know, after we'd been shot to pieces, we were ordered to advance again. Advance! When everybody about you is dead. And poor Ike! He never had time to pull a trigger!"

"Roland's gone to hospital in Chinchon. He may pull through."

Sam's eyes seemed mesmerised by the flame of the lamp beside the bed. "They ordered us to advance . . . Not Wintringham. The big-whigs at the back, playing with their toy soldiers.

"Advance! It was crazy. We could have held them without advancing, I tell you, all England died today! For olive trees and grass . . . Oh Jarama, Jarama!"

Will piled five sugars into a mug of tea for Sam. He wanted to ask about Federico but feared to prompt more unbearable news.

"Now you must rest, Sam."

He seemed to accept Molly's good advice, but only for an instant. "No!" A memory galvanised him into action. He wrenched his eyes from the lamplight. "We're needed!"

"No more fighting for you just yet."

"Not fighting . . . There are wounded—many!"

"We've been bringin' in the wounded," informed Griff, proud. "Fifty or sixty of 'em, eh, Will?"

"Not those, others! Thirty, possibly more." He swayed and had to put his hand on Will's shoulder to steady himself. "Horrible, horrible! Fred and me, we happened on them in the dark. Wounded, horribly wounded, lying there—been there all day, for hours and hours! Down the sunken road."

It was clear that Sam was suffering from more than grazes. He could hardly stand. "Fred's stayed with them, doing what he can. We've got to go!"

"Not you, Sam."

"I'm going! I know exactly where they are. And I promised." He shook confusion from him. "Where's Peg? We'll take her."

Stubborn brother encountered stubborn sister. "In your condition, Sam, you'll just faint away on top of them. They'll need immediate attention. Charlie—get me bandages, everything."

"Not you, Molly, it's too dangerous."

"Let me decide that."

Charlie agreed with Sam. It was folly, he said, for a woman to take such risks; but when he realised he could not dissuade her, he agreed to stand in for her till she returned.

"Dr Diaz will be back from the lines shortly. Tell him what to expect."

"If Molly's going, so are we," declared Will.

"Right," agreed Griff. "It's our job. An' mebbe one day they'll pay us them ten pesetas a day they owe us."

Charlie had the look of someone saying goodbye for ever. "Talk about mad dogs! Christ, I love you all! But watch that track. It winds." He clutched Molly's hands tight between his own. "All the luck in the world, Little Blue Eyes!"

"And to you too, Yankee Diddle Brandy!"

CHAPTER EIGHT

"I'll not make it!" Candy Sam had tried to forget his wounds but they refused to forget him. Will had watched him struggle to push Peg's gearstick into reverse. He winced in agony.

"Let me drive, Sam—please!"

"You're under age and probably as flogged as I am." Nevertheless, Sam moved over. "Care for some barley sugar?" He knocked on the cab wall. "All right, you two in there? Hold on!"

Darkness. Distant flashes of green light. Stars but no moon. Peg shaking, slithering over hard earth. Upwards, evenly, without headlamps. Through the open window, the smell of sulphur.

"Left now, sharp. Good driving, Will. Keep her along that line, not too fast. It's way down the sunken road, where nobody bothered to look."

Descending, quicker, Will touching the brake, easing Peg back into third gear, then second.

"We're practically there . . . slowly—and halt!"

They spilled out into the night, with torches, water, bandages and stretchers. Federico rose to meet them as though from a grave. His violin hung below his shoulder.

The sight that greeted them in that dim luminance of stars surpassed in horror anything Will had experienced. He remembered, long ago, Grandpa Viljoen being brought home with half his side burnt away by molten steel; but this was worse. The victims lay in twisted shapes along the sunken road, mutilated almost beyond human recognition by artillery shells and machine-gun bullets.

Several were already dead, others only moments away from death. Molly passed among them. There was little she could do but hold their hands before their final breath escaped into Spanish air. In those moments Will felt the last

of his boyhood drain from him. His youth had blossomed
and died as swiftly as the mayflower.

The wounded were given water. They were calm, resolved. No one cried out. No one gave voice to the extent of
his pain. They were lifted into Peg until she could carry no
more. "We'll need at least another trip. Explain to them,
Molly, will you? We'll be back for them."

The black, cavernous silence was all at once pierced by a
distant, ghostly wail, a pathetic, desperate and tragic cry for
help. "One of ours!" But out there, lying between the opposing lines, a broken voice, sobbing, pleading for someone to
come to him, mad with loneliness, begging for water.

"We've got to bring him in."

"No, Will." Fred held him back. "Is too far and too late.
One step out here, and machine-gun it spill your guts.
Listen, already he stop."

They waited. They heard nothing more, and Will was
suddenly resolved. He wanted none of this war. He had had
enough. There must be other ways to win justice, protect
liberty.

He would fulfil his duties—and then he would get out,
anyhow, any way.

Thin blankets of cloud had stretched across the stars. Will
released the clutch and pressed Peg's accelerator. His instructions were—ahead and then sharp left. Griff was beside
him while Candy Sam and Fred helped Molly with the
wounded.

Will's anger at the waste of good lives, at the senselessness
of such human conflicts, reflected in his driving, in the speed
he demanded of Peg, in the haste with which he took the
dark bends. His one thought was to get these ravaged men
to warmth and care.

"Are you sure we're goin in t'right direction, Will?"
asked Griff after several corkscrew turns, dips and climbs.

Will shared Griff's doubts. "It's all these slopes crossing
one another." He slowed. He had to veer right when instinct
told him he should be bearing left. Yet the contours of the

landscape demanded it. Eventually he did turn left. But had he compensated sufficiently for all those yards that spiralled right?

Peg bumped over ribs of rough earth. Then her tyres found smooth ground, almost good enough to be a road.

"We're 'eadin' down'ill, matey!"

For half a minute, false comfort. The road climbed. "We've just got to be right." Such words tempted fate and fate was feeling unkind. The road dipped more sharply.

Will braked hard, and as he did so a spray of bullets buried themselves into Peg's side.

"Christ almighty!" Griff plunged back in his seat. The darkness was sundered by beams of torchlight. "We're bloody surrounded!"

Will closed his eyes. He prayed that this was not really happening. He opened his eyes. The nightmare had not passed away. Moroccan troops approached, with starlight dancing on their bayonets.

There was a sharp rap of command on Peg's door. Will and Griff were ordered down. "Las manos arriba!" Hands up. "No os movais!"

For the first time, Will looked into the faces of the enemy. He was sweating in spite of the cold wind. These men had spent the day killing. They were smeared with blood and dirt. Will did not dare move his eyes.

Peg's rear doors were swung open. "Wounded, wounded!" protested Molly in Spanish. "Red Cross!" Will turned his head a fraction. Candy Sam and Federico were bundled out and Molly was dragged, with a vicious tug, from the clasp of one wounded man.

"Las manos arriba!"

Sam and Fred were then ordered to carry all the wounded on to the roadside. Though they were harried by abuse and threatened with bayonets, they treated their comrades with the utmost gentleness. They did not understand, could not understand, the Moroccans' purpose—until they were commanded to step clear.

Molly screamed a warning. She moved in towards the Moroccan guns only to be hurled into the ditch. "No! No!"

The Moroccans emptied their rifles into the helpless wounded; then they bayoneted them. Candy Sam defied the order to remain still but he had not gone more than two paces before a rifle butt crashed into his face and toppled him on to the ground.

Federico did not move, but his voice rose in furious condemnation. He was grabbed. He was held. He was shot through the knee. A bayonet point was in Will's back. For an instant, he thought he too was about to be shot. All the blood in his body, all the water, suddenly seemed to have dried up; and all the breath left him.

But the Moroccans indicated that Will and Griff lift Sam and Fred into Peg. Molly alone seemed unafraid. She had climbed from the ditch. She pushed forward between the menacing rifles. "Let me help! Steady!"

They were locked in, with a Moroccan guard riding up with them. He refused to allow Molly to give assistance to Fred and Sam until she gave him a mouthful of abuse and waved his rifle aside. He yawned. What did he care if she wasted good bandages on condemned men? He lit a cigar and permitted Molly to bind up Fred's shattered knee while Will wiped the blood from Sam's face.

Peg was driven through the night, first along bone-shaking tracks, then on rutted, unrepaired roads. There was a change of drivers and on went Peg, hour after hour, airless, smelling of blood and of liniment and the foul stink of the Moroccan's cigars.

Will blamed himself. If he had not taken the wrong turning, if he had checked his eagerness to get the wounded back to the farmhouse, they might now be alive and his friends safe from harm. He could hardly wait for Sam to recover consciousness. When he did, Will accused himself.

"What do you mean, lost your way?" Sam was almost cheerful. His left eye had almost disappeared into swollen flesh but gratefully his nose was not broken. "We were practically home and dry, man. Old Howard would've been proud of you! Another quarter of a mile and we'd have been eating grilled steak with the rest of them. Don't worry!"

Will knew he lied to be kind, but he said nothing.

"No, that was a slice of terrible luck. Somebody must've forgotten to say his prayers. If anybody should be apologising, it's me, for getting you into this funfair in the first place."

Federico had given no hint of the agony he was suffering. He had begun to nod, then smile. He sniffed the freshening air. "We go north," he announced. "I feels it in my elbones. See, we finish the mountain climb, we say hello to the windy plains."

He nodded and the pain burnt through him. " 'Ow good 'eavens and dear oh dear me, as you Eng-leesh say! Guernica —I smell it on wind! You see, I read the horror scope: these nice butchers, they feel sorry for ruddy awful trouble they cause and now they give us free hitchhawk to the Basque Cow-ntry. From Bilbao, you sail 'ome, eh?"

Will fell into a sleep of narrow walls and prickly dreams. When firm but friendly hands shook him into wakefulness he was no longer lying with a rolled blanket under his head but in a dark room.

Sam and Griff stood to his right, propping up Federico. They were in a row like schoolboys about to get a thrashing from the headmaster.

His eyes were dazzled by a bright lamp, turned up and towards them, on a desk in the corner of the room. Through the light, Will could see a new guard, a Spaniard this time, leaning against the wall, half asleep.

They waited—and waited. Will's throat was sandpaper. He told himself not to swallow: save saliva. Yet once the idea was in his head, his swallowing went wild. More than anything else in the world at this minute, he wanted one of the barley sugars in his pocket.

He waited, sweating. He watched the guard and his hand climbed inch by inch to the zip of his windjammer. He made room for one finger, then poked downwards, hooking up four barley sugars.

They were in his hand, free of his pocket, when Will almost jumped out of his boots with fright as the guard suddenly came to attention. The barley sugars skidded across the floor, all eyes resting on them.

Immediately the guard levelled his rifle at Will. They exchanged stares, one fierce, the other shocked. Then the guard nodded. Will must pick up the barley sugars. Now he had gathered them, what was he to do with them? Again eyes met, questioning.

He could not believe it, for the guard was going to let him keep the sweets. Will glanced at his friends. Could he?—yes! He passed them round.

He was overwhelmed by this unexpected act of kindness. He felt again in his pocket. There was one barley sugar left. He offered it to the guard. "Por favor!"

The Spaniard hesitated. He looked from face to face. He smiled—and he accepted the barley sugar. "Good?"

"Bueno!"

"English," said Sam. "Bad for the teeth but easy on the gastric juices."

"Si?" If the guard was mindful to confer with his prisoners, the opportunity passed when, from overhead, came the roar of heavy aircraft preparing to land.

There were other sounds too indicating that the survivors of the Seven Bells Brigade had been brought to an airfield and military camp. Will heard the movement of trucks and, very faintly, voices and laughter. The language was German.

After a further endless wait, a jeep pulled up outside and the Spaniard straightened his clothes, his back and his rifle. An officer entered the room escorted by a second Spanish guard. Without a glance at the prisoners, he went to the desk and sat down. His face was concealed behind the glaring white light.

He paused, unhurried, taking papers from a briefcase.

"You are English, I believe, captured at Jarama." He spoke in an immaculate Oxford accent.

"You sound as though you were born under an English heaven too," replied Sam.

"Silence! You will speak only when addressed. I alone stand between yourselves and summary execution. Kindly remember that as the interrogation proceeds."

The officer removed his military cap. His black hair was cut very short. He had a tiny stub of a moustache. His face was long and narrow, reminding Will of a dog that had once bitten him.

Candy Sam could not stop himself: "You're English! It can't be true—fighting with Franco!"

The second Spanish guard was less friendly than the first. He advanced, his rifle poised to strike Sam down. "Wait!" The English officer waved the guard back. "It is no less astonishing to me, Mr Hannington, to find an Englishman, an artist of your reputation, disgracing your birthright and fighting with the Communists."

"Who are you? How do you know my name?"

"Kindly allow *me* to conduct the questioning . . . I am Lieutenant Faradyne of the Requetés." He spoke proudly, vainly. He raised his officer's riding crop from the table, running his fingers along its length, as though touching it gave him a sense of mastery. "Official English interpreter to Captain Robles, our Spanish commandant.

"Arriba España!"

His words prompted the guards to salute. "Arriba España!" they responded.

"To business!" Faradyne leaned back, locking his fingers in front of him like a much older man. "You are accused, all of you, of being enemies of the people of True Spain, of aiding those—namely the Communists—who have subverted justice and by armed revolution conspired to overthrow the rightful government of Spain."

"Green bananas! It was Franco who took to arms against the elected government—and you well know it."

"Be silent!" Faradyne was beginning to lose his initial calm.

"Then don't treat us like half-wits."

"You are Communists!"

"No!"

"Then why did you fight on the side of the Reds?"

"We fought for the Republic."

"Reds, Republicans, they are one and the same."

"Now I see who you are, Faradyne. You're one of Mosley's Blackshirts. To them, everybody that disagrees with their hateful notions is a Red." He knew he was very close to being beaten but he went on: "You ask why I fought for the Republic. I'll tell you—because any cause blessed by Adolph Hitler and his gang of cut-throats is an evil cause."

Faradyne's composure completely vanished. He struck the desk with the flat of his hand. "You are condemned out of your own mouth! Clearly you understand nothing of events. Be assured, one day the glorious ideals of the Führer will rule us all!"

"Cheeps and feesh!" interrupted Federico.

Lieutenant Faradyne thrust forwards through the light, nodding vengefully. Federico was a marked man. He would pay dearly for his insolence.

He took out a gold-topped fountain pen. "Names and details, if you please."

"First we demand to know what has happened to the Red Cross nurse who was captured with us."

"Demand?"

"Request, then."

"That is better. I assure you Nurse Hannington shall go unharmed. She will be useful in our own small hospital. I dare say a few of our men might sustain wounds before the Basque country finally submits to General Mola."

"Never!" ventured Federico. "The Basques, they send you cotton picking with two bogs of spit!"

"The Basque country will fall within the month." Faradyne had recovered confidence. "Out there are the finest bombers and fighter planes the world has ever seen. How many aircraft have the Basques to defend their skies—half a dozen? And do not presume, my Red friend, that we have never heard of the Cinturón, the famous Ring of Iron the Basques are so fond of boasting about."

He smiled. His cheeks swelled like a toad's. "Two hundred miles of trenches, barbed-wire and concrete machine-gun posts—impregnable? Ha!"

His pride conquered discretion. "Such fortifications might indeed have presented General Mola with a headache or two, had not a certain Major Goicoechea seen the light of truth, not to mention the writing on the wall. He turned traitor to his Basque comrades, bringing with him the entire plans of the Cinturón." Faradyne gave the Fascist salute. "Arriba España!"

"Arriba España!" chanted the guards.

Will had fallen asleep on his feet. It seemed for an hour but perhaps it was only for a few seconds. He leaned into Candy Sam who linked his arm in his.

"I will repeat, Hannington, what is the strength of the Republican forces at Jarama?"

"And I repeat, if we're supposed to have been beaten to kingdom come in that battle, why do you want to know such irrelevant information?"

"The battle is not quite over."

"You mean the Fascists have been held. Admit it, Franco's stubbed his jackboots at last!"

Faradyne's voice rang through the room. "What is the strength of the Republican army? How many tanks, how many guns? If you want to save yourself, speak—at once!"

"To be completely honest, we've not the slightest idea. And we wouldn't tell you if we knew. All I can remember is tripping over a lot of dead Moroccans."

Lieutenant Faradyne tried another tack. "For your Spanish friend here, there will be no mercy. He will face the firing squad at seven this morning, but you, Mr Hannington, you have a chance to prolong your life."

"That is not my wish."

Faradyne stood up. "I am reluctant to order the execution of fellow Englishmen, even if they are Reds." He drew out a typed form from his briefcase. "I am going to give you a chance. You will sign this declaration. It states that you were forced to take part in the battle of Jarama: that you were lured into the ranks of the Red armies by officers of the Communist party in London."

"Lured? How are we supposed to have been lured?"

Faradyne mistook Sam's tone. He believed he was beginning to make progress. "You were offered a job in Spain . . . er, as a . . . cartoonist, designer—anything."

"And somehow found myself with a rifle in my hands struggling up Suicide Hill?"

"Exactly!"

Candy Sam laughed. "Then you'll pass on this confession to the British press and the whole nation will read about it?"

"Sign!"

"I would appreciate it, Lieutenant Faradyne, if you would insult me no further in this matter."

"I am under instructions. You must sign! You will not be alone, I assure you . . . Well?"

Slowly Candy Sam stepped forward. He held out his hand for the declaration. He cast his eyes over it once, then screwed the paper into a ball and dropped it at his feet.

Will expected Faradyne to leap up in fury. Rather he seemed to shrink in his chair. "If this puts you into difficulty, Faradyne," said Candy Sam in a sympathetic, almost friendly voice, "I'm sorry."

"Me? In difficulty? Nonsense. I am trusted here, I . . . No Spanish sluggardliness for me. My superiors require results, on the dot. And they get them!"

"How many deaths are on your conscience, Faradyne?"

"None. Those that have died were Red vermin, enemies of the True Spain." He flicked the lamp away from the accusing faces before him. "Hannington, you have thirty minutes in which to change your mind."

"Will my confession save Federico here?"

"What, spare one of those who have burnt down the churches, shot priests, raped nuns? Impossible!"

"Then you already have my answer."

"Thirty minutes, Hannington!"

There was no sleep left in Will. He was alert. His eyes searched in every detail for something to anchor himself to, something to distract his mind from the dreadful probability of what would soon happen to him.

To be shot.

Once he had seen it at the pictures, an execution by firing squad; how they had blindfolded the victim, how he stood, infinitely alone, against a blank wall; and how quickly, how torturedly, he had fallen when the volley came.

Along a dark corridor and—mercy!—into fresh air and the first grey light of morning, To his left, hangars, planes on the runway. All round, a barbed-wire fence, single, not very high. Could be climbed, given half a chance.

One sight cheered them all. Stabled with the other trucks was old Peg. So near, waiting faithfully. If they all, at a given signal, thought Will, made a dash for it . . .

Too late. They were escorted inside a brickbuilt cell-block. Their prison was a cold, damp box no more than six feet square. It stank. There was a small slit window at the top of the wall too high for anyone but an eight-footer to see through.

Yet some former inmate, desperate for a view of the out-side world of graceful wooded hills had chipped a toe-hold between brick and plaster. The cell looked out on to a small exercise yard surrounded by brick walls topped with barbed wire.

Each prisoner in turn surveyed the scene. Each noticed the end wall of the yard. Each remained silent about the bullet holes gouged from the brick.

Candy Sam asked Will and Griff for their forgiveness. "I brought you into this mess. That is my first sorrow. My second is that I've been no use to my sister."

"What'll 'appen to us, Sam?"

"If you're asked to sign the declaration, sign it. Faradyne has no alternative but to have Fred and me shot, but if I'm any judge, he's no monster. Misguided rather than wicked. He's as caught up in his situation as we are."

"Then why don't *you* sign, Sam?" asked Will, with little hope.

"Aye," came in Griff, "it's just a scrap o' waste paper."

"And if the *Daily Mail* gets hold of it, plasters it all over the front page that the Republic is forcing men into its ranks at bayonet point or by trickery? Never!" He smiled. "And in any event, I'm not so trusting in Fascist honour to think that they would spare me after I had signed. I would, like so many other victims of Franco's barbarity, be reported shot while escaping."

Sam chose to concentrate his thoughts on those he would leave behind. For them he forged a dream of escape. In that dream perhaps he would escape, momentarily, the reality of his own death. He told Will and Griff where to find a hidden ignition key to Peg, where there was a concealed pistol, where there were bars of chocolate to beat starvation on a long and hurried journey.

Federico too grasped at this fragile blossom of future life. "It take no Spanish Shylock 'Olm-es to snuff out this place. North—it is Vizcaya. My throat of the woods as you Eng-leesh say. The Basque people, they make you safe. And after they feast your bellies big with steak and wine, they wave you bye-bye on Eng-leesh ship from Bilbao. And before you speak Jack Robertson, you 'ome and dry."

He ignored the hundred-and-one hazards that might prevent such an escape. In his condemned mind he saw only open doors and empty roads winding ever homewards. "You go to Guernica, eh?" He emptied his pockets. He produced a curled and torn photograph of his family. "I write the

street on 'ere. You go. You tell thems 'ow Federico he die for
España. Free Spain! Give my dog Vasco da Gama a pat on
'is sto-mach. 'e like that!"

With a splitting heart, Will received Fred's possessions.
This was not happening, not to him, not to friends he had
come to love; it could not happen. Something, surely, would
turn up.

"Everything I left behind me in Sussex, Will, is Molly's,
but if you can grab it, my sketchbook is for you. Peg belongs
to whoever can get her home.

"At the back of my sketchbook, you'll find the last known
addresses of the Seven Bells Brigade. Tell them, if the chance
comes—Ike's old mother, Howard's father, Roland's wife,
Ben's brother in St Helen's . . . Tell them of the sacrifice
they made."

He paused. "As for me, say only this to Molly, that my
love and admiration know no limits. Tell her I shall meet her
beside the Long Man of Wilmington. Together, we'll walk
over the Downs to the sea. Tell her!"

The heavy fall of boots sounded in the passage outside. A
key jarred in the lock. The lock's mechanism was slow to
respond. The door swung open. The kind guard stood back
for the unkind guard who ordered out the prisoners.

"All of us?" protested Sam in Spanish. "Surely not these
two—but they're just boys!"

"All!" repeated the guard, and the kind guard nodded.
There was no mistake.

They were marched into a morning grey with mist, and
numbingly cold. Now the drums were beating in Will's
chest. He was going to be shot. He was going to be executed.
He would stand against *that* wall.

The Seven Bells Brigade were held at bayonet point in the
empty yard. Soon it would be like Tuesdays in Jarrow, after
the cattle had been brought in for slaughter and the blood
ran out from under the butchers' back doors.

From a far gate, reinforced with slats of iron, emerged
ten militiamen, rifles slung carelessly over their shoulders.

"Spaniards to shoot a Spaniard!" murmured Sam. He held out his hand to Federico. "It has been an honour and a great pleasure to have known you, Fred the Basque man. May Free Spain live!"

Lieutenant Faradyne arrived with a Spanish officer. They stood together flicking the air with their riding crops.

"You have decided to sign the declaration, Hannington?"

There was no reply. From the rainless sierra came a dry, shivery wind. "You are keeping Captain Robles and his firing squad waiting."

"Have I time for a bite of candy?"

Sam's calmness irritated the impatient Faradyne. "What is your answer, Hannington?"

"Barley sugar!"

The experience of death was already in Will. He sensed the slow departure of mind from body until it was an unanchored, distant thing, recording events as if they were the concern of another person in another time.

Captain Robles' riding crop cracked petulantly against his knee-high boot. The prisoners were herded towards the bullet-sprayed wall. The firing squad lined up in front of them.

Faradyne stepped forward. "In the name of the Commander of the Nationalist Army of the North and in the name of the people of True Spain——"

"Faradyne!" Sam had not finished. His voice could have been heard a quarter of a mile away. "These boys! They are no part of this. May you roast in hell if you allow them to fall with us this day."

"Then sign the declaration!"

There was silence, a century long.

Faradyne advanced on the prisoners. There was no blood in his face and his hands trembled as though he himself were condemned. He stared into Candy Sam's fierce eyes. "You will go through all this in the cause of the Reds?"

"In the cause of the Spanish Republic. For her freedom, and for the freedom from tyranny of every man."

"For God's sake, sign!"

"Never!"

"I do not want this!"

"Then save my young friends."

Faradyne retreated a step. He glanced over his shoulder at Captain Robles, at the militiamen ready for the order to take aim. Then he descended on the prisoners. He grabbed Will by the collar, Griff by his windjammer, and hurled them away, out of line of the firing squad.

He was brisk now, determined. "Captain Robles!"

Federico called out, "Por favor?"

"Yes?"

Fred slipped his violin from his shoulder. "Bullets, they play bad music. Please, you permit the boy to take it."

Will felt the warm wood of the violin in his hands, the strings taut under his fingers. He looked at Candy Sam.

"Goodbye, Jarrow, so long gingertop. Take care of Molly for me."

Faradyne had saluted smartly. "At your pleasure, Captain!"

CHAPTER NINE

He had seen his friends die. He had seen them stagger and fall in blood. He had witnessed the villainy of the world and now he was locked in the stinking cell, alone. He had appealed to the kindly Spanish guard: "Let us stay together!" But orders had to be obeyed. Griff was taken down the passage. Door slammed on their anguish, leaving them black walls on which to project the last images of those they would never see again.

Will had sat on his bunk, staring into shadow; and as he stared, refusing to blink, refusing to avert his gaze from the emptiness before him, the tears darted from his eyes. He did not wipe away the streams from his cheeks. He did not raise his hand or move his weary, shock-stiffened body; he did not lift his head, bowed by the picture no tears would ever wash away.

It would have been better, yes by far, to have stood with Sam and Fred, died with them, than be their lonely mourner, who saw no further reason for his existence and who, in a spasm of anger, dropped to the ground and struck the brick floor with his fists. He was untouched, unscathed, but he would suffer like Sam and Fred, like Howard and Roland, and like Ben whose self-sacrifice had earned him a driftwood cross on a forgotten Spanish beach.

Will was upright. He hurled himself at the cell door, battering his forehead against the flat ribs of studded iron. And the blood he wished for flowed. He crashed again into the door. He spun over, collapsed on to his knees, eyes wet with blood, and found what he most desired—the oblivion of unconsciousness.

Yet if he had foreseen the nightmares that pursued him into writhing sleep he would have chosen to stay awake. He remained for hours, unmoving, his wounds congealing in the cold air, until discovered by the guard when he brought a

tray of soup and black bread. For a dazzling instant, he
hoped they might call for Molly, but the guard brought
water and bandages and proved himself a considerate and
skilful nurse.

You must make no trouble, Will was told, be as a mouse
and you might live a little longer. "I do not want to live,"
was Will's response. He repeated the words after the guard
had left and, curiously, they gave him comfort. He did not
want to live, therefore it followed that there was nothing the
enemy could do that would frighten him.

His sleep was less disturbed. He awoke refreshed and
strengthened. "I do not want to live," Will said aloud. Beneath the layers of sorrow, he sensed a dim spark of pride.
His captors believed that life was so precious to him that
there would be nothing he might not do to preserve it. He
almost laughed. If they threatened him, he would demand
their worst punishment.

At first, as the hours passed, he refused to conduct himself
in any way that might suggest he retained a will to survive.
He lay as though already in his coffin. He refused to watch
the thin beams of sunlight penetrating his cell; closed his
ears to the song of birds outside. Days passed. He ate little
and refused to exercise his body. He lay in the ante-room of
death—and nothing happened, no one came but Manuel
the guard; no one threatened him.

Manuel was friendly and cheerful. He talked through
Will's stubborn silence, about the farm he helped his brother
run south of Pamplona, about his wife and children, his love
of the good earth, and little by little Will began to relent.
Manuel's simple friendship—and the ever-comforting words
of Da's letter—restored him. He slowly succumbed to the
urge to plan and dream.

Having given way to a trickle of the life force, Will's true
nature reasserted itself, and the trickle became a flood. He
wanted to live—a hundred times yes! He would fight to live
and even in this miserable cell he would learn good reasons
for surviving. To begin with, he had treated all days and all

times of day as the same. Now time was of value again and he noted its passing.

He scratched the days on to his cell wall, yet not in simple marks but in the initials of his friends. He, Will Viljoen, realised his task. He was the living testimony to his dead comrades. Their heroism must be remembered and eventually recorded. So each day was re-Christened—Sam's Day, Ben's Day, Ike's Day, Roland's Day, Howard's Day and Federico's Day. Sundays, when Manuel returned glowing from Mass, was reserved as Da's Day, and shared by absent friends—Molly and Griff.

Manuel allowed him a small, broken-runged step-ladder so that Will could stare out of his cell window in comfort. There, each day without fail, he bathed his face in warm sunlight. He watched winter dissolve into spring; he saw banks of crocuses under the faraway trees and smelt the tang of fresh grass.

He struggled to keep his brain alert, remembering all the songs his Da had taught him, itemising every detail he could recall of the places they had visited together—Bamburgh Castle, Durham Cathedral, Holy Island, and five unforgettable visits to watch Newcastle at St James's Park.

Even so, when he had listed every street name in Jarrow, every face from his childhood, every film he had seen at the pictures, the nickname of every club in the football league, when he had drawn up his Hundred Best Meals, his mind remained unsatisfied. He begged Manuel to ask Lieutenant Faradyne to provide him with books.

After a fortnight of waiting, Manuel arrived with a pile of old copies of the English *Daily Mail*. The reports stung Will to anger. They were so biased against the Republic, so bitterly opposed to the International Brigades. He had been present at Jarama, yet in the *Mail* Will read:

BRITONS LURED TO DEATH IN SPAIN. SENSATIONAL DISCLOSURES BY 35 OF REDS' VICTIMS. PROMISED WORK THEN PUT IN FIRING LINE. OBJECTORS SHOT.

It was all lies! But for his courage and judgment, Candy Sam's name might have been among them, for the world to see. Will then sent Lieutenant Faradyne a letter composed of type from the newspapers. He made three requests: for information about Molly, for daily exercise outside in the yard, and to share a cell with Griff.

Sam's Day came and went, came and went, and Will heard nothing. Da's Day, however, proved lucky. Manuel brought Will breakfast and, sharing his delight, led him out of his cell. For the first time in weeks, he stood with the sky above him and the spring breeze bustling round him.

" 'ere comes little Adolph," said Griff before the two friends could start a conversation. Faradyne strutted towards them, as usual flicking his riding crop against his boot.

"I would like you two to know," he began, with a hint of nervousness, "that your friends received a proper burial, despite their being enemies of the state. They were stubborn and foolish, but I have come to think of them as brave men too. It was not my wish that one of England's most promising artists be cut down so sharply in his prime." He waited. There was no response. "We are all victims of circumstance —do you understand that? Never masters of ourselves."

"Can we see Molly Hannington, Mr Faradyne?" asked Will boldly.

Faradyne walked in a small circle as if deep in thought. "She has demanded to see you. It is difficult to deny such a head-strong young woman, particularly as she has tended our wounded with great efficiency.

"But I am afraid . . ." He stopped. He smoothed and nipped the ends of the moustache he was growing Spanish-style. "Miss Hannington has not yet been informed of her brother's death. She is under the impression that he was transferred to Burgos for further questioning. She must not be told the truth, not for the present anyway."

"What've they got up their sleeves for us, Mr Faradyne?" Griff asked.

Faradyne was uneasy. He looked away when he spoke.

"That is the business which has brought me here this morning." His riding crop no longer tapped his boot but fell like a cane across his palm. "The brief answer is that I do not know. Soon I shall be posted. I have no idea what Captain Robles has in mind for your future, or Miss Hannington's."

He tried to smile. "My father would have been better able to advise you. He successfully escaped from the Germans during the Great War. A very daring exploit!"

"If you were us, Mr Faradyne, would you try to escape?" Such a question might have earned a whipping, but Will risked it. He sensed that Faradyne was worried for them.

"Escape? That would be difficult." He paused. "Though not impossible, of course. Myself, as a matter of pure conjecture, you understand—I would be tempted not to delay." His laugh was forced. "The Basque Country will fall to the Army of the North within days. Then there would be no hope of catching an England-bound ship."

Faradyne was leaving when he checked his stride. "Oh, another thing. I am afraid that Manuel will no longer be your guard. It is not of my doing, but he has been arrested, suspected of having Republican sympathies. A relative brought charges against him. I'm sorry."

"That's senseless!" protested Will bitterly.

Faradyne turned away. "I suggest you address such remarks to Captain Robles. Here comes your new guard. Ask him no favours and do not trust him."

As they were escorted back to the cells, Will and Griff thought only of escape. "If old Faradyne wasn't givin' us a 'int as big as 'ouses, then I'm a bleedin' Aborigine. I mean, they're lax, these Spanish. Dozy devils. Likes their sleep an' their vino. If we could just get out the cells, it'd be as easy as training up a flea circus."

"I'd have thought that was difficult."

"I've got one goin' in t'cell. They'll do anythin' for a blob o' warm 'uman blood. I've tight-rope walkers, clowns and fleas that ride on one another's backs. It's the greatest show on earth! They'll be comin' wi' me in a matchbox when we escape."

The two friends expected to meet each day to discuss their plans for escape but the new guard, sour-faced, resentful, who refused to talk or answer the simplest of questions, chose to override the prisoners' privileges. He would either take them out for exercise at odd times or not at all.

Will's determination to escape increased; it gave him no rest, prodded him, haunted every waking moment, whispered along the strings of Fred's violin as Will struggled to make music out of it. He thought up many plans but each one fell foul of his resolve not to leave without Molly. Somehow he must persuade his captors that he needed her.

He had begun to suffer from a skin infection—swelling, aching, suppurating. Infection? Will suddenly had what seemed a bright idea. Battering his head against the cell door had been the wrong tactic. Any soldier worth his salt could bandage a wound; but would he be so confident treating a spreading army of germs?

Will remembered spending Christmas Eve on the Aragon front reading one of Candy Sam's medical books, called *Medicine for Nurses*. He had been intrigued by a very odd photograph in which a man suffering from deadly meningitis lay with his leg stuck up in the air, his knee helplessly locked and his neck stiff as a ramrod. That, the book had explained, was Kernig's sign.

Now meningitis was one of those highly infectious diseases that make jittery folk run a mile to avoid. Will decided to wait till nightfall before contracting the disease. He lay on his bunk. He cleared his throat—and then let fly a piercing scream, just as the book recommended. His "meningitis cry" would have done justice to a true sufferer and the Spanish guard came at once. Whether or not he diagnosed this cry as a sign of an increased formation of the cerebrospinal fluid in the skull, his alarm was immediate.

He brought Lieutenant Faradyne, who was not amused. "Feigning sickness, my young friend, could put you in front of the firing squad again." Yet he was uncertain. Will squinted up at him. He yelled out when the light went on, exactly as the book advised. Faradyne remained at the door. "For God's sake, put your leg down. Look, if I find . . ." He relented. He ordered the guard to fetch Nurse Hannington. "This is what you were angling for, isn't it? You will say nothing of her brother's death, understand?"

Will concentrated on making vomiting noises.

"As a matter of fact, I was on my way here." Faradyne was plainly nervous, tensed-up. "With a story you and your cockney friend might appreciate. Yes, about what happened at Jarama to one of your machine-gun companies. Quite a joke, really." He glanced closer.

Will pretended delirium.

"Our intrepid Moroccan troops crept up on them in the dark. Crafty as foxes, they began to sing the Internationale—the hymn that stirs you Reds to a fever. Snake charmers, you see! Thinking they were being greeted by their comrades, this Harry Fry and his dunderheads surrendered without firing a shot. Best joke of the war, what?"

The glaring cell light was eclipsed by a head of dark curls and the blue glow of cornflower eyes. Despite his resolve, Will abandoned his squint. He had never seen anything so beautiful as Molly's smile.

"Nurse, I would advise you to urge this young malingerer——"

"Of course he's sick! Are you suggesting he's used stage make-up to acquire these suppurations?"

"I will be straight with you. If it is infectious, Captain Robles will have him shot in his cell."

Will's meningitis took an abrupt turn for the better. His knee unlocked, intracranial pressure eased, progressive drowsiness was set in reverse and photophobia disappeared completely.

"It must be scarlet fever," he murmured.

"I diagnose escapitis, Nurse Hannington."

Molly held Will's hand. "Do you blame him, Lieutenant?"

"It's the least I would expect from a tough Tynesider. You mistake my beliefs if you think I do not love my own race." He retreated a step towards the door and pushed it to. "In a way it is convenient that we meet like this. For it will be the last time. I travel to Burgos tonight." He came to attention, clicking his heels. "I will bid you goodbye."

He opened the door. "You will remain here, Nurse, to treat Viljoen's rash. The guard will escort you to your quarters when he returns for duty in ten minutes' time." He paused. "I shall have a final word with Griffiths."

He gave the Fascist salute. "To the Land of Hope and Glory!" He turned. "And good luck!" He was along the passage, at Griff's cell, for less than a minute. They heard Griff's door slam. They listened to Faradyne's receding footsteps. To their astonishment, he began whistling as he left the building.

"Whistling? Him? He must have got a touch of the sun."

Will sprang up. "What's that tune?" It sounded again, from outside, before being drowned by the throb of Faradyne's jeep. "Dee, da-da, dee, da-da, dum-dum-dum!"

Molly's eyes widened. "It's . . . Good God!—Run, Rabbit, Run!" They stood facing each other, electrified with excitement. Run, rabbit, run? "Surely he'd not——?"

Will crossed towards the door. He tried the heavy iron handle: the door opened. "What did he say—about the guard?"

"He'd be coming back for me in ten minutes." For a moment they were dumbfounded. A crevasse, teeming with vipers of fear and danger, had opened up before them. All that they desired lay on the other side, but would there be strength enough in their leap?

"Shall we risk it?"

Molly switched off the light. "Try Griff's cell." In five heart-whirring seconds the three of them were squatting in the dark, too nervous even to whisper.

Then from Will, cradling Fred's violin which no escape

bid would persuade him to leave behind: "We'd not get far on foot. Peg's our best bet."

"She's still where they left her. But wouldn't we wake the camp?"

"Aye, but we'd be off quick as lightnin'."

"Yes, and heading north to Vizcaya—the Basque Cow-ntry. Molly, what's the main gate like?"

"Oh, flimsy. They don't expect to be attacked. There's just a pole with a halt sign hung on it."

"Guards?"

"Two, perhaps three."

"How many other trucks are there with Peg?"

"Several. Sometimes guarded."

"Are we agreed, then?"

At the end of the passage was the guards' room. A rifle had been left carelessly against a table. There was a bottle of wine on a tray and an uneaten supper of bread and cheese which Griff stuffed into his pockets. "Like old times, eh, Will?"

The outer door was ajar. The night air was balmy, the sky full of stars. In front of them, a black desert of space reached to the distant aircraft hangars. From the barrack huts came the sound of a concertina and a spirited German chorus.

"Any guards around the trucks?"

They were no more than thirty yards away. Hopes dived towards despair. Right in front of Peg, one guard brought another into vision by lighting his cigarette.

"They're moving off!"

"Here goes, then." Will reached out his hand for Molly's. They sprinted across the open ground. The white horse of Pegasus shone in greeting. The cab handle clicked as Will pressed it down. There was a soft whine as the door's hinges awoke for the first time in weeks.

Molly and Griff were aboard. Will followed Candy Sam's instructions. Under the driving seat he located a metal plate. He slid it sideways. "One pistol, six bars of chocolate and one ignition key!" There was also a scout knife in a leather sheath. "Just hang on a minute."

"Blast it, where're y'goin'?"

Will had slipped from Peg. He stooped towards the truck next to her. He knifed its front tyre. He raced to the other three vehicles, disabling each one.

He was back, turning the key in the ignition. "Fingers crossed!" He pulled out the choke as far as it would go. His foot was hard down on the accelerator. He didn't dare consider the possibility of a flat battery.

He released the handbrake. "Do your stuff, Peg!" The engine fired once, then petered into silence. Will tried again —again a breath of life, dying. A third tug on the starter brought no more luck.

Will's fingers were shaking so violently he could hardly grasp the starter.

"You can only keep trying," said Molly soothingly.

He pulled the starter for the fifth time. "She's alive!" First gear, slowly forward. Second—almost jammed it; but rolling nicely.

"Faster!"

"Give her time!"

Five miles an hour on the clock. Ten. Trundling towards the camp gate. "We'll do it!" Foot right down, engine snorting, going straight for the pole across the entrance. All at once, movement. Alarm. Figures, dark, white-faced, skidding from the guard hut; behind them, the tumbled remains of a card game; wine glasses overturned.

In front of Peg, a guard, arms outstretched, shouting.

"Move!" The guard twisted aside as Peg charged on like an avalanche. The white pole snapped and flew. Abreast of them, barbed wire. Now behind them. "We've made it!"

They were almost away, almost ready to cheer, when a single shot rang out. It fractured glass, passing through the passenger's window. It lifted Griff off his seat as though he had been a plank of wood, badly stacked. He rose, his knees seeming to press him into a standing position. Then he flopped against the dashboard. He sank on glass.

"Griff?"

He had not made a sound. As Will drove, Molly fought to lift him on to the seat again. "Where, Griff? Where's it hit you?" He did not answer. Molly guessed it was his shoulder or the side of his body. Her arms were round him. His head fell against her and all at once, in the terrible darkness, she was drenched.

"He's . . . Oh—God!" She raised her hand to Griff's face, to his head that hung like a stone in a sack.

Will had turned on Peg's headlights. Left out of the camp. At the forked roads, bear right—Manuel had told him that much. North, beyond the pine-fringed hills, was Vizcaya, loyal to the Republic. "We'll drive all night. Hide up somewhere during daylight . . . Griff, is he bad?"

Molly held Griff tightly to her. His head-wound continued to soak her hair, her clothes, yet she did not put him from her. She stared along the beams of Peg's eyes at the rough road climbing across the black sierra. She stared and the tears welled up from her lids till the lights multiplied before her and shot away in glistening arcs, till her lashes soaked up the tears and cast them one by one down her cheeks.

"He's dead, Will."

The blow almost made Will bring Peg to a total halt. She slowed. Her engine complained. "He can't—he can't be! Look at him again—please, Molly!" He needed to change to a lower gear. He tried to look. After the execution of Sam and Fred he had thought he could withstand any shock. Yet this death was to devastate him worst of all. "It's not possible. Not Griff!"

Peg was demanding concentration. Will was shattered. Griff's death knocked the heart out of him. "What do we do, Molly?"

She did not move her head. She made no attempt to wipe away her tears or Griff's blood, but her strength was that of the mountain. "We drive on."

CHAPTER TEN

They buried Griff at first light on a hill slope ringed with pines. Will dug the grave with the spade the Seven Bells Brigade had used to deepen the trenches on the Aragon front and to prepare Ben's last resting place. With Sam's knife, he shaped two arms of a wooden cross and bound them in place with rope.

"There were times when I hated him. That first night in Aragon, I'd have killed him, given the chance. But what use is there in remembering those things!" His own tears were flowing. "In the end I came to love him . . . And to think, he never got one of those ten pesetas a day promised to every militiaman. Not one!"

Below them stretched a lake of white mist. It seemed to be spreading southwards, swallowing the land. Out of its soft, glowing turbulence appeared the deep green of forests. Will knelt down beside the grave. "Molly, there's a secret I can no longer bear to keep." He did not look at her as he spoke. "Sam wasn't taken off to Burgos for questioning."

She had stooped towards him. She put her hands affectionately, reassuringly on his shoulder. "Do you think I don't know that? They took me out of camp, miles away—but I still felt the bullets. Later, Manuel—good, kind Manuel—confirmed the truth. Did Sam say anything, leave a message?"

"He said he would meet you by the Long Man of Wilmington." Till this instant Molly had borne her grief. Now, at these words, it flooded her defences. She threw her arms round Will's neck and wept.

For his part, he felt an abominable weight go from him. The death of Sam was no longer a shadow between them; it was a bond as strong as death. "We'll manage, won't we?"

Her head rested for several seconds on his shoulder. "This would be a grand storybook ending to the tale of Will and Molly, wouldn't it?"

His reply was not what either expected. "We're being watched!" Very slowly, he raised his face into the sun. "We mustn't frighten him off."

A youth sat on the hill high above them, surrounded by his goats whose bells tinkled brightly in the clear air. He carried a sapling staff and wore a goatskin cloak around his shoulders.

"Buenos dias!" called Molly.

The statue moved, though only to his feet, wary of the strangers. "Buenos dias!" Whose side? was the question written on all three faces—Republican or Fascist? When Will took a step nearer, the goatherd took his guard, his staff held threateningly out in front of him; but Molly climbed up the rocky escarpment towards him.

She spoke quietly to the goatherd in Spanish. They both started to smile. Molly turned round to Will. "Would you believe it? Lady Luck's showing her soft spot for us at last. We've got ourselves a guide. José here lives in Guernica. He says he'll be glad of a lift."

Lady Luck did indeed seem to be in a generous mood: José the young Basque goatherd was to prove that he knew every road and track, hill and wood in this part of Vizcaya. Without his help, Will and Molly would have been caught in the advancing ring of Fascist armies.

First he showed them a cooling spring, where they washed; then he fed them with bitter-tasting black bread and delicious goats' milk. There was no time to delay. The Basque country was encircled; the main roads were blocked every few miles by Mola's troops; the skies were rarely empty of German planes. Several days following he had seen bomb smoke on the northern horizon.

In his turn, José was grateful to his new friends in their flying horse. Now, care for his goats must give way to care for his people. He must go and fight for Vizcaya. He unfolded an enemy leaflet he had found on the road below. Molly translated the cruel words of warning by Franco's commander in the North, General Mola:

I HAVE DECIDED TO TERMINATE RAPIDLY THE WAR IN
THE NORTH. THOSE NOT GUILTY OF ASSASSINATIONS
WHO SURRENDER THEIR ARMS WILL HAVE THEIR LIVES
AND PROPERTY SAVED. BUT IF SUBMISSION IS NOT
IMMEDIATE I WILL RAZE ALL VIZCAYA TO THE GROUND,
BEGINNING WITH THE INDUSTRIES OF WAR.

His last words were no idle boast:

I HAVE THE MEANS.

The threat had been delivered, and the people of Vizcaya
had ignored the threat.

Peg swooped into lush, tree-filled valleys. She took cart
tracks, crossed meadows, cut through orchards. She sheltered
in pinewoods to let enemy convoys pass. She skirted road
blocks, and José announced that they would be in time for
the market at Guernica. Afterwards, he would show them the
famous old oak tree near the Casa de Juntas, where the kings
of Vizcaya swore to uphold the liberties of the people.

"The Freedom Tree!" Will was thinking of the words
Count Philippe had called after the Seven Bells Brigade, so
long ago: protect the Freedom Tree! He was remembering
Federico's surprise at such a task. "Protect?" he had said.
"From who, amigo—the greenfly? There is no Spaniard
alive-o who dare touch the Oak of Guernica. No!"

"If I come out of this war with nothing else, Molly, I
want an acorn to plant in Jarrow. She could do with a
Freedom Tree."

Eventually José permitted Will to turn on to a recognisable
road. The tide of war was behind them. Ahead were signs of
a people still at peace—farmcarts pulled by oxen and piled
high with produce for market. The Basque peasants walked
backwards in front of their oxen, gently urging them on with
the occasional tap of a stick on the horns. They talked to the
oxen and the oxen seemed to take in every word.

Will drove slowly through the fine, leafy streets of Guernica to the market place in the town centre. Soon they would

search for Federico's home, but first they bought food. Will had never felt so close to his own home in Jarrow since his travels had begun. He had thought his childhood gone for ever, but in that timeless market, the tough armour of his manhood melted as if it had never existed.

He was the boy who had played under the stalls at Jarrow market, whipping sweets from the open counters, begging for the bad apples and swapping his precious halfpennies for horse-chestnuts sizzling in blue smoke. Yet they did not stay long. Molly and Will did not have a peseta to split between them and José had only enough to buy three small white loaves and a bottle of wine—which he practically emptied in three laughing gulps.

"We Basques," he said, "love money, wine and God—in that order!"

The Oak of Guernica seemed to beckon them from its quiet solitude. It was like walking out of the bustle of Jarrow centre, thought Will, to the holy silence of Bede's Well; a similar pilgrimage. They stood before an oak tree like other oaks, not bigger, not grander; yet a special oak.

Beneath the spread of its branches there were wooden seats carved with the arms of Vizcaya—a tree and lurking wolves. "Smell the sea, Molly? It can't be far away."

"I'll remember this for ever."

The early evening sunlight filtered through the dark branches as José described how, when the rights of Vizcaya were declared, trumpets were blown and bonfires lit on hill-tops all over the province. The hum of the market did not drown the soft rustle of the leaves. A breeze carried rose petals along the ground.

"Peace!"

Then, from across the town came the sound of a church bell. It struck single chimes, and the look of contentment on José's face vanished. "San Juan!"

"What's he saying, Molly?" José was dragging them away. Will was hearing words his mother had never taught him. "What's happening?"

"Air raid!"

General Mola was keeping his word.

The three of them ran. And then they stopped running, for where was there to run? They stood still. They waited. The bell of San Juan struck again and again and again, stirring apprehension into fear.

"We can get out—now!" It was for Molly to decide. Peg awaited orders.

"We promised Federico. We'll never be back." They hesitated. They listened. The even murmur of the market had become disjointed. People were running. First, the solitary sprinters, with only themselves to save. Then parents with children, and the elderly forcing along their slow limbs.

"Hear anything?"

Above the squall of voices close by, the shouts, the clatter of panicky feet, there came a faint, drumming roar. Will and Molly knew that sound well enough. "It could be they'll pass over—on their way to the factories in Bilbao." They took comfort from this possibility. After all, what strategic significance had this sleepy market town?

Echoing Federico's words, José declared that no Spaniard would give orders for the bombing of Guernica. Yet his fingers pressed round the empty wine bottle till they were white.

A single plane, blunt-nosed, with the outline of a killer whale, skimmed the town. "Heinkel!" The bombs were clearly visible. They glided through the rays of evening sunlight. One . . . two . . . three . . . four, and the ground shook, the air flashed. A blistering wind swept the rose petals over the dusty earth.

Five . . . six, followed by the crack of grenades.

Will gripped José's arm. Were there any anti-aircraft guns in Guernica? The young Basque replied that there were no guns and no troops either; scarcely a rifle to aim at the sky.

Having delivered its load, the German Heinkel 111 banked towards the west. José beat his fist against stone. He had heard rumours, he said, of other bombings, at Durango and

Elgueta, at Ochandiana and Elorrio. Perhaps this was just a warning. Perhaps a single pilot had a few bombs to drop to fulfil his quota. Perhaps the Heinkel was the first and last.

Will remembered his Granda Viljoen describe how the German Zeppelins bombed Jarrow during the Great War. They had gone straight for Palmer's who built battleships for the British navy; seventeen men had been killed and sixty-one injured in the engine erection shop. The rest of the town had been left untouched.

An aching pause. Optimism rising, then fading as a second Heinkel traced the path of the first, its target the town centre. It completed its unchallenged tour of destruction with a burst of machine-gun fire.

José advised that if a full air-raid came, they must look for the sign REFUGIO where they would find shelter behind sandbags.

"Look!" A lone shadow crossed the street ahead of them. "A priest carrying the sacraments."

Ten minutes passed. Eleven. Twelve. The sky was clear and smiling. People were venturing out of their shelters, calling nervously to one another. "Is it possible they're going to spare us after all?" asked Molly.

"We'll wait five minutes," said Will, "and if there's nothing else, we'll look for Federico's house. Then away to Bilbao."

Thirteen minutes. Fourteen. On the fifteenth, silence died. The thunder of man rolled across the eastern horizon.

"Tranvias! Tranvias!" The call spread down the street. "Tranvias!"

"What are they on about, Molly?"

"Trams! José says that's what people've nicknamed the Junkers . . . Junker fifty-twos."

"They're well named."

The temporary peace was shattered by the clanking roar of huge, ugly, clumsy monsters that hardly seemed able to hold their positions in the air.

"Too late for a refuge. Quick, against the wall!" Will had

had this nightmare before, of planes blackening the sky till there was no sky left, of bombs so big, so close, they appeared to have been released from the ceiling. Yet in the nightmare the bombs fell, struck him, but never exploded. Now there would be no Da to clasp hold of when the dream became too fearful to bear.

His hand searched for Molly's. They watched the bombs fall in a single, streaming cascade. They saw whole streets shudder with the impact of high explosive. Houses split in two, lifted from their foundations. Great walls keeled over into the streets. Solid brick and stone disintegrated. Plumes of black smoke shot upwards through the jagged ruins.

José had Molly and Will by the arms. "Refugio! Refugio!"

"But where?" José had no idea.

"We're staying put—next to Peg." They were alone in the deserted streets. Will did not know what to do. His concern was for Molly. The population was indoors, hiding in cellars —should they run, risk it?

More bombers. Wave upon wave of them. Precise, in line, their bombs patterned for maximum destruction. Will observed the first trickle of fire, the lick of flames. Smoke enveloped whole streets in acrid coils.

The trenches held no terror like this terror. In the trenches you could duck, hide, be confident in the protection offered by mother earth. This was a new kind of war, no longer soldiers against soldiers, but the deliberate extermination of civilians. And Will wondered, when solid stone could resist attack no better than a sandcastle survives the lapping sea, what future was there for man?

He watched the bombs falling, tilting in line, sometimes spinning. He saw them plunge to the very heart of the houses. Roofs collapsed into upper storeys, upper storeys on to the floors below, ground floors into basements.

"What price the Refugios now? People'll be buried alive."

"We must help!"

"Wait, Molly." He was sick with fear. He could hardly breathe. He felt Molly trembling. Equally shaken, José prowled. He refused to stand with his back to the wall. He advanced into the road. He retreated. He snarled abuse at the sky.

The streets were deserted no longer. For the people, their refuges threatened to become stone coffins. They fled from battered and unmolested homes alike. They would take their chance in the open. The town was doomed. They must escape from it.

Better the open fields where only a tree could fall on them than remain under hurtling tons of stone.

Will held Molly from the crush. He watched their faces, blank with terror, contorted with terror. He thought of those less fortunate who had been left behind, the mangled dead, those buried alive.

"We've got to do *something*!" cried Molly.

"When the time comes. They've not finished with us yet."

The bombs had driven reason and sense from all minds. José had stepped in among the crowds. He tried to rally them, turn them back as though a barricade or ranks of determined people would frighten the German aircraft away.

"Gara Euzhadi Eskatuta! Gara Euzhadi Eskatuta!"

"What's he shouting, Molly?"

"It's the Basque freedom cry . . . Long live free Euzhadi."

"Tell him it's no use, he's getting in folks' way."

José confronted the old and limping. He thrust out his arms at parents fleeing with infants in their arms, at those loaded with their most needful possessions, at scampering youths, at children separated from their families.

Solely in the direction of the people's flight was there no confusion. They knew their way—the Bermeo road, the sea and the protection of their mother city, Bilbao.

Molly too was in among the crowd, her intention to assist those who stumbled and fell. No one did, the risk was too great. Only Molly tripped. She was carried headlong in the rush and Will had to lift her out of the dust.

"Take it easy, Florence Nightingale, or you'll end up being the Lady with the Wooden Leg."

The panic of the townspeople was evidently part of the grand scheme of the enemy, for close on the heels of the Junkers came an escort of Heinkels—51s this time, new planes, pin-nosed, the sharks after the killer whales.

Will dragged Molly to the wall. He called José, but José was staring upwards, transfixed.

The Heinkels, with their characteristic split wheels, were flying so low that Will could see the faces of the pilots. He suddenly felt his fear die and be replaced by anger. Behind the flashing steel, the heartless machines, were humans enjoying a day of bestial killing. What did those pilots feel?

He shared José's mad desperation. He would have done anything to bring one pilot down, to rip him from the metal walls that made him immune and indifferent to the agony he caused. He saw everything, foresaw everything, remembered everything—but understood nothing.

The Heinkels dived. They could have been no more than six hundred feet above the roofs of the town. They carried no bombs. Their target was not wood and stone and glass, but running flesh. They dived. They machine-gunned.

"Down flat!" Will cast his body in an arch around Molly's head, his arms crossed over her shoulders. Somewhere behind him, he heard José yelling up at the German pilots, defying them. Was he actually dancing in the road, waving his hand and his empty wine bottle? Was he out of his mind?

Twice, three times, the Heinkels swooped over the streets. "Molly—into that doorway!" They alone in this world of terrified motion, remained still. Through hands clapped over eyes like frail visors, they became spectators of the daring exploits of pilots with nothing to fear but cramp in their firing thumbs.

They witnessed a massacre: a young mother and her baby sent to eternity by a single burst; an old man, scarcely able to hobble, robbed for ever of the need to go on trying; a dark-eyed, handsome boy of seven or eight, that afternoon having played with brothers and sisters for the last time—decapitated an arm's length from his father.

Scores fell. Yet before they fell they were carried off their feet, beaten upwards by the impact of lead and flung in the direction they were running; blasted into death, not sleekly, not silently as in a Western, but messily, screamingly.

Through his arms, Will felt all Molly's horror as well as his own. He tried to blanket the scene from her, but she held away his fingers. She would see everything. She would remember.

More Junkers ripping the streets apart. More smoke from growing fires. More bombs, more and still more. Heinkels devouring every morsel that threatened to survive, spraying walls and windows with wasteful bullets, rising, searching out the human mice spread away below them.

On the perimeter of the town, the hunting pack sniffed blood, circled, dived—destroyed. All that people found in the meadows was more space to die in.

"José, come back!"

The young goatherd was in the centre of the street. He was advancing in the direction of a lone Heinkel coming in from the east, diving low, furrowing the stone ground with machine-gun fire. He was a sleepwalker. He had stepped out of his living skull. Rage was his only instinct.

José paused. He looked over his shoulder at Molly and Will. He raised his fist in salute as if to say thanks, as if to say —goodbye.

"José!"

He held his bottle like a club. He cursed the Fascists. He cursed Franco. He walked almost into the shadow of the Heinkel.

"Gara Euzhadi Eskatuta!"

He waited, yet one more David against Goliath, bottle against machine-gun. As the Heinkel reached the lowest point of its dive, José emulated David. He cast his bottle, spinning, flashing, at the plane's propeller. Yet he was not blessed with David's good fortune.

In return for his impertinence, he received the multiple blows of death. The bullets carried him across the street.

They left him a punctured carcass beside the front wheels of Peg, as yet untouched.

There followed a savage tug-of-war. "Let me go, Will!"

"He's dead—what can you do?"

"There are others. Listen to them! We've bandages, we've——"

"Wait!" She fought so hard she pushed Will off his feet. But he held on to her. They were both on the ground, kicking at debris, creating their own storm of dust.

Another Heinkel had followed, in search of pickings, emptying gunbarrels into the dead. Will was over her, shielding her, and she struggled. "One martyr in your family's enough!" He slapped her so hard his hand stung. She winced with pain, but she relented.

"*We* haven't got to die. Not yet!"

After the Heinkels, the Junkers; after the Junkers, the Heinkels. Will and Molly were back on their feet. The building that had protected them had been hit. They ran out into the centre of the street, only to return to the spot they had left as houses opposite were demolished.

One wall and one precious doorway had been left standing. Hands over mouths, they stumbled through a whirlwind of dust. They were cut by showers of cement and glass. They could not see the street, but they could see the sky, the continuing shapes of aircraft passing through it, and there was enough power left in their smarting eyes to witness a change of programme.

In place of the usual hundred-pounder bombs, silver canisters now showered the town. The ground did not shake when they exploded, yet their effect was equally devastating.

An instant after the fall of the canisters, huge columns of flame shot above the housetops. "Fire bombs! This time we've got to move."

Silver fish descended through the grey smoke tides and Guernica was transformed to crimson and scarlet.

"Grab my hand. Hold on!"

"But where?"

"In Peg."

"The streets though—the bodies."

"The dead'll not remember."

Down to their left, a row of once-stately houses, already ruined, were alight as though at the press of a switch. The fires did not lick and grow. They did not spurt and waver as natural fires do, allowing a few seconds between infancy and manhood. They leapt full-grown into all-consuming life. They became impenetrable walls whose flames knew no points.

Will threw open Peg's door for Molly. He pushed her aboard. "Head down, all the way."

"We could make for the hospital. Help them."

"Don't know where the hospital is."

"Look for it, then!"

"It'll have been bombed with the rest."

"What does that matter?"

When Molly tried to raise her head, Will thrust it below the dashboard. "We're getting out. We're too small. We've nothing to offer but a lift."

"I'm not afraid of dying."

"Well I am—and I made a promise to your brother." They were moving. Second gear was all Will could risk. He skirted bodies. He drove between them. Then it became impossible to continue for them.

He closed his eyes. He pressed the accelerator. "Please, God, forgive me!"

A sheep, wild with terror, almost rushed onto Peg's bumper. Other animals than humans scattered to the winds: cattle, oxen, rabbits, dogs, cats and poultry.

Will could not keep Molly from looking. "Ahead of us, those kids! Stop for them."

Will nodded. He was slowing. He glanced into Peg's wing mirror. The Heinkels were coming. "The next lot's for us, Molly. Get right down!" The plane was half a street away. "We're a sitting duck. Come on, Peg—fly!"

Will swung the truck towards a stretch of clear pavement.

Down came a wall in front of him. He hit rubble. He
swerved. He hit bodies. Bullets tore through Peg's roof and
walls. They sprayed around her. They ripped open the
street pavings. They ricocheted from side to side like sparks
of steel.

An entire housefront capsized immediately behind them.
The draught washed forward past Peg. She rocked. Will spun
the wheel one way then the other. His chest was bursting;
his ears were bursting.

For a second he thought he was hearing rifle fire, only to
realise that this was the crack of red-hot tiles. Several times
he was brought to a halt by blazing cars and trucks, by new-
fallen walls, by beams and flying stones tippling into lakes
of fire.

Peg crushed over furniture that had been blown through
gaping walls; her shadow darkened the limbs of the dead
protruding from the rubble of their homes.

The children Will and Molly had marked out for rescue
had vanished. The horror was too much for silence. Will's
voice swelled against the roar of destruction. He howled out
his fury, his helplessness, his defiance:

"M-U-R-D-E-R-E-R-S!"

The tumbling stones had voices: murderers! The crashing
roofs had voices: murderers! Over and over the accusation
was repeated, as insistently as the wheels of a train clatter
over the rails.

Murderers! Murderers!

CHAPTER ELEVEN

Guernica was one gigantic furnace. The stench of high explosive mixed with the effluent of sewers. The air had been turned to midnight black by smoke and brickdust. Plaster had been stripped from the fronts of the houses like torn curtaining.

Peg's way was jammed. She had reached the outskirts of the town. Will braked. "We'll never get through." Hundreds of survivors spread darkly into the fields. Some kept close to the road, despite the bodies that lay there as testimony to its extreme danger. Others hastened for the woods.

Molly jumped down among them. "We'll take the young ones."

Will lowered his window. He heard no planes. He too climbed down. He opened Peg's rear doors for Molly. "Bilbao first stop! All aboard!"

There was no squabbling, no fighting. One man volunteered to clear a route for Peg. "Standing room only, full on top!"

Molly pushed two children into the cab. "That's the lot." She rode on the running-board. They were moving, out into the open. There was green in the meadows. Spring flowers grew. A stream passed behind distant trees, peacefully unaware of the fire and destruction a few hundred yards away.

"Any sign of them, Molly?"

"Not yet. Haven't they done enough?"

Once again, hope simmered and hope died. Shrieks of warning rippled through the crowd. The cold sea of the helpless surged on, scattering for the trees, for dips in the ground that sloped from either side of the road.

Heinkel 51s, fins aslant, cut through the twilight. Fingers touching the cannon. Fingers pressing the cannon. How ugly, how pathetic, how lacking in "nobleza" as Franco's supporters among the gentry might say, is the human body riddled with bullets.

The attack produced a score of victims. It scoured the earth with criss-cross furrows. It caused the furrows to run with blood.

Will heard the gush of air. Peg settled lopsidedly on a flat tyre. Another sound—trickling. He sniffed. Petrol! Peg still moved. The engine had been struck by bullets rebounding off the road.

After circling above the smoke and flames of the town, the Heinkels sped back for more scalps. They would be singing over this tonight, these bright boys from Frankfurt, from Dusseldorf, from Oberhausen, these veterans of Durango where the priest and his congregation had been blown to pieces in the church of the Jesuit Fathers; they would be cracking their glasses in celebration at the Hotel Fronton in Vitoria, toasting the Führer and the Fatherland.

Now perhaps the lazy Spaniards would learn how to conduct a war.

Will felt Peg's strength draining from her. They wouldn't make another hundred yards. "Let's get out!" He lifted the two children into the road. He thrust them towards the ditch.

The Heinkels were coming again. With Molly, he raced round the back of Peg. They did not have to explain to the trembling occupants their lift to safety and sanity was at an end.

The young passengers ran where instinct took them. There was no time to think, to look around, only to dive to earth as the Heinkels pierced the drifting palls of smoke.

"Will!"

He had returned to Peg. He lunged over her bench seat. He emerged with Candy Sam's sketchbook and Fred's violin. "The bastards are not getting these!"

He also carried in his hand Sam's pistol.

They ran together. They reached the edge of a bomb crater. "It's too open, Will."

"Better than nothing."

They plunged into the crater the moment the Heinkels

began firing. Bullets hit the soil above them. There were screams close by. A woman who seconds before had been in Peg, nursing a toddler, whose step had been nervous, hesitant, now departed this world, leaving the toddler alone and sobbing—the only creature on two feet in that meadow of death.

"Another coming!" Will climbed out of the crater. Molly made no motion to stop him. She tried to follow him. He wheel-barrowed her over into the bottom of the crater. "Me, just me!"

He felt utterly exposed, as if the German pilots could not only see him but hear his thundering heartbeat. Yet he ran, doubled to his knees, skipping over the bodies in his way.

"Here, kid!" He was ten paces from the child. Ten paces between life and death: his own life and the death of the child. The bullets split the orphan in two. Gone, fallen, scarcely pieces to pick up.

Something had become unlatched in Will's brain. It blazed with lightning flashes. He was José. Nothing could hurt him, therefore nothing could frighten him.

He sensed Candy Sam speaking through him:

"No pasarán!"

The Heinkels dived. He was still. He raised his pistol. He straightened himself. He fired. One for José. Again: one for Griff. One for Sam. One for Fred. One for the rest of the Seven Bells Brigade. Finally, one for Da.

And when his pistol was empty, he shook his fist at the sky.

The enemy's bullets passed over him. He spun round. He dropped the pistol. He saw trusty old Peg the victim of a direct hit. She exploded into a roaring bonfire in the fading light.

"Poor Peg!"

The white horses of Pegasus leapt onwards for a few seconds, then dissolved in flames. The fire reflected on Will's face. He bent his head, witnessing the funeral pyre of Candy Sam's expedition in the name of peace and freedom.

Tears blinded Will's vision. The task of bringing home the

Golden Fleece had proved too much for Sam's modern
Argonauts.

There was a breathing space. He looked about him.
People were rising from their living graves, hurrying away.
Will's eyes searched for strays. He had lost one by seconds.
His anger commanded that he save others.

He ran back to Molly. "We'll call them. Those with nobody to look after them. We'll fetch them here, to the crater."

Together Will and Molly roamed the meadow. They
called and the call was answered. One, two, three, they
came: a boy covered in blood, perhaps not his own; two
girls of about five and six, caught while playing by the
stream when the first bombers darkened their evening
games; the two children they had carried in the cab—twins,
brother and sister, whose hands were so tightly clasped they
might have been riveted with steel.

Again and again came the Heinkels. Each time Will and
Molly shielded the lost children of Vizcaya as hens protect
their chicks. Again and again drummed the bombers, dropping incendiaries upon incendiaries.

They remained flat as bullets spit over the grass. They
watched light slink into darkness. They waited: one hour,
two hours.

All at once there was an eerie silence. Lessons had been
learnt and no one moved. Molly got the children to count
the seconds before the next attack. Their little voices joined
in slow rhythm: uno, dos, tres, cuatro . . . On they went:
veinte, veinte y uno, veinte y dos.

At a hundred, the counting stopped. Will raised his head.
He got to his knees. He stood up. He nodded and the children
too were on their feet, huddled around Molly, listening, all
listening.

They heard the crack of flames. They heard the fall of
masonry. But they heard no more planes. It was 7.45 p.m.
The attack on Guernica was over.

The survivors held their breath, and the skies were silent.

With their ragged procession, Will and Molly headed for the town. Miraculously, the children slipped away, discovering if not their parents or relatives, neighbours who would welcome them in to what was left of their homes.

They entered Guernica, once the pride of Vizcaya. They heard the slither of wreckage crashing from the houses, followed by showers of glass.

"See, Will! People are returning. They're not going to be beaten!"

Rescue teams were out in force. Two men approached, carrying a stretcher. They wept aloud. They bore a dead girl of startling beauty. She was laid on the ground with the other dead.

Will and Molly exchanged no words: none would suffice to describe this unparalleled tragedy.

Two refugees were left—the twins, still with their hands bonded together. Molly asked them to lead the way to their home. It was not far, they said. They skirted giant piles of rubble. They walked in the middle of the road for the pavements were carpeted with smouldering coals.

At the end of their street, the twins stopped. The housefronts stood almost undamaged save for shattered glass; but the rooms behind them were completely gone.

Will glanced up at the street name. "No! It can't be!" He caught Molly's arm. "This . . . this is Federico's street!" That this was a coincidence, impressed him; that the children should stop in front of Federico's very own house, made him gasp with amazement and with foreboding.

The house was totally destroyed. On the doorstep, a dead dog.

"Vasco!" The children ran to it. They had spilt no tears. Now they flowed. The little girl lifted the dog's head from the hot ashes. She nursed it against her, spurning her brother's efforts to tug her away from the heat of the fires still burning inside the house.

Were Federico's nephew and niece to find themselves orphans too?

Suddenly the boy skipped out into the road, treading up a cloud of ash. He called to his sister. His eyes shone. He was looking down the street, beginning to run. His arms were outstretched.

"Mama! Mama! Papa!"

Brother and sister turned to their rescuers. They hugged them with wiry little arms. They rained kisses on their cheeks. Then away they dashed, feet dancing over the ground, towards the longing hands of their loved ones two hundred yards away.

Will had no need to check on the photo in his breast pocket of Federico's family to recognise his friend's married sister, his granda and gran, his slender, black-clad mother.

He waved, but he did not go forward. "This isn't the time." He would not spoil their brief joy. "Some day, I'll come back. Their bad news can wait."

Molly slipped her hand into Will's. "At least there's been this." Her face was as smoke-grimed as a chimney sweep's. "What now?"

"The Fascists will come streaming in by morning. So I reckon it's another Jarrow March."

Molly smiled. "Via Bilbao? There'll be things for us to do there, Will. Spain's not finished with us yet."

Will was leading her away, but not as the crow flies to Bilbao. "Bear with me for a minute or two, Molly. There's something I want to make sure of."

They ignored the fires, the walls leaning giddily outwards into the streets. They passed the burning ruin of the church of San Juan. They did not pause until the Casa de Juntas came in sight. The building was scarcely damaged.

"Fingers crossed!"

Will looked up and his heart was a bell striking a glad sound. "The oak, Molly—it's still standing! All those bombs and not one of them, not one of them touched her!" He was laughing. He was crying. The tears dripped down his cheeks.

"This is what they came for, once and for all, to kill the Freedom Tree. But they failed!"

He went towards the Oak of Guernica. He reached out to it with the palms of his hands, stroking the rough texture of the bark with the tips of his fingers. He was thinking of blind Count Philippe, and in the gnarled trunk he was seeing the faces of his friends—Griff, Candy Sam, Ike, Roland, Howard, Ben, Federico and José.

He was seeing too his Da, and in the mists of memory, his Spanish mother; he was seeing the folks of Jarrow blighted by a disaster of another kind—hunger and worklessness; he was seeing the lads of Jarrow marching to London for the cause they believed in so passionately.

He called to them across the silent, deserted square:

"The Freedom Tree still stands! Can you hear, Sam? No pasarán!"

He stooped down. His hand had been a fist. He opened his fingers towards Molly. "An acorn from the Freedom Tree." He sniffed back his tears. "One for Jarrow!"

Will took Molly's hand. He raised it high in the air. His shout rose into a scream of attack, of victory.

"Gara Euzhadi Eskatuta!"

HISTORICAL NOTE

The story of the Spanish Civil War after the destruction of Guernica and the death of eight hundred of the town's population in April 1937, was one of inevitable and tragic defeat for the Republican armies. The governments of Britain and France stood aside, their hands over their eyes, refusing assistance while Germany and Italy provided Franco's Insurgent troops with manpower, aircraft and guns.

Only Russia and Mexico supplied arms to the Republic, but in no way enough. However, though Britain and France were afraid to prevent the death of democracy in Spain because they might offend Adolph Hitler, thousands of volunteers from all over the world came to fight in the Republican ranks.

They could see, as it seems the British and French governments refused to see, that if naked and illegal force were to prevail in Spain, the rest of Europe too must suffer—fears all too swiftly fulfilled in the Second World War.

Despite the valour of her armies—their repulse of the Fascists at Jarama, their victory over the Italians at Guadalajara, their prodigious sacrifices at Brunete; despite the fact that her soldiers often fought on even when their ammunition had long run out; and despite the contribution of the International Brigades, whose bravery earned them undying fame—the Republic wavered, retreated and was overwhelmed.

The might of the Fascist sword triumphed everywhere and the victors were to show the vanquished little mercy. Spanish earth ran with the blood of the executed and thousands of men, women and children fled from their homeland, many never to return.

Hundreds of children from the Basque country settled in Britain after the fall of Bilbao; hundreds marched with their forlorn and desperate parents across the Spanish borders into

France or journeyed to foster-homes as far away as Moscow and Mexico City.

On 11th March 1938, as the Spanish Civil War was nearing its close, Hitler's armies occupied Austria. Soon the Führer was to bully his way into annexing Czechoslovakia— this time with the active connivance of Britain and France. Later, Warsaw and other cities were to suffer devastation similar to that which left the proud little town of Guernica a skeleton of stone.

Edmund Burke, the English philosopher, wrote: "All that is necessary for evil to thrive is that good men do nothing about it." For such a belief, men left their jobs, their families, their homes, to fight and die in Spain. If fate had granted them victory, all that followed might have been averted.

Daniel Bird

The Pocket Essential

ROMAN POLANSKI

First published in Great Britain 2002 by Pocket Essentials, 18 Coleswood Road,
Harpenden, Herts, AL5 1EQ

Distributed in the USA by Trafalgar Square Publishing, PO Box 257, Howe Hill
Road, North Pomfret, Vermont 05053

A CIP catalogue record for this book is available from the British Library.

ISBN 1-903047-89-7

2 4 6 8 10 9 7 5 3 1

Book typeset by Pdunk
Printed and bound by Cox & Wyman

Jan Lenica (1928-2001)

Acknowledgements

Thanks to Jez Adamson, Paul Buck, Professor Richard Gregory, Mike Hart, Maxim Jakubowski, Andrzej Klimowski, Jan Lenica, Michele Salimbeni, Helle Schoubye, David Thompson, Stephen Thrower and Pete Tombs.

CONTENTS

1: Introduction: Anatomy Of The Devil

> "...and so, who are
> you, after all?
> - I am part of the power
> which forever wills evil
> And forever works good."

> *- Faust*, Goethe

> "Where would your good be if there were no evil and what
> would the world look like without a shadow? Shadows are
> thrown by people and things. There's the shadow of my sword,
> for instance. But shadows are also cast by trees and living
> things. Do you want to strip the whole globe by removing every
> tree and every creature to satisfy your fantasy of a bare world?"

> *- The Master And Margarita*, Mikhail Bulgakov

Roman Polanski was born in Paris but spent most of his youth in Cracow, Poland, during the 1940s. Around the same time, across the border
in Stalinist Russia, a Devil was being committed to print. A dying
Mikhail Bulgakov was putting the final touches to a literary bombshell,
The Master And Margarita. Flash forward almost half a century later.
During the last days of the Eastern Block, Polanski – by now having
firmly established himself as a major film-maker of international standing – is putting the final touches to his most ambitious project, a film
adaptation of *The Master And Margarita*.

It was not the first time Polanski had filmed the Devil, nor would it
be the last. In 1968 Polanski adapted Ira Levin's *Rosemary's Baby* for
the screen, whilst his most recent film was based on Arturo Pérez-
Reverte's labyrinthine novel *Il Club Dumas* (filmed as *The Ninth Gate*,
1999). 1989 marked the fall of the Berlin Wall. Communism was now
officially dead and the ghost of Stalin (integral to Bulgakov's novel)
was fading. Ironically, Polanski's financiers, Warner Brothers, dropped
The Master And Margarita for a more prosaic reason. Money.

Nonetheless, Polanski described *The Master And Margarita* script, which he wrote alone, as the best adaptation he had ever done, something all the more remarkable given the novel's 'unfilmable' reputation. As Joseph Strick's *Ulysses* (1967, after James Joyce), Bernardo Bertolucci's *The Sheltering Sky* (1990 after Paul Bowles), David Cronenberg's *Naked Lunch* (1992, after William Burroughs), *Crash* (1996, after J G Ballard) and Raul Ruiz's *Time Regained* (1999 after Marcel Proust) show, a book with an unfilmable reputation never stops filmmakers from trying.

However, no matter how daunting the project may have appeared, it is easy to see what attracted Polanski to *The Master And Margarita*. Bulgakov's novel epitomises Polanski's major concern, the mechanisms and confrontation of evil.

To say that Polanski is no stranger to evil would be an understatement. His generation of Poles endured the holocaust only to find themselves 'freed' under the ever-watchful eye of another totalitarian regime, though one belonging to the other extreme of the political spectrum. When the Manson family murdered Polanski's second wife, Sharon Tate, in 1969, many commentators implied that what "goes around comes around" – that Polanski, a film-maker who fantasised about sex and violence, had finally paid the price.

It's easy to play Cassandra with the benefit of hindsight (and many of Polanski's commentators do) but it is difficult to make a distinction between life and art. However, by constantly using events from his own life as raw material for genre or at any case distinctly non-autobiographical films, Polanski has made such a distinction even more difficult to make. Usually life can never match the form or the symmetry of art, but Polanski has gone out of his way to bind up his films with elements from his very public personal life. Polanski claims in *Roman By Polanski*, his autobiography, that for him the line between reality and fantasy has always been blurred. Indeed, one cannot watch *Macbeth* (1971) without being goaded by parallels with the Manson murders, nor can one watch the violent seduction of *Tess* (1979) without being struck by the irony of it being a film directed by someone fleeing charges for raping a minor in a foreign country. The more pressing issue is whether or not Polanski's films hold up without the ironic *frisson* generated by knowledge of the director's off-screen life? Or rather, how much weight do the horrific (and reckless) events in Polanski's life impinge on the nature of his films? Sainte-Beuve and Proust quarrelled over the question whether appreciation of a novel is deepened by knowledge of its author's life. Sainte-Beuve said "Yes." Proust, however, said "No" on the grounds that an author's work comes from a place too deep even for self-knowledge – 'le moi profond'. The anecdote is not a moral, just a warning: Polanski's films are open to *auteur* interpretations that reduce every one of his films to aspects of a single psychodrama, just as one can throw away the peach and noisily suck the stone.

Polanski, like another Hollywood exile, Stanley Kubrick, has developed a body of work dedicated to charting the mechanics of evil. Contrary to the judgements of a large faction of critics, Polanski is not amoral. His work reflects a Western world in which the black and white moral landscape painted by once-oppressive Judeo-Christian religions is dissolving, whether we like it or not, into ever finer shades of grey. Above all else, Polanski's films depict a Godless world in which the good do not always triumph, the outsider is always persecuted and the innocent is always abused.

Evil

In her excellent biography of Polanski, Barbara Leaming suggests that his work lacks a "moral tone" and that his films are "amoral." However, a distinction needs to be drawn between a moral film-maker and one who moralises. *Chinatown* (1974) ends with the abused Evelyn being shot and her evil, incestuous father, Noah Cross, gaining custody of his daughter. The protagonist, detective Jake Gittes, handcuffed to a member of the Police force that once employed him, is left as an impotent bystander to the spectacle. His plan for Evelyn and her daughter to esc ape to Mexico has gone badly wrong. However, it's absurd to think that Polanski condones Cross' actions and condemns Evelyn. Though Polanski doesn't moralise, his films are, nonetheless, moral. It's just that Polanski's vision – here expressed via the fate of Jake Gittes – is frankly pessimistic. Just as Czeslaw Milosz wrote of the Holocaust poet Tadeusz Borowski in *The Captive Mind*, if Polanski comes across as a nihilist in his stories, then his nihilism is the result of an ethical passion, from a disappointed love of the world and of humanity.

9

The sense of despair in which *Chinatown* climaxes is typical of Polanski's films, although unusually political. Polanski more commonly expresses despair in everyday situations, as in *The Tenant* (*Le Loctaire*, 1976), *Tess* or *Frantic* (1987). However, sexual despair dominates Polanski's sharpest films including his debut *Knife In The Water* (1962), *Repulsion* (1964), *Cul-De-Sac* (1965) and *Bitter Moon* (1992). Whatever the form, despair in Polanski's films stems from a broadly existential moral aspect which, conversely, depicts an absurd, meaningless world. Polanski's characters behave in a perverse, though nonetheless truthful manner, for their actions are often self-serving (specifically in terms of sexual and material greed, both of which Polanski equates with power) and don't necessarily tend towards good. Polanski knows only too well that such good intentions last only so long as civilisation lasts. Polanski's films end on the brink of the collapse of civilisation or the eve of a new tyranny, either satanic (*Rosemary's Baby*, *The Ninth Gate*), political (*Macbeth*, *Chinatown*) or even one ruled by vampires (*The Fearless Vampire Killers*, 1967).

Chinatown ends with the implicit idea that atheistic doubt, or at least the feeling that we no longer live in fear of being judged, does not license amorality. Just as Bulgakov reiterated Goethe's ethics, Polanski's films present goodness and evil existing in equal measures. Polanski's vision is unacceptable from a Christian standpoint because, for Polanski, evil cannot be reduced to the flesh. It is a social phenomenon: a fundamentalist religion, like totalitarian rule, is merely another force organised around engulfing/crushing non-conformists, though one which proceeds through the labelling of people and things as evil. Christianity arrived in Poland in 966. Caught between Rome and Byzantium, the conversion to Christianity of Polish pagan tribes was a political manoeuvre to consolidate the fledgling state and curb the Eastward expansion of the German Roman Empire. By operating on the edges of Rome, Polish Catholicism developed in a highly conservative, not to mention combative spirit. Anything that threatened the Catholic State acquired a demonic profile.

The Devil's Polish reputation developed in the rich, ethnically diverse folklore that comprised Polish culture at that time: Lithuanian, Ukrainian and Byelorussian. According to Wiesiek Powaga, native Polish folklore brimmed with pagan devils and demons. The *upiór* (a bodiless spirit, now associated with vampires) took on all forms, like *strzygi*, bloodsucking owls, or *zmory*, creatures that suffocated their victims.

Mythologies owe their system entirely to the inquisitors. Just as witches developed their demonic mythology out of what Trevor Roper describes as "peasant credulity and feminine hysteria," the Nazis assembled their own systematic mythology of ritual murder out of prejudice and scandal and propagated a global conspiracy against Judaism. The Nazi occupation of Poland was replaced by another tyranny, however, the Neo-Stalinist mythology of applied dialectical materialism was no less systematic. Witchcraft and vampirism were, like religions of any sort, excluded from Soviet ideology, thus prompting Bulgakov's recourse to the fantastic on the one hand and the banning of Constanin Erchov and Gueorgui Kropatchev's adaptation of Gogol's witch story, *Viy* (1967), on the other. Even in the United States Polanski was 'officially' condemned by the US Roman Catholic Office before being scrutinised for his very public lifestyle. In art and life, Polanski is an outsider, so what better figure to identify with than the Devil?

Painting Birds

If Polanski's films explore the disparity between moral behaviour and what is perceived as evil, then they find an analogue in the novels of the Polish writer Jerzy Kosinski. The paths of Polanski and Kosinski crossed many times until Kosinski's suicide in 1992. Both share many characteristics, not to mention obsessions. At one point Polanski was scheduled to direct a film adaptation of Kosinski's novel *Being There* (later successfully filmed with Peter Sellers in the lead role). However, whereas Polanski dispensed with any of the responsibilities associated with highbrow artists, Kosinski retained his credentials as a social scientist and often overextended himself as a social critic.

Kosinski met with fame upon the publication of his first novel, *The Painted Bird*. It was often rumoured that Kosinski had, in fact, based the story upon Polanski's childhood. However, the origins and intentions of Kosinski's novel are in need of some clarification. Kosinski had first met Polanski in Lodz during his film school years. As Kosinski's biographer James Park Sloan argues, it's more likely that Kosinski drew his inspiration from Unuk and Rodmska-Strzemecka's *Polish Children*

Accuse, a collection of testimony by children who had wandered and suffered during the occupation.

Implicit in Kosinski's *The Painted Bird* is the humanist idea of the scapegoat's role in the functioning of society. Society fears the outsider and tries to destroy him. Paradoxically, society needs the outsider and, if necessary, creates one so that by labelling him as evil it can confirm itself as good. Kosinski's story hinges around a violent incident involving the painted bird of the title. The boy's sexually frustrated mentor grabs hold of a strong bird, paints its wings in bright colours and takes it into the forest. The bird's twittering attracts a flock of the same species. They release the bird, which then flies up into the sky amongst its flock. The flock inspects the painted bird before attacking it.

Kosinski's novel is very much a product of the Sixties: the idea of the outsider is a violent expression of lingering existential concerns revitalised from a social humanist perspective. The notion of the 'other' – the outsider – resonated in the writings of renegade psychiatrist, R D Laing, author of *The Divided Self*, whilst the Hungarian psychiatrist Thomas Szasz, writing in *The Manufacture Of Madness*, likened the painting of the bird's wings to how "psychiatrists discolour their patients, and society as a whole taints its citizens."

Polanski, of course, has repeatedly identified with the 'outsider'. Polanski has often cited Carol Reed's *Odd Man Out* (1947) as the film that probably had the most influence on his youth. As Polanski wrote in an issue of *Positif*, Reed's film is about a fugitive: "during the war I was a fugitive from the ghetto. Twenty years later, in London, I was a fugitive from Stalinism. And today I am still a fugitive!" However, the 'other' takes many forms and roles in Polanski's films. For example, persecuted heroines like Carol in *Repulsion*, Rosemary or Simone Choule/Trelkovski in *The Tenant*, or a misanthropic idealist like George in *Cul-De-Sac*. If these characters are burdened with madness, paranoia or extreme cynicism, Polanski's most accessible films, such as *Rosemary's Baby* or *Frantic*, operate by switching the tables on the viewer, having an average protagonist succumb to an insane, cynical world where paranoia becomes a distinct advantage. Being labelled paranoid doesn't mean that people aren't out to get you; rather, as Kubrick said, to be paranoid is to be in possession of all the facts. However, as the protagonists of *Rosemary's Baby*, *Chinatown*, *The Tenant* and *Frantic* would testify, to possess the facts, whether through detection or obsession, is to confront a distinctly grimmer world than the one in which they started.

Concentration

The 'outsiders' in Nazi Occupied Poland or Stalinist Russia found themselves in a "concentration universe," to use Czeslaw Milosz's chillingly apt phrase. It's a term that has particular resonance in the films of Walerian Borowczyk, particularly *Angels' Games* (*Les jeux des anges*, 1964) and *Goto, Island Of Love* (*Goto, l'île d'ámour*, 1968). However, concentration can also occur through less dramatically sinister means. In films as diverse as *Nashville* (1975), *Prêt-À-Porter* (1996) and *Gosford Park* (2001), Robert Altman consistently uses location or an event to precipitate drama. For *Psycho* (1960), Hitchcock used the Bates Motel as a crucible of a sick consciousness. This "terrible building," as Robin Wood put it, would become a crucial device of Seventies horror films, most notably in Tobe Hooper's *The Texas Chainsaw Massacre* (1974). "Claustrophobia" is the adjective usually applied to Polanski's films. In *Knife In The Water*, three disparate characters find their nerves shredded on a yacht whilst profoundly oppressive apartments contain *Repulsion, Rosemary's Baby* and *The Tenant*. These locations may be urban, but they could easily be an island, as in *Cul-De-Sac*, or a foreign country, as in *What?* (1972) or *Death And The Maiden* (1994).

Concentrating the drama reveals an absence of selflessness amongst the incarcerated characters. People are reduced to animals with a desire to live. Yes, Polanski's films are cynical, but let's not forget that the 'cynic' refers literally to what is 'dog like'. As a cynic, Polanski's choice to 'play the dog' creates havoc for any moral discourse, since humans are traditionally defined by their place in both nature and civil hierarchies. When civil hierarchies collapse, as in the concentration camps that underpin totalitarian rule – but also Macbeth's castle, Chinatown and the seedy district depicted in *The Tenant* – cynicism re-evaluates man' s place in nature and society. The idea finds its most explicit expression in Ben Kingsley's climactic confession in Polanski's film of Ariel Dorfman's play, *Death And The Maiden*. Sigourney Weaver plays a victim of the state torture in a South American dictatorship. She later conducts a violent and humiliating mock trial of her abuser. Though *Death And The Maiden* never quite rids itself of its stage origins, the actions of Paulina, like Carol in *Repulsion* and Trelkovski in *The Tenant*, illustrate the single ethic by which the persecuted outsider lives: it's permissible to harm others, provided they harm you first. Beyond this, everyone saves himself the best they can. However, as Wladyslaw Szpilman's *The Pianist* (the subject of Polanski's most recent film scheduled for release in 2002) goes to show, just as many educated, respectable middle-class people behave in a weak manner in the concentration camp scenario. In fact, the so-called crooks and rogues were often brave and the most helpful.

Broadly Darwinian in his survival of the fittest mentality, Polanski's predisposition for the absurdity of these situations springs from a feeling of the pervasiveness of violence and a Germanic (Schopenhauerian/ Nietzschean) pessimism. To man, the herd animal, as to his non-human ancestors, safety lies in similarity. That is why conformity (biological and social) is good and deviance is evil.

The Left of the West

Though Polanski is most famous for the films he has made in the West since the 1960s, he had already established himself as a major film-maker in Central Europe prior to his departure. If Polanski had turned to the commercial market place of the West for greater artistic freedom, during the Sixties the critical community in France, especially *Cahiers du Cinéma,* found itself looking towards the East for political inspiration. Therefore, Polanski's early films, especially *The Fat And The Lean,* were subject to an often muddled, left-leaning trend in evaluating Iron Curtain cinema from the comfort of the West.

The debate concerned 'progressive' versus 'reactionary' and the merits of 'realism' versus 'non-realism'. Both forms proved to be radical and controversial within the existing production context. For example, it wasn't 'new wave' style techniques that worried the Polish authorities in the case of *Knife In The Water* but its decidedly non-communist message expressed within a realist format, similar to Jarmoil Jires' *The Joke* (Czechoslovakia, 1967), Milos Forman's *The Fireman's Ball* (*Hori, ma Panenko,* Czechoslovakia, 1967) and Jiri Menzel's *Larks On A String* (*Skrivanci na niti,* Czechoslovakia, 1969). Conversely, the 'non-realism' of the fantasy structures of Polanski's early short films, such as *Two Men And A Wardrobe* and *Where Angels Fall*, contains no social concern whatsoever. In the case of Vera Chytilova's wonderful *Daisies* (Czechoslovakia, 1966) and Dusan Makavejev's *WR: Mysteries Of The Organism* (Yugoslavia, 1970), their formal experimentation was condemned as elitist and, ironically, valued only in the West. Interestingly, as Milos Foreman pointed out, not one of the communist countries could financially sustain the number of films produced annually during the Sixties and the high output of aggressively artistic films was solely a response to demand from Western markets.

Not surprisingly, there have been frictions between Polanski and the left-wing community of critics and film-makers in France. During the darkest days of *Cahiers du Cinéma*, politics sullied film criticism to the point of absurdity. The nadir surely being Luc Moullet's dismissal of Jan Nemec's harrowing *Diamonds Of The Night* (*Demanty noci*, 1964) on the ludicrous grounds that it had 'reactionary' aesthetics and was generally "deprived of all social and human value." However, Polanski's finest moment came at the 1968 Cannes Film Festival with *Rosemary's Baby* when he pulled up on the Croisette in a flamboyant sports car only to learn of the outbreak of the infamous May riots. Truffaut and Godard, the latter now well into his Maoist phase, attempted to close the festival. However, Polanski violently protested and publicly condemned Truffaut and Godard as a bunch of so-called new wave directors "playing at being revolutionaries." There was a row and Godard told Polanski to "fuck off back to Hollywood."

Like Milos Forman and Jan Nemec – both in attendance at the festival – Polanski had first-hand experience of living in countries where a Communist philosophy had been gradually displaced by totalitarian rule. Speaking in a recent *Guardian* interview of his own confrontation with student radicalism in Berkeley during the late Sixties, Czeslaw Milosz expressed his sadness to see that every stupidity he had experienced in Poland was being recreated in the West. Andrzej Zulawski's *Diabel* (*The Devil*, 1971) painted a very different picture of the student riots in Poland in 1968: "part of the Communist establishment wanted to seize power. In order to do this they devised a very clear trick. They provoked youth – innocent, naïve university youth especially – to start a series of protests on the streets against censorship, lack of freedom.

They did it on purpose. Then the Communists turned to the Russians, the landlords, saying ' this government in Poland cannot control the population. So you have to fire them and take us because we know how to deal with them.' To show this – because they were from the police, what you'd call KGB Polish branch – they organised a savage repression of the Polish young people in March 1968. And in May 1968 in France, to this day they talk of their French revolution; they burned a car – one."

Polanski must have had the last laugh when Jean-Luc hilarity reached new heights with a ridiculous rosy postcard of post-invasion Czechoslovakia, *Pravda* (1969).

Sexual Violence

Towards the end of Louis-Ferdinand Céline's *Journey To The End Of The Night* (*Voyage au bout de la nuit*, 1932), the narrator, Ferdinand Bardamu, asserts that his "friendly feelings" towards his friend/doppelganger Robinson and his fiancée have taken an insidiously erotic turn: "Betrayal". The erotic aspect of Polanski's best work, *Knife In The Water*, *Cul-De-Sac*, *Rosemary's Baby*, is always a function of betrayal. Betrayal or the need to betray is thrown up by the sexual tension that is the result of the incongruity of this existence with idealistic conceptions (Christian or communist) of social contract, transactions amongst equals and mutual benefit. As Raymond Durgnat points out in relation to Polanski's films, if sexuality was the Victorian obscenity then violence is ours.

If the totalitarian oppression of Poland – from both the East and West – operated through violence and the threat of violence, then it also engendered a deep cultural preoccupation with the act of surrender. Andrzej Zulawski's *Third Part Of The Night* (*Trzęcia czesc nocy*, 1970), for example, makes surrender mystical whilst Polanski, like Witold Gombrowicz (*The Marriage*, *Pornography*) and Bruno Schulz (*The Book Of Idolatry*), renders it erotic. From the absurd slapstick of *The Fat And The Lean* and *Mammals*, through the acute observation of *Knife In The Water* and *Cul-De-Sac*, to the blatant vulgarity of *What?* and *Bitter Moon*, victim and victimiser exist in reciprocal affairs of ascensions and submissions.

The violence of *Knife In The Water* is an expression of sexual jealousy, violence in *Repulsion* is the climax of Carol's sexual disgust. George and Oscar are sexually humiliated through a succession of stylised violent acts in *Cul-De-Sac* and *Bitter Moon* respectively, despite playing fantasy roles of being the victimiser. It's no cliché to talk of rape as an act less about sex than power. But in Polanski's films, especially *Tess*, sexual relationships are only about power, no matter how loving. Violent seduction is the norm in even his most whimsical films such as *The Fearless Vampire Killers* or *Pirates*. With *Bitter Moon*, Polanski pushed the sexual power play into a new contorted form that precariously balanced on the edge of self-parody. The result was unashamedly voyeuristic, more than a little mischievous and very funny. By contrast, thanks to Ariel Dorfman's stage play origins, *Death And The Maiden* offered a smartened-up, politically correct chamber piece about revenge. *Death And The Maiden* is both more liberal in tone and lacking any sense of humour, for it is about 'serious' issues in world affairs. The result, however, is at best too simplistic, at worst a little po-faced, and ultimately unconvincing. However, the blame lies solely with Dorfman; Polanski no doubt took on the project as a jobbing director happy with the opportunity to work with both Sigourney Weaver and Ben Kingsley. Left to his own devices, if Polanski were to deal with the same source material, I'd hazard a guess that the result would move perilously close to Liliana Caviani's *Night Porter* (1974).

Voyeurism

Polanski's obsession with watching violence is evident in his first short film, *Murder*. Polanski's eye on violence is unflinching. Paradoxically, an unflinching camera isn't necessarily the most revealing. Polanski's glory lies in what he doesn't show; he's a master manipulator of the mind's eye. The grotesque shock in Polanski's early short film *Smile* is that a voyeur expects to see a young woman in a bathroom, though he's actually confronted with an old man. In Polanski's most famous film, Rosemary's baby is conspicuous by its very absence. Through a brief superimposition of a cat's eyes which Rosemary had dreamed of earlier, the viewer thinks it has seen the baby's demonic eyes. Though it turned out to be an unrealised project, Polanski had conceived two short films for Kenneth Tynan's erotic revue *Oh! Calcutta!*

These films perfectly illustrated his voyeuristic strategy. Both shorts were static single takes. In one, a girl would appear and strip naked, although her breasts and crotch would be obscured by furniture. Another girl would enter, strip, and the two girls would make love, reaching orgasm for reasons the viewer could only dream about. The other short involved another sexual scenario, but a window frame was to be used as a similar editing device.

Like Michael Powell's *Peeping Tom* (1960), a favourite film of Polanski's, *Repulsion* opens with a close-up of an eyeball. The credits cut horizontally across this image, recalling the infamous eyeball slicing scene in Buñuel's *Un chien andalou* (1929). Ironically, when Catherine Deneuve went on to star in Buñuel's *Belle de jour* (1967), the famous scene in which she spies through a peephole in the wall of a brothel was more typical of Polanski than Buñuel. Polanski himself plays the voyeur in *The Fearless Vampire Killers*. His character, Alfred, is equally delighted to see Sarah bathing herself and being spanked by her father. The most disturbing case of voyeurism in Polanski's filmography occurs in *The Tenant*. Polanski plays Trelkovski, whose recently acquired apartment has a clear view into the toilet across the courtyard. Believing h e has seen the dead former tenant unbandage herself in the toilet, Trelkovski ventures across the hallway. Staring back out of the toilet to his own apartment window, he finds himself staring back.

A Dionysic Uprising

Walerian Borowczyk's short animated film *Renaissance* (1962) reveals a decimated room gradually reconstructing itself, as if time were going backwards. The final object to materialise is a hand-grenade which then explodes, destroying the room. Renaissance works through an antagonism: order against disorder. This Nietzschean tension haunts Polanski's cinema too, though here the entropy is inverted, in Dionysus' favour. Social and moral order gives way to violent insatiable erotic frenzy through the dream of a more orgiastic world composed of vampires, Satanists and crooks, in *The Fearless Vampire Killers*, *Rosemary's Baby* and *Chinatown* respectively. Even psychological order is brought tumbling down in *Repulsion* and *The Tenant*. Rosemary may dream nostalgically of the Sistine Chapel, but her real fantasy is of the decadent life of the millionaire on the Kennedy yacht. Maybe Rosemary's social repulsion is the result of a tension between her own desires for a more orgiastic, materialist life and a heightened awareness of its immorality. In speaking o f the 'other' and of violence and voyeurism, it may no longer be necessary to resort to the devil in order to speak of their sexual aspects (as Todorov argues in *Structural Approach To The Fantastic*) but it's nonetheless effective in the films of Roman Polanski.

2: Sex, Violence And Surrealism (1957-1962)

Roman Polanski was born in Paris on August 18, 1933. He was the only son of Ryszard Polanski and Bula Katz. Ryszard had been living in Paris for several years, working for a record company. A native of Cracow, Ryszard discarded his original family name, Liebling, as well as his first wife whom he had divorced in Poland. In France Ryszard fell in love with the Russian Katz. Katz was married and she also had a child, though she divorce d and married Ryszard. Ryszard, Bula and Roman lived at 5 rue St. Hubert in the 11th arrondissement, near the Père Lachaise cemetery.

In 1936, the family moved to Cracow. On September 1, 1939, the Nazis invaded Poland. Only five days later Cracow was taken. Five years later only 50,000 of 3,350,000 Polish Jews remained in Poland. Four million people, including Katz, died at Auschwitz alone. Having watched his mother being rounded up by the Nazis, and separated from his father, Roman fled into the ghetto. Roman's small build made him ideal for smuggling food and medical supplies in and out of the ghetto. Three years later Ryszard was caught. A Catholic family hid Roman, a crime that the Nazis punished by death. Later, under the name Romek Wilk (Wolf), Roman stayed with another Catholic family in the Polish countryside until his return in 1945.

Reunited with his father after the war, Roman couldn't play the role of the obedient son. Ryszard remarried again in 1947. His new wife, Wanda Zajaczkowska, loathed Roman and gave Ryszard an ultimatum: either Roman went or she would. Ryszard opted for the former and placed Roman in a boarding house.

Roman began acting in the theatre. His first major part was in the Russian play, *Son Of The Regiment*. In 1949, he played a street urchin in *Circus Tarabumba* at the Cracow Puppet Theatre. In 1950, Roman abandoned his technical studies – against his father's will – and entered the Cracow art school where he studied painting, sculpture and graphics. After his studies, Roman resumed his acting, appearing in *Three Stories* (a compilation film made by a group of students at the Lodz State Film School), *The Magic Bicycle* (Silik Sternfeld), *End Of Night* (Julian Dziedzina), *Sunken Ships* (Ewa and Czeslaw Petelski), *Phone My Wife* (Jaroslav Mach), *See You Tomorrow* (Janusz Morgenstern) and

Beware Of The Yeti (Andrzej Czekalski). However, Polanski's crucial break came when he played 'Mundek' in Andrzej Wajda's seminal *A Generation* (*Pokolenie*, 1954). Wajda played a major role in shaping Polanski's ideas about film and film-making.

A Generation and Andrzej Wajda

Andrzej Wajda (born in Suwalki, 1926) was the son of a cavalry officer killed in the Second World War. He fought in the Resistance from the age of sixteen. After the war he briefly studied painting at Cracow alongside Walerian Borowczyk before studying film direction at Lodz. Wajda's first film, *A Generation* – referring to Wajda's own, the 'lost generation' – was the first part of the War Trilogy: the second part, *Canal* (*Kanal*), arguably Wajda's best film, followed in 1957, and the Trilogy was completed in 1958 with *Ashes And Diamonds* (*Poiol i diament*).

A Generation and Andrzej Wajda are significant for several reasons. First, *A Generation* marked the beginning of the Polish School of the Fifties which included films by Andrzej Munk, Jerzy Kawalerowicz and others that were formally influenced by De Sica and Rosellini's Neo-Realism and thematically preoccupied with the Second World War Polish Experience. Secondly, Andrzej Wajda was instrumental in forwarding the acting career of the "Polish James Dean" Zbigniew Cybulski, who made his debut in *A Generation* in the role of Kostek, as well as the directing careers of Polanski, Jerzy Skolimowski (born in Lodz, 1936) and Andrzej Zulawski (born in Lwow, 1940).

Besides *Lotna*, Polanski acted in Wajda's *Innocent Sorcerers* (*Niewinni Czarodzieje*, 1960) and *Samson* (1961). Skolimowski was a young poet when Wajda asked him to collaborate on the screenplay and act in *Innocent Sorcerers*. Zulawski served as Wajda's assistant on an episode of the portmanteau film *Love At Twenty* (*Milosc Dwudziestolatkow*, 1962) and *Samson* and *Ashes* (*Popioly*, 1965). Both Zulawski's *The Third Part Of The Night* (1971) and *Possession* (1981) end with an homage to the jaw-dropping staircase set piece that ends *A Generation*.

In his autobiography, *Roman By Polanski*, Polanski recalls how *A Generation* suffered badly from pre-release problems: "Some scenes had to be re-shot to reinforce their ideological content; others, including a spectacular fight scene between Cybulski and me, were cut altogether.

The *Generation* ultimately shown and admired around the world was a pale shadow of Wajda's original version." *A Generation* does suffer from oversimplistic idealism and a harsh polarisation of nationalist villains and communist heroes, though this is more a reflection of restrictions imposed on pre-Gomulka Polish cinema, than of Wajda's artistic shortcomings.

The Lodz Film School
(Panstwowa Wyzaza Szkola Teatraina Filmowa)

Polanski was accepted on the directing course at Lodz upon Wajda's recommendation. Between 1957 and 1959 Polanski completed six short films during his studies.

The Bicycle/Rower - Incomplete (1956)

Cast Roman Polanski, Adam Fiut.
Crew Cinematography: Nikola Todorow.

According to Polanski, a Bulgarian student, Nikola Todorow, had been assigned to make an exercise film in colour. Polanski persuaded Todorow and his teachers to turn the footage into a dramatic short. Polanski and Todorow travelled to Cracow to make a film based on an episode from his childhood. After the War Polanski bought and sold bicycles and spare parts. On one occasion, he was duped during one prospective purchase and a thug bludgeoned his head with a rock and stole his money.

Polanski produced, directed and acted in the short, as well as serving as "wardrobe mistress, continuity girl, and make-up man." His stepmother's nail polish stood in for blood. According to Polanski, half of the raw footage was lost in a processing mix-up at Film Polski and he reluctantly abandoned the film.

Murder/Morderstwo (1957)

Crew Cinematography: Nikola Todorow. 1½ mins. approx.

Story Total darkness. A door opens. The light reveals a man asleep. Another man enters, visible only from the waist down, carrying a pocket knife. Opening the knife, he stabs the sleeping man before leaving.

Verdict As a State Film School short, *Murder* stands out as lacking any social consideration, revelling in private fantasy, the ultimate crime in a Communist state. Probably the most memorable aspect of the film is just how discreet it is. There is little editing, let alone any moral. *Murder* simply introduces themes that would obsess Polanski for the next forty years: voyeurism and violence.

Teeth Smile/Usmiech zebiczny (1957)

Cast Nikola Todorow.

Crew Cinematography: Henryk Kucharski. 2 mins. approx.

According to Polanski, *Teeth Smile* was an exercise set by his supervisor. It shows a voyeur, played by Nikola Todorow, peering lecherously through a bathroom window at a naked girl drying herself. Nearly caught in the act, he retreats. He goes back for a second look, only to find an ugly old man brushing his teeth. The old man sees the voyeur in the bathroom mirror and turns to give him a toothy smile.

Break Up The Dance/Rozbijemy Zabawe (1958)

Crew Cinematography: Andrzej Galinski, Marek Nowicki. Music: Krzysztof Komeda. 9 mins.

Apparently Polanski arranged to film the annual student dance at Lodz. Having done that, he then coerced a group of thugs to 'break up the dance'. As planned, the thugs arrived and proceeded to beat up the unsuspecting students. According to Thomas Kiernan's (admittedly unreliable) *The Roman Polanski Story*, Polanski was imitating the documentary style of his Lodz mentor, Andrzej Munk. More of an anecdote than a success.

Two Men And A Wardrobe/Dwaj ludzie z szafa (1958)

Cast Jakub Goldberg, Henryk Kluba, Roman Polanski.

Crew Director: Roman Polanski; Screenplay: Roman Polanski; Cinematography: Maciej Kijowski; Music: Krzysztof Komeda. Production: Polish Film Academy (PWSF) (Lodz). 15 mins.

Story Two men, one short the other tall, bearded and balding, lug a decorative wardrobe out of the sea. They stagger across a deserted beach into town to offer the wardrobe to various people. A girl isn't interested in their offering, and what's more they aren't allowed onto the tram with it. They are heckled out of a café with the wardrobe. However, the wardrobe is put to good use when they use it as a table for lunch. The pair pass an empty pavilion. A group of thugs are about to molest the girl, but she sees their reflection in the mirror and moves on. The thugs attack the two men instead and smash up the wardrobe. The group then stones a kitten to death. With the wardrobe between their legs, the two retrace their steps through the town back to the beach, carefully avoiding a field of sandcastles, before disappearing back into the sea.

Origins The actual premise of *Two Men And A Wardrobe* is borrowed from Stefan and Franciszka Themerson's comparatively obscure avant-garde *The Adventures Of A Good Citizen* (*Przygoda Czlowieka Poczciwego*, 1937). Sadly, only two 16mm copies of *The Adventures Of A Good Citizen* exist, one in London, the other in Warsaw.

Surreal Violence Two Men And A Wardrobe – the title itself evokes surrealist wordplay. It is overtly pre-occupied with violence, though on a number of levels. Most prominent is Polanski himself who plays the thug who attacks one of the two men. Then there is the stoning of the kitten. Above all, *Two Men And A Wardrobe* is about violent juxtapositions – *Two Men And A Wardrobe* in the sea, on the beach, in a café, etc. A fish in the sky – actually lunch laid out on the wardrobe mirror. By playing the thug, Polanski identifies with the victimiser rather than the victim of violence in a world that refuses to make such a distinction.

Avant-Garde Success Polanski conceived *Two Men And A Wardrobe* as an entry for the 1958 Brussels Experimental Film Festival. The Belgium manufacturer of film stock, Gevaert offered $10,000 for the first prize, and $5,000 for the second. Out of the 400 submissions, 133 were selected. *Two Men And A Wardrobe* placed third and was awarded a bronze medal. Another Polish entry, *Dom* (House), the third and final collaboration between two brilliant poster artists, Walerian Borowczyk and Jan Lenica (see below), won first prize. Amongst the other entries were Stan Brakhage's *Loving* and Agnes Varda's *L'Opèra Mouffe*.

The Verdict Two Men And A Wardrobe is a deeply pessimistic parable: two men find themselves in absurd circumstances and fail to find a place in a corrupt, violent and cruel world. Polanski's treatment is, however, hilarious. 4/5

Krzysztof Komeda

From *Two Men And A Wardrobe* through to *Rosemary's Baby*, all but one of Polanski's films feature remarkable jazz soundtracks by Krzysztof Komeda. Komeda's scores are 'cool' both in timing and execution. His untimely death in 1969 earned Komeda the reputation as the "Lost Leader of Polish jazz." Komeda was born Krzysztof Trczinski-Komeda in Poznan and trained as an ear, nose and throat specialist. Komeda became one of the most prominent Jazz musicians during the post-war thaw in Sixties Poland, though Komeda was a stage name employed to divert the attentions of both the political and medical authorities, neither of whom would have taken kindly to his extra-curricular activities. In 1956 Komeda made his musical debut at a small, semi-official jazz festival at the coastal town of Sopot in Poland, the forerunner to the now annual Jazz Jamboree in Warsaw. Komeda completed his masterpiece in 1965, *Astigmatic*, widely regarded to be one of the best Jazz records of all time. By that time Komeda had with him a gifted group of musicians including the trumpeter Tomasz Stanko, Zbigniew Namyslowski on alto sax, Gunter Lenz on bass and Rune Carlsson on drums. In 1969, shortly after completing the haunting soundtrack for *Rosemary's Baby*, Komeda had a fall and badly injured his head. He returned home to Poland from the United States in a coma from which he never recovered. Komeda also regularly composed music for Jerzy Skolimowski – *Barrier (Bariera,* 1966*)*, *Hands Up! (Rece do gory,* 1967/1981) and *Le Départ* (1967) – and for the animated films of Miroslaw Kijowicz - *Usmiech* (1965), *Klatki* (1966), *Sztandar* (1965), *Rondo* (1966), *Laterna Magica* (1967) and *Wiklinowy Kosz* (1967).

The Lamp/Lampa (1958)

Crew Cinematography: Krzysztof Romanowski. 15 mins.

According to John Parker's *Polanski*, *The Lamp* is about a doll maker whose shop burns to the ground through faulty wiring after he installs electricity. Apparently it wasn't a success and Polanski himself omits it from his own filmography.

Basia Kwiatkowska

Polanski cast 17-year-old Basia Kwiatkowska in his next film, *When Angels Fall*. Kwiatkowska was a former shepherdess from the mountain village of Szulechow. Her film break arrived when she won a contest staged by a magazine "To Get Beautiful Girls On Screen." Polanski met her when Tadeusz Chmielewski cast her in *Eva Wants To Sleep* (1958). Polanski proposed to Kwiatkowska and they were quickly married on September 9, 1959, in Lodz. The poor couple stayed with Krzysztof Komeda and his wife Sofia in Cracow before moving back to Polanski's room in Lodz. Kwiatkowska left Polanski during one of his early visits to Paris. She later married Carl Boehm, ironically, the star of one of Polanski's favourite films, *Peeping Tom* (1960).

When Angels Fall/Gdy spadaja anioly (1959)

Cast Barbara Kwiatkowska (as Barbara Lass), Andrzej Kondratiuk, Henryk Kluba, Roman Polanski, Andrezej Konstenko, Jakub Goldberg.

Crew Director: Roman Polanski; Screenplay: Roman Polanski, based on a short story by Leszek Szymaeski; Cinematography: Henryk Kucharski; Set Design: Kazimierz Wisniak; Music: Krzysztof Komeda. 22 mins.

Story A wrinkled old woman works as an attendant in a public lavatory. She looks back upon her life – her son, her seduction by a cavalryman, the death of her lover. Her memories are interrupted by the chores that make up her present life. She is reunited with her lover, an angel crashes through the skylight, killing her, thus setting her free.

Origins Polanski's graduation film, less confrontational than *Two Men And A Wardrobe*, is a much more intriguing work. In his autobiography, Polanski recalls that the idea originated in a newspaper article about an elderly lavatory attendant who had a mystical vision. For Polanski, the lavatory attendant's life seems to epitomise vacuity, drudgery, monotony: " Nobody would ever look at an old crone in a public lavatory, with her pathetic saucerful of coins and her vacant, impersonal air, and conceive of her having had a life imbued with passion and drama."

The Influence of Naïf Painting When Angels Fall is Polanski's most 'Polish' film to date and one that is rooted in Polish naïve painting. When Jean-André Fieschi and Michel Delahaye interviewed Polanski in *Cahiers du Cinéma*, he elaborated: "I tried to ballast the flashbacks with certain references, among others, to Polish naïve painting, especially that of the nineteenth century, Jacek Maichewski, for example."

Polish Themes With the exception of *The Pianist*, *When Angels Fall* is the only one of Polanski's films to deal with ' Polish themes', the brutality and absurdity of wartime experience. The juxtaposition of age and youth is reminiscent of Gombrowicz's *Pornography*. The old woman, seemingly straight out of a similar scene in *Ashes And Diamonds*, was found in a home for the elderly.

Drag Cameo Polanski himself plays the old woman in middle age. He would return to drag in *The Tenant*. It is typical of Polanski and comparable to Woody Allen's early films: acting in front of the camera goads us to see the story as loaded with personal meaning, but its execution (unashamed drag) is so theatrical that it conceals more about Polanski than it actually reveals.

The Verdict Polanski's most atypical film, *When Angels Fall* is easily the most audacious as well as personal of his short films. Though less overtly innovative than its predecessor, *Two Men And A Wardrobe*, *When Angels Fall* is definitely worth seeking out. 4/5

Andrzej Munk

After graduating from Lodz, Polanski became an assistant director with Kamera, one of Poland's eight production companies, working with the French television director Jean-Marie Drot on a series of documentaries on Polish culture, then as assistant to Andrzej Munk. Though Andrzej Munk's films shared the same concern as Wajda's, his treatment was much more ascetic. His sceptical approach as well as his ironic treatment of both the grotesque and the absurd bear comparison with Polanski's early shorts. Polanski worked on *Bad Luck* (*Zezowate szczescie*, 1960), a film about a political opportunist beset by failures, the controversial moral being that people should start thinking for themselves. Sadly, Munk was killed in a road accident during his subsequent film, the harrowing *Passenger* (*Pasazerka*, 1961).

In March 1960 Polanski went to France for about eighteen months. He arrived in Paris with only a change of shabby clothes, a print of *Two Men And A Wardrobe*, a feature-length script he had collaborated on with Goldberg and Skolimowski, another short script developed with Goldberg, and the screenplay he had tried to write for his wife. His earlier contact with Drot enabled Polanski to work on another short, *The Fat And The Lean*.

The Fat And The Lean/Le gros et le maigre (1961)

Cast Andre Katelbach, Roman Polanski.

Crew Director: Roman Polanski; Screenplay: Roman Polanski, Jean-Pierre Rousseau; Director of Photography: Jean-Michel Boussaguet; Editor: Roman Polanski; Music: Krzysztof Komeda. Production: Claude Joudioux/APEC (Paris). 16 mins.

Story A grotesquely obese man sits outside his ramshackle house waited on by a tiny servant who tires himself out performing menial tasks and entertaining his master. When the servant threatens to leave for the city, the master pacifies him by making him a gift of a goat. However, the goat is tied to the servant, and it becomes even more difficult for him to rush about at the fat master's bidding. The master removes the goat and the servant is so relieved that he works faster than ever before.

A Gross Misunderstanding The critical success of the film relied particularly on the fact that *The Fat And The Lean* was perceived as a fable of the inequalities of the capitalist class system. However, given Polanski's outright contempt for 'clever' art, not to mention his own experience in post-war Poland, it seems unlikely that he travelled all the way from communist Poland to Paris to ridicule the class system. Conversely, Polanski treads similar ground as he did with *Two Men And A Wardrobe*, though austere absurdity displaces outright surreal effects. If anything, Polanski leans heavily on Beckett, Lucky and Pozzo on loan from *Waiting For Godot*. 3/5

In 1962 Polanski returned to Poland to do his first full-scale direction job for Kamera. However, Kwiatkowska had by now left Polanski, leaving him in deep depression. According to Jerzy Skolimowski, the assignment was given to Polanski by Andrzej Munk in order to divert his attention away from his marital break-up.

Mammals/Ssaki (1962)

Cast Henryk Kluba, Michal Zolnierhienicz

Crew Director: Roman Polanski; Screenplay: Roman Polanski, Andrzei Kondratiuk; Cinematography: Andrzej Kostenko; Editor: Halina Prugar, J Niedzwiedzka; Music: Krzysztof Komeda. Production: Film Polski/Studio Miniatur Filmowych Se-Ma-For (Lodz). 11 mins.

Story Mammals portrays two male characters travelling across the snowy Polish landscape. One sits on a sleigh while the other pulls it. Then they change positions and continue to take turns. The one who pulls tries constantly, by faking different ailments, to take the seat in the sleigh – to be pulled and not have to do the pulling. Finally they fight, and while they are preoccupied, a third man comes along and steals the sleigh.

Cartoon Characters Though thematically very similar to *The Fat And The Lean*, *Mammals* is a more kinetic affair, its rhythm closer to that found in animation. The white background not only anticipates the opening of *The Fearless Vampire Killers* but it also pares down the drama to formal elements – two men fighting over a sledge. *Mammals* finds company in an early live-action short by Borowczyk, *Gavotte* (1967). 4/5

After *Mammals*, Munk told Polanski, Goldberg and Skolimowski that he would help them get clearance and money from the state film board to make *Knife in the Water* – but only once the script was ready. With the advice of Gérard Brach, Polanski's screenplay was put into production under Munk's supervision.

Knife In the Water/Nóz w wodzie
(1962; aka *The Young Lover, The Long Sunday*)

Cast Leon Niemczyk (Andrzej), Jolanta Umecka (Christine), Zygmunt Malanowicz (The Student).

Crew Director: Roman Polanski; Screenplay: Roman Polanski, Jerzy Skolimowski, Jakub Goldberg; Producer: Stanislaw Zylewicz; Cinematography: Jerzy Lipman; Editor: Halina Prugar; Music: Krzysztof Komeda; Sound: Halina Paszkowska. Production: ZRF Kamera (Warsaw). 8,460 ft. 94 mins.

Story An attractive young woman, Christine takes the wheel of an enviable French car belonging to her partner Andrzej, a sports columnist. Whilst Andrzej criticises her driving skills, a reckless student leaps out in front of the car. Andrzej instigates a challenge, hoping to relieve Christine's boredom and elevate his own self-esteem. Andrzej not only gives the student a ride, but also insists on him accompanying them on their yacht trip. Attracted to Christine, the student becomes increasingly clumsy. He spends his time jabbing the point of a pocket knife rapidly between the fingers of his other hand. Andrzej argues with the student, who topples overboard, vanishing into the lake. Andrzej dives in to save him, though he fails to find the student and swims ashore. Despite an earlier claim that he couldn't swim, the student manages to hide behind the nearest buoy. Later he returns to the yacht to find Christine. The student seduces Christine before leaving. Later on land, Christine catches Andrzej on his way to the police, and assures him that the boy is alright. Andrzej's complacency in supposing that she may be lying in order to put his mind at rest goads her to hint at her own infidelity. Andrzej is left uncertain as to whether or not to believe that he is guilty of drowning the boy, or whether his wife has been unfaithful to him.

Collaborative Tensions On the surface *Knife In The Water* is a story of sexual jealousy, though its depth is the product of separate collaborative tensions between Polanski, Jerzy Skolimowski and (uncredited co-scriptwriter) Gérard Brach. *Knife In The Water* links violent threat with sexual possession in both narrative and more abstract social forms.

Dramatically Impoverished Knife In The Water is not so much absurd, rather dramatically impoverished, pared down to the point where we perceive only machismo competition in terms of athletic skill, technique and sexual prowess. The jarring incongruities of *Two Men And A Wardrobe* are absent, but what's left, as in Pinter's plays, is no less ridiculous.

Sexual Trespassing As with *The Fat And The Lean* and *Mammals*, *Knife In The Water* is about power, though reiterated in sexual terms. Significantly, there is never an explicit sexual conflict between Andrzej and the student over Christine. It seems probable that Andrzej no longer cares about Christine, their passion long since dissipated. Andrzej is only interested in affirming his territory and possessions, both sexual and material. Andrzej perceives himself in terms of his job, his yacht and his wife. His confidence is undermined by the student's apparent nonchalance, his lack of admiration. Envy or jealousy would be fine, but the student's indifference arouses Christine's interest and threatens Andrzej's self-esteem.

Class Antagonism If Andrzej's sexual jealousy is aroused by Christine's attraction to the student, then *Knife In The Water* operates on two sets of antagonisms, one between two generations – those either side of Wajda's 'generation' – and class antagonism. This Polish dimension smacks of Skolimowski's concerns, here succeeding where Wajda failed with *Innocent Sorcerers*.

Youthful Nihilism Despite the Freudian connotations of the knife, the student's game, as Raymond Durgnat suggests in *Sexual Alienation In The Cinema: The Dynamics Of Sexual Freedom*, is a focussing of the mind preoccupied by the exasperated aimlessness of everyday life. The knife game, like sailing (not to mention the game Andrzej initiated by picking up the student), depends on the satisfaction gained from the ascendancy of skill over danger. The student's impulsive and ultimately destructive momentum smacks of youthful nihilism. When Andrzej throws his knife overboard, the student rises to the challenge, only to get knocked into the sea. Andrzej is physically stronger than the student, though the student masochistically exaggerates his disadvantage – claiming he is not able to swim – turning it into a definite advantage over Andrzej, who is now obliged to rescue the helpless crewmate in the eye's of their judge, Christine.

The plot thickens when the student swims to a buoy and dives underwater, terrifying Andrzej into thinking he has drowned. The underdog lies low, tricking Andrzej. He is not what the materialistically superior

Andrzej thinks he is. The student risks himself under the car and when he hides behind the buoy it is without any plan, just animal cunning. As Durgnat points out, though the student is awkward in society, he is a 'natural' in his instincts, sabotaging the writer's natural order. Andrzej fails at life-saving – he can't even find the student's body – nor does he suspect the student is hiding. Both failures would be normal enough, but Andrzej is shaken by the loss of control incurred by this chance accident.

Verdict Christine tells the student that he and her husband are actually two of a kind. As Jean-Paul Torok observed, her bitter tone reminds us that the boy's ironic self-deprecation is no less false and destructive than the writer's pomposity. Not only is *Knife In The Water* an outstanding debut, it is unique in Polanski's filmography as, on the one hand, the only feature shot entirely in Poland and, on the other, exhibiting a social concern, typical of Skolimowski's subsequent films but generally absent from Polanski's own. 4/5

3: Power Plays Abroad (1963-1966)

Despite creating frictions with the Polish authorities, *Knife In The Water* became an art-house success abroad. The film was nominated for an Oscar (honourably losing out to Fellini's *8½*, 1962) and there was talk about a remake starring Warren Beatty, Richard Burton and Liz Taylor, in the roles of the student, Andrzej and Christine respectively. Having tasted Hollywood, Polanski set his sights on getting a film deal in the US. However, the English language was a problem and Polanski returned to Europe, though to France not Poland.

World's Greatest Swindles/Les plus belles escroqueries du monde (1963; aka *The Beautiful Swindlers*, *The World's Most Beautiful Swindlers*)

Episode: *The River Of Diamonds/La rivière de diamants*
Cast Nicole Karen, Jan Teulings, Arnold Gelderman.
Crew Director: Roman Polanski (other episodes by Claude Chabrol, Ugo Gregoretti, Hiromichi Horikawa); Screenplay: Roman Polanski, Gérard Brach; Cinematography: Jerzy Lipman; Editor: Rita van Royen; Music: Krzysztof Komeda. Production: Ulysses Productions, Primex/Vides/Caesar/Lux Films/Toho/Towa (Amsterdam/Paris/Rome/Tokyo). 33 mins.

Story Polanski went to Amsterdam to shoot his section of this portmanteau film. *The Best Swindles In The World* is, like *RoGoPaG* (*Laviamoci il cervello*, 1962) and *Love At Twenty* (*L'amour à vingt ans*, 1962), one of several international portmanteau films produced during the early Sixties. The title refers to a stolen necklace. Struggling to balance his traditional notions of film-making against the avant-garde French style, soon ran into directorial dilemmas. Polanski wrote in his autobiography that for him "a film has to have a definite dramatic and visual shape...as opposed to the rather flimsy shape that a lot of films were being given by the *nouvelle vague*...it has something to be finished, like a sculpture, almost something you can touch...it has to be rigorous and disciplined."

Verdict Portmanteau films are by nature uneven affairs, one part exacerbating its strength or weakness against the others. Polanski's episode is arguably the best, though that's not really saying much. 1/5

Returning to Paris, Polanski wrote the scenario for *Do You Like Women?* with Gérard Brach, based on a novel by Georges Bardawil. Jean Léon directed the film, though in terms of theme and execution it's typical Polanski.

Do You Like Women?/Aimez-vous les femmes? (1963)

Story Jérôme discovers that an exclusive vegetarian restaurant turns out to be merely a front for a clandestine cult of high-class cannibals. Beautiful girls prepared with seasoning are served to members with silver service. Jérôme is torn between twin sisters in white PVC. He falls in love with one, while the other turns out to be the villain of the piece. Though he never quite works out which one of the sisters he's rescued, he loves her anyway.

Cannibalised Surrealism Twin sisters, one good and bad, an emblem of Sade (Justine and Juliette). Sadomasochistic fantasies are played out in a nightclub where girls are apparently stripped through the cuts of a bullwhip. Jerome is sewn up in sheets. Guido Crepax recycles the cannibalistic feast set piece several times over in his erotic surrealist comic strip *Bianca*.

Love Hurts Raymond Durgnat saw Jérôme's predicament as leading straight into a tangle of paradoxes about eroticism, masochism, personal loyalty and orthodox morality: "Is love love if it isn't masochistic? Is it ever the real person whom we love, or merely a persona which may well be superficial, and yet so precious to us as still to be worthy of our love? Insofar as everybody has his secrets, can we ever love a real person?" Or, as Sonya (Diane Keaton) consoles her love-sick sister (Jessica Harper) at the end of Woody Allen's *Love And Death* (1975), "...to love is to suffer, not to love is to suffer, not to suffer is to suffer, to suffer is to suffer..."

Verdict The prospect that Polanski could have directed *Do You Like Women?* makes the flat direction of the film doubly frustrating. Despite some fantastic imagery, this black comedy would have been better risking outright bad taste by being even more excessive. 2/5

After scripting *Do You Like Women?* Polanski was particularly depressed and preparing to return to Poland to avoid being drafted into the French army, despite the fact that he was now certain to be drafted into the Polish army. However, a Polish American producer, Gene Gutowski, tracked Polanski down and urged him to come over to London and direct in English. Polanski accepted.

Gene Gutowski

Born in 1923, Gene Gutowski was a Polish-American who had escaped Poland during the last weeks of the war and established himself with an American army OSS unit in southern Germany. As Gutowski spoke German, he assisted in the interrogation of captured German military personnel. A year later, he was sent to the US, given an American Army rank, and assigned to a Pentagon intelligence unit. Gutowski later married and had a family, which he was to leave in the mid-1950s to become a film producer based in London. Gutowski was aware of Polanski's eagerness to break into Hollywood, as well as his weak English. When Polanski moved to London, Gutowski acted as both his agent and executive producer. Gutowski rejected offers from other producers for Polanski to direct for them, instead forming a company with Polanski, Cadre Films, to produce their own projects. Polanski was most eager to direct a script that he prepared in Paris with Gérard Brach, a project later realised as *Cul-De-Sac*. Looking to raise money for this project, Gutowski turned to Compton Films. Compton specialised in sexploitation films, and they said no to Polanski's script. However, they did express interest in him directing something a little more exploit-ative, like a horror film. Polanski and Gutowski decided to shoot a horror film to raise the money for *Cul-De-Sac*. If only all capital raising ventures were as imaginative as *Repulsion*.

Repulsion (1965)

Cast Catherine Deneuve (Carol), Yvonne Furneaux (Helen), John Fraser (Colin), Ian Hendry (Michael), Patrick Wymark (The Landlord), Roman Polanski (A Spoons Player).

Crew Director: Roman Polanski; Screenplay: Roman Polanski, Gérard Brach, David Stone; Producer: Gene Gutowski; Cinematography: Gilbert Taylor; Art Director: Seamus Flannery; Editor: Alastair McIntyre; Music: Chico Hamilton; Assistant Director: Ted Sturgis; Sound: Stephen Dalby; Executive Producers: Michael Klinger, Tony Tenser; Associate Producers: Robert Sterne, Sam Wayneberg. Production: Compton/Tekli. 9360 ft. 104 mins.

Story Carol Ledoux is a withdrawn Belgian girl living with her sister Helen on the top floor of a rather dingy flat in South Kensington. She works as a manicurist in a beauty salon. Before Helen holidays with her (married) lover Michael, she prepares a rabbit for Carol. Carol evidently loathes Michael, she bins his clothes when he tries to embrace her. Carol lies transfixed in bed as she hears her sister climax in the adjacent room. Left alone, Carol starts to go to pieces, she sees the reflections of men in the wardrobe mirror, wanders aimlessly around South Kensington, cuts a customer's finger in the Salon. The plaster cracks, molesting hands plunge out of the walls and the ticking of clocks become deafening. When her boyfriend Colin turns up to find out if they still have any sort of relationship, Carol bludgeons him with a candlestick. She drags his body into the bath, full of cold water she's forgotten to empty. Carol frantically barricades the front door, lending her some comfort, while she sews and sings to herself. Michael's wife calls and, mistaking Carol for Helen, insults her. Carol cuts the phoneline with a razor before slashing the sleazy landlord. Helen and Michael return to find Carol hidden under the bed, the flat in chaos and a rotting rabbit. Michael carries the catatonic girl out of the flat, past her neighbours. The camera pans around the flat before closing in on an old family photograph, ending with Carol's eyes...

Modern Horror Like other European horror films (or those with European sensibilities at least) of the Forties, Fifties and Sixties – Jacques Tourneur's *Cat People* (1942), Henri-Georges Clouzot's *Les Diaboliques* (1955), Georges Franju's *Eyes Without A Face (Les yeux sans visage*, 1959), Michael Powell's *Peeping Tom* and Hitchcock's *Psycho* (1960) – *Repulsion* doesn't rely upon the supernatural. Rather, it reiterates the staples of gothic horror, particularly the haunted house, in a post-Freudian consciousness. However, as Hitchcock's cod-Freudian denouncement of Norman Bates at the end of *Psycho* goes to show, it is the absolute certainty of psychiatrists that is really frightening. To use the old saying that Milosz uses as a preface to *The Captive* Mind: "When someone is honestly 55% right, that's good. If someone is 60% right, that's wonderful. But when someone is 75% right, there's call for suspicion and if someone's 100% right they're simply lying."

Psycho Inside Out Raymond Durgnat pointed out that *Repulsion* is *Psycho* turned inside out. Polanski's protagonist is a woman, through whose eyes we see the outside world, with whom identification is consistent and of whose mental processes any explanation is conspicuously absent. The haunted house is inside Carol's head and is made all the more frightening because she can't escape. *Psycho* introduces us to a structure of motivations, whereas *Repulsion* takes that as read and offers us the experience, the snapping of a mind, not in one grandiose convulsion but quietly, progressively. However, both *Psycho* and *Repulsion* end on a pair of blank, catatonic stares.

A Woman Possessed Carol is haunted or 'possessed' by sexual disgust. Sex is the modern-day Devil, and so *Repulsion* makes *The Exorcist* (1975) appear medieval BY comparison. The lineage of *Repulsion* includes both Jerzy Kawalerowicz's *Mother Joanna Of The Angels* (*Matka Joanna od aniolow*, 1961) and Zulawski's delirious *Possession* (1981). Kawalerowicz's film is based on Jaroslaw Iwaszkiewicz's historical novella set in 17th-century Poland. The drama is an effective, mystical study of a priest-exorcist who comes to exorcise a group of convent nuns, based on the same Loudon trial documented by Huxley, dramatised by John Whiting and filmed by Ken Russell in *The Devils* (1971). Whilst the gothic horror of Kawalerowicz's film is brought out on purely an aesthetic level, the 'possession' by sexual insanity in *Repulsion* is closer to Zulawski's. At heart, the 'horrors' of *Repulsion* and *Possession* are existential conundrums: Carol's sexual disgust and the psychotic behaviour of Anna, the protagonist of *Possession*, do not arise from physical desires or orgasms. Rather, the fear they share is that of being possessed by another. Anna's crisis arises during marital infidelity, Carol's during burgeoning sexuality – their breakdowns find a curious Sartre-esque expression: characters entering or trapped in sexual relationships who nonetheless refuse to give up their freedom, which is impossible.

Reinvigorated Expressionism The cracked walls and lascivious corridors in *Repulsion* constitute an attempt to reinvigorate the stream-of-consciousness aesthetic of Expressionism. The natural ascendant of Carol's madwoman's-eye-view décor *à la The Cabinet Of Dr Caligari* (1919). However, the grotesqueries of George Grosz and Max Beckmann infiltrate less overt scenes, such as the one in which Carol walks through South Kensington past crab-like disabled buskers (one of which is played by Polanski) and lecherous old men. Raymond Durgnat suggested that Carol's isolation and violence is only a climactic form of all the reciprocal repulsions that make up our 'sane' society. *Repulsion* is certainly not *Family Life* (1971; aka *Wednesday's Child*), though Polanski's picture of madness as a social product is in keeping with the Sixties radical psychiatrist R D Laing. Ingmar Bergman relied upon similar expressionist shock effects for his own 'breakdown' period – *Persona* (1966), *Shame* (*Skammen*, 1968), *Hour Of The Wolf* (*Vargtimmen*, 1968), *The Passion Of Anna* (*En Passion*, 1969). Polanski has been criticised in both *Repulsion* and its spiritual successor, *The Tenant*, for resorting to these "overblown facile effects." He is not alone: the same critics suggest that Kubrick should have dropped all allusions to the supernatural in *The Shining* (1980) and confirm Tarkovsky's regrets about clinging to the SF premise of *Solaris* (1971). At best such critics are genre snobs, at worst it reveals a conception of cinema where the inner and outer world should be kept cleanly on two separate plates.

There's Always Freud Expressionism enjoyed a particularly close, and occasionally collaborative, association with psychoanalysis. *Repulsion* also falls into a clear oedipal pattern: elder sister as mother, every male caller as father.

Pessimism Durgnat argues that the society in *Repulsion* cannot but accommodate the violence which each of us inflicts on others by the very fact of our existence and which we undergo at the hands of others, a violence which makes nonsense of individualism and reformist idealism alike.

Verdict Repulsion is excellent. A harrowing performance from Catherine Deneuve and brilliant use of décor and photography compensate for the occasional dated line to make *Repulsion* an all-time classic, not just of horror but cinema, full stop. 5/5

Between *Repulsion* and the final draft of *Cul-De-Sac*, Polanski had written, in collaboration with Brach, a story of a divorced American dentist who decides he is sick of American women and travels through Europe in search of a more congenial wife. According to Ivan Butler, the black comedy was to have been called *Cherchez la femme* and Larry Gelbart was engaged at one point to Anglicise and revive the script. *Cherchez la femme* would have been the second film made by Cadre Films and Filmways. However financing could not be found and the project was sold to MGM, never to be realised.

Cul-De-Sac (1966)

Cast Donald Pleasance (George), Françoise Dorléac (Teresa), Lionel Stander (Richard), Jack MacGowran (Albie), Iain Quarrier (Christopher), Jacqueline Bisset (Jacqueline).

Crew: Director: Roman Polanski; Screenplay: Roman Polanski, Gérard Brach; Producer: Gene Gutowski; Cinematography: Gilbert Taylor; Art Director: George Lack; Special Effects: Bowie Films; Editor: Alastair McIntyre; Music: Krzysztof Komeda; Assistant Director: Ted Sturgis; Sound: Stephen Dalby; Executive Producer: Sam Wayneberg. Production Company: Compton/Tekli. 9990 ft. 111 mins.

Story A broken-down jalopy is pushed along an endless roadway on either side of which lies sand and water. The car is pushed by a bulky, gravel-voiced man, Richard, whilst a lean, bespectacled passenger, Albie, handles the steering. The two have escaped from a bungled armed robbery. Both have sustained injuries, Richard has been shot in the arm whilst Albie has received more serious wounds in the stomach. Leaving Albie in the car, Richard follows some telephone wires to a small castle. A beautiful girl, Teresa, lies in the sand dunes with her lover, Cecil, whilst her husband, George, flies a kite. George is a short, bald, middle-aged man who has sold his business, left the city and his family to live with Teresa, a French nymphomaniac. Richard breaks into the castle and tries to telephone his boss, Mr Katelbach. Teresa, meanwhile, is busy helping George into her nightdress. Richard holds them both at gunpoint and forces them to push the jalopy to the castle. The jalopy crashes into George's car and Albie soon dies. Albie is buried and a car arrives with some of George's old friends. Richard reluctantly plays George's butler in order not to arouse suspicion. A boy uses a rifle to put through a castle window, which George uses as an excuse to get the group off his island. Richard spanks Teresa with his belt when she places pieces of paper between his toes and lights them whilst he's sleeping. Katelbach calls to say he's deserting Richard. Teresa gets hold of the rifle. George accidentally shoots Richard. George returns to his castle to discover that Teresa has ran off with Cecil. George is left perched on a rock as the tide comes in calling for his wife Agnes.

Victim as Victimiser Richard, the victim of a bungled bank robbery, assumes control over George and Teresa. However, in order to remain inconspicuous to guests from the mainland, Richard plays at being George's butler. Richard is once again the victim, this time of Teresa's sadistic tricks, but retaliates with his considerable bulk and strength by spanking her over his knee with his belt. Richard is then the victim in an accidental shooting, whilst George, now in control, is left nonetheless powerless as Teresa leaves with Cecil under his nose.

Sexual Humiliation Submission in *Cul-De-Sac* is equated with an almost infantile sexuality. George consents to his humiliation in Teresa's cross-dressing game. As the 'man of the house' George, guarding his territory, creeps downstairs, only to be caught by Richard dressed "like a little fairy." No wonder George so readily relinquishes authority to Richard's effortless challenge. Upon being caught in the middle of her cruel but nonetheless provocative trick, Teresa pays the price and is punished by Richard. However, Richard doesn't rape Teresa, rather he takes her over his knees and spanks her like a naughty child, much to George's delight. Even when George "acts like a man" (i.e. threatens Richard at gunpoint), Teresa sexually rejects him in favour of Cecil.

Beckett Goes to Lindesfarne The original title of *Cul-De-Sac* was *When Katelbach Comes* which alludes to Samuel Beckett's most famous play. The title *Cul-De-Sac* suggests a very British take on existential matters, Sartre's *No Exit* 'up North'. Polanski had already made clear his plans to film *Waiting For Godot*, though nothing came of it.

Casting Beckett regular Jack MacGowran in the role of Albie must have been some consolation. *Cul-De-Sac* is the crowning achievement of Polanski's numerous forays into the absurd. The opening sequence with the scruffy Richard struggling to push Albie in the clapped-out jalopy is no less ridiculous than the poor goat in *The Fat And The Lean* or the sledge fight in *Mammals*. On the other hand, the incoming tide makes their efforts just as futile as the lives of Lucky and Pozzo in *Waiting For Godot* or the relationship of Fernando Arrabal's *Fando And Lis* (*Fando y Lis*, 1967). The dramatic structure of *Cul-De-Sac* hinges around a visitor instigating and participating in a series of misapplied actions as well as self-deceptive role-play comparable with Gombrowicz's *The Marriage*.

The Sad Fate of a Misanthropist Françoise Dorléac, Catherine Deneuve's sister, plays Teresa, though her character could not be more different than Carol in *Repulsion*. Whereas Carol is frigid, repelled by sexuality, Teresa is a nymphomaniac. If anything, it's George who is closer to Carol. Teresa acts more like a prick-teasing big sister. Rather than incarcerating himself in an urban flat, George uses money from the city to retire to a castle on Holy Island. George's life is the ideal of the Englishman's home taken to an extreme, which in turn reveals just how ridiculous it is. George's castle is his house, its walls and moat a defence against society. There's no romance either, only hate. By choosing a partner whose beauty is matched by her sexual infidelity, not only is George in denial over his hatred of friends, but his lover as well.

The Verdict Arguably Polanski's most original film, *Cul-De-Sac* is the culmination of a preoccupation with the absurd that was fostered in his native Poland but only reached maturity in England. Secondly, *Cul-De-Sac* exhibits Polanski's tremendous skill for handling pared-down, rigorously composed sexual dramas. However, the most remarkable aspect of *Cul-De-Sac* is Polanski's use of location, arguably the most imaginative in all British films to date. Finally, the UK television version of *Cul-De-Sac,* occasionally screened on BBC2, is significantly longer (and superior) to the current UK video release. 5/5

Jan Lenica

Immediately after the international success of *Knife In The Water*, *Sight And Sound* interviewed Polanski. He was asked to name his favourite film-makers. Polanski's first choice, Wajda, was unsurprising, though his second, Jan Lenica (born in Poznan, 1928), may have seemed a little obscure. However, Lenica's absurd graphics and Komeda's music played integral roles in establishing how 'cool' Polanski's early films were.

Besides producing the title sequence for *Cul-De-Sac* Jan Lenica created the poster artwork for *Repulsion* (1965) and *Cul-De-Sac* (1966). Both are childlike gouaches, verging on the abstract, though immediately distinctive. Like Polanski films, Lenica's career in poster art and set-design cultivated associations with the absurd, a preoccupation that culminated with a series of remarkable animations during the Sixties and Seventies. Together with another poster designer, Walerian Borowczyk, Lenica produced several short animated films *Once Upon A Time* (*Byl sobie raz*, 1957), *Education Days* (*Dni oswiaty*, 1957), *Banner Of Youth* (*Szalandar Mlodych*,1957), *Striptease* (*Strep-Tease*, 1957), *Requited Sentiments* (*Nagrodzone uczucia*, 1958) and *Dom* (1958), arguably their most brilliant animation. Dom is composed of several absurdist episodes using a number of different techniques (cutouts, pixilation and object animation), exploiting the full potential of film animation. Lenica's first solo film was *Monsieur Tête* (1959), narrated by Eugène Ionesco. Afterwards, Lenica was invited back to Poland, where he produced a Henryk Sienkiewicz animated pastiche, *New Janko The Musician* (*Nowy Janko Muzykant*, 1960). In 1962 Lenica created *Labyrinth* (*Labyrint*, 1963), a self-consciously Kafka-esque tale of a winged lonely man literally devoured by totalitarian rule. Along with Jiri Trnka's *The Hand* (*Ruka*, 1965), *Labyrinth* is considered to be one of the finest political animations ever made.

In 1962, Lenica moved to the Federal Republic to make a wordless condensation of Ionesco's *Rhinoceroses* (*Die Nashorner*, 1963). *A* (1964) was a formally austere pessimistic tale of interrogation. Between 1966 and 1969 Lenica laboured single-handedly on a remarkably ambitious feature length animation *Adam 2* (1968). Lenica returned to making shorter films, most notably *The Flower Woman* (*La femme fleur*, 1969), a poem to Art Nouveau with a commentary by André Pieyre de

Mandiargues and music by Georges Delerue. *Fantorro, The Last Arbiter* (*Fantorro, le dernier justicier*, 1971), *Hell* (*Enfer*,1973), *Still Life* (live action, 1973) and *Landscape* (1974). In 1976, Lenica returned to animation, choosing Alfred Jarry's *King Ubu* (*Ubu roi*, 1976) as the subject for a medium-length feature project. In 1979 he edited this German production into a later French production of two other Ubu plays, *Ubu cocu* and *Ubu enchâiné*, a venture which resulted in the feature-length *Ubu et la grande gidouille* (1979), the only one of Lenica's films to rely on dialogue. Lenica died in 2001.

4: Vampires And Devils (1967-1968)

Sharon Tate was born into a military family in Dallas in 1943, the eldest of three daughters. After winning a number of beauty contests as a teenager she acquired an agent, Martin Ransohoff. After a television series, *Petticoat Junction*, Tate starred in an occult horror film, *Eye Of The Devil* (1965), alongside David Niven and Deborah Kerr. She was introduced to Polanski at a London party and he cast her in the role of Sarah in his next film, *The Fearless Vampire Killers*, with Ransohoff acting as co-producer. Polanski and Tate became lovers during the making of the film. Polanski photographed a *Playboy* spread of Tate titled, unsurprisingly, *The Tate Gallery*.

The Fearless Vampire Killers
(1967; aka *Dance Of The Vampires*)

Cast Jack MacGowran (Professor Abronsius), Roman Polanski (Alfred), Alfie Bass (Shagal), Jessie Robins (Rebecca), Sharon Tate (Sarah), Ferdy Mayne (Count Von Krolock), Iain Quarrier (Herbert).

Crew Director: Roman Polanski; Screenplay: Roman Polanski, Gérard Brach; Producer: Gene Gutowski; Director of Photography: Douglas Slocombe; Production Designer: Wilfred Shingleton; Art Director: Fred Carter; Costumes: Sophie Devine; Editor: Alastair McIntyre; Music: Krzysztof Komeda; Choreography: Tutte Lemkow; Makeup: Tom Smith; Titles: André François; Assistant Director: Roy Stevens; Sound: George Stephenson; Executive Producer: Martin Ransohoff; Production Manager: David W Orton. Production: Cadre Films/Filmways. 9654 ft. 107 mins.

Story Professor Abronsius, an undervalued scientist and author of *The Bat And Its Mysteries*, is on a sacred mission with his one and only faithful disciple, Alfred. A sleigh carries them to an inn. The Professor is frozen solid. The innkeeper, Shagal, and his wife, Rebecca, thaw out the Professor. The Professor and Alfred are vampire hunters and excited by the sight of garlic hanging around the room. Upon inquiring about a nearby castle, their host goes numb. The Professor suspects that this is where the chief vampire, Count Von Krolock, resides. Alfred falls in love with Shagal's beautiful daughter, Sarah, a compulsive bather. Trying to impress her, Alfred heats some water for her to bathe in. Alfred spies on Sarah bathing through the keyhole. Suddenly, Krolock sweeps down, revealing his vampire fangs. Alfred, helpless, watches Krolock disappear with Sarah through the skylight. Abronsius finds Shagal's body drained of blood, but still the locals doubt his explanation, preferring to heap the blame on wolves. Shagal returns from the dead as a very Jewish vampire in search of a servant girl, Magda. The Professor and Alfred raid Krolock's castle, fail to infiltrate his crypt and wind up in his library searching through old sex instruction manuals and telescopes in search of Sarah. Herbert, Krolock's camp vampire son, takes a shine to Alfred, whilst Krolock confronts Abronsius. The film ends with Abronsius and Alfred's clandestine pursuit of Krolock and Sarah in a spectacular vampire ball. They manage to escape with Sarah. However, she bites into Alfred's neck and Abronsius carries them both away, blissfully unaware that he is about to spread the vampire plague.

Vampire Parody The Fearless Vampire Killers is a very self-conscious parody of the vampire genre, in particular *Kiss Of The Vampire* and *Brides Of Dracula*. However, Polanski's references extend beyond Hammer horror. The film opens with a loose pastiche of the opening of Carl Dreyer's sombre *Vampyr* (1932, based on J Sheridan le Fanu's novelette *Carmilla*) and ends up satirising the vampire's aristocratic credentials with Richard III and the Duchess of Tyrol on the guest list of Von Krolock's ball. Quoting Puccini's *La Bohême*, Alfred's melodramatic last words to Sarah compare vampirism to consumption. Polanski also derives a number of gags by dragging out the latent homosexuality in vampire films with Krolock's camp vampire son, Herbert. More obscure is the Eastern European sensibility that Polanski imports into the film, particularly evident in a scene when a Jewish caricature, Shagal, about to lunch on Magda, is confronted with a crucifix and laughs "you got the wrong vampire!" Shagal alludes to Chagal, who in turn mythologised Vitebsk, a Polish town destroyed by the Nazis.

Pessimism Alfred and Abronius are both outsiders, rejected by the village community. Whereas the villagers in Terrance Fisher's Hammer films triumphantly storm the castles of the imposing vampire aristocracy (satirised by Paul Morrissey in *Blood For Dracula* (1974; aka *Andy Warhol's Dracula* in which Polanski had a cameo role), Polanski's villagers resign themselves to the futility of their situation, submitting to the shadow of Von Krolock's castle. With the villagers stuck in a rut, Abronsius' idealism only makes things worse, as his expedition ends up spreading vampirism to the wider community. The film ends on a curious note: Sarah is lost to Von Krolock and Alfred and Abronsius have unwittingly smuggled vampirism out of the village, fulfilling Krolock's ambition. With Sarah's bite, Alfred too has become a vampire and part of a growing community of vampires. As a living member of the cast, Abronsius' hours are now numbered.

Voyeurism Sarah is the object of both Alfred's and Von Krolock's desire in *The Fearless Vampire Killers*. Two shots of Sarah take place as Alfred peers at her body through a keyhole as she takes a bath. One of them culminates in her father spanking her and the other with Von Krolock ravishing her in the bathtub. Alfred is helplessly excluded in the latter, much like Jeffrey Beaumont in Dorothy Valence's bedroom wardrobe in David Lynch's *Blue Velvet* (1986). Both scenes have the person being spied upon submitting to violence, both are charged with an infantile sexuality thanks to their voyeuristic set-up. Another more ambiguous shot is one in which Sarah is framed through the window of the Inn as she watches Alfred build a snowman outside. Children destroy the snowman and Alfred, now humiliated under Sarah's gaze, consoles himself by groping a barmaid's breasts.

But why are the exteriors shots so grainy? Polanski originally intended to shoot the film in the Panavision 2.35:1 aspect ratio but MGM insisted that Polanski shoot using the cheaper 1.85:1 ratio. When the production was forced into the studio (the production was to be shot on location in a castle in the Dolomites) because of the lack of snow, Polanski insisted that the rest should be shot using the 2.35:1 ratio. To match the aspect ratios, Polanski simply cropped the 1.85:1 exterior shots and stepped them up at the printing stage.

The Musical In 2000 Polanski adapted *The Fearless Vampire Killers* for the Viennese stage with librettist Michael Kunze and composer Jim Steinman. William Dudley's elaborate stage design recreated the snowy landscape of Polanski's original film as well as a dilapidated village pub and a huge horror palace with bizarre halls complete with a gallery of ancestral portraits, library, bathroom and crypt. Sue Blane was responsible for costume design and Hugh Vanstone lit the production.

The Verdict Vampire myth not only hints at coercive sexual betrayal (*Knife In The Water*, *Cul-De-Sac*), but relationship dominance is expressed as cannibalism (*Do You Like Women?*). As a macabre parody, *The Fearless Vampire Killers* is too restrained. If the success of Morrissey's *Blood For Dracula* lay in excess, the sexual elements in Polanski's film, like many Hammer films, are too prudish. His choice of allusions is at best obscure, at worst merely coy. If the intense, macabre atmosphere of *Repulsion* demanded audience involvement, the facetious gags of *The Fearless Vampire Killers* make it impossible. However, if *The Fearless Vampire Killers* looks and sounds fantastic thanks to exceptional photography by Douglas Slocombe and arguably Komeda's best film score. 3/5

Rosemary's Baby (1968)

Cast Mia Farrow (Rosemary Woodhouse), John Cassavetes (Guy Woodhouse), Ruth Gordon (Minnie Castevet), Sidney Blackmer (Roman Castevet), Maurice Evans (Hutch), Ralph Bellamy (Dr Sapirstein).

Crew Director: Roman Polanski; Screenplay: Roman Polanski, based on the novel by Ira Levin; Producer: William Castle; Cinematography: William Fraker; Production designer: Richard Sylbert; Art Director: Joel Schiller; Set Director: Robert Nelson; Costumes: Anthea Sylbert; Editors: Sam O'Steen, Bob Wyman; Music: Krzysztof Komeda; Assistant Director: Daniel J McCauley; Sound: Harold Lewis; Associate Producer: Dona Holloway. Production: Paramount/William Castle Enterprises. 12290 ft. 137mins.

Story Rosemary Woodhouse and her husband Guy take a flat in the Bramford, a dingy block of flats in New York City, once the site of a witchcraft scandal according to an old friend, Hutch. It is home to the cannibalistic Trench sisters and Satanist Adrian Marcato. Rosemary meets a young girl, Terry, in the basement laundry. They discuss an odd silver charm around Terry's neck. Rosemary is repulsed by its smell. Shortly after, Terry leaps to her death. An odd, noisy as well as nosy couple invite Rosemary and Guy to dinner. Roman Castevet takes a distinct interest in Guy's career. Rosemary notices that all the. pictures have been removed from the wall. Rosemary finds herself pregnant after a bizarre nightmare in which she is being raped by the Devil in the middle of a black mass. Guy's acting career takes off when a rival candidate for a Broadway show suddenly goes blind. The Castevets recommend an exclusive doctor, Sapirstein, who prescribes Rosemary a drink which makes her pale and drawn. Hutch is struck down, left in a coma and Rosemary grows sick of Guy's preoccupation with the Castevets as well as the pain in her stomach. She becomes convinced that she is surrounded by a coven of witches when she is given a book left to her by Hutch, *All Of Them Witches*. With the aid of Scrabble letters, she discovers that Steven Marcato, Adrian's son, is an anagram of Roman Castevet. Convinced that her child is to be part of some Satanic ritual of which Sapirstein is a part, Rosemary runs to her old Doctor. To Rosemary's horror, Dr Hill turns her over to Sapirstein. Unable to escape, Rosemary gives birth. She is told that her baby has died at birth but she soon realises that the milk which is being drawn from her breasts is being given special care. In the end, Rosemary, knife in hand, finds her baby and like its father, it has goats' eyes. Unfortunately for Christianity, Rosemary 's maternal feelings prevent her from destroying her the child.

A Satanic New Testament Rosemary should have listened to Pope John Paul who reminded us that behind the initiation to sensual pleasure there loom narcotics. However, the US Roman Catholic Office did in fact deliver the most acute insight into *Rosemary's Baby*. Polanski's first Hollywood film was condemned because of "the perverted use which the film makes of fundamental Christian beliefs and its mockery of religious persons and practices." If *Repulsion* opened a sane eye on an insane world, Polanski turns Christian faith inside out and back to front in *Rosemary's Baby*. To make things worse, the film ends not on an apocalyptic note but on one of triumph as the witches' coven give thanks to their lord that, after 2000 years of the torture and persecution of Satanists, the world is about to enter its new era. The Devil worshippers at last have their Christ, its father, ironically, an actor. Their Virgin Mary is, appropriately enough, raped and prostituted by her own husband. Even Vidal Sassoon gets in on the act, fashioning Rosemary's hair like Rene Falconetti's in Carl Dreyer's silent film of another religious martyr, *The Passion Of Joan Of Arc* (*La passion de Jeanne d'Arc*, 1928). Adding insult to injury, the end of the (Christian) world is brought about by a disturbingly prosaic wish of Guy's. For the Devil has promised that his acting career would prosper sufficiently to enable him to give up making television commercials and appear in films worthy of his artistic talent.

Psychosis or the Devil? Polanski's film of *Rosemary's Baby* is superior to Ira Levin's source novel because Rosemary's ordeal is all the more effectively expressed through an unresolved tension between two different interpretations of events. On the one hand, Rosemary is defiled and prostituted by inherently evil people and gives birth to the Antichrist. Slightly less exciting is a humanist reading positing Rosemary, like Carol in *Repulsion*, as a healthy mind persecuted by sick perverts with a shared hang-up for group sex. However, it's a humanist reading in reverse. Psychiatrists advocate psychopathological theories of witchcraft, maintaining that witches were mentally ill women. Persecution *per se* is the result of economic uncertainty, apprehensions about physical security and deflecting antisocial impulses against a single group. However, in *Rosemary's Baby* it is the witches who appear to be persecuting Rosemary.

Erotic Witchcraft The inquisition's Devil myth hinged upon his connection with sexual license and, conversely, the repressed sexuality of faithful Christians. Though Rosemary isn't particularly religious, she is not sexually repressed. If anything, Rosemary is the liberated girl next door. Raymond Durgnat points out that the sexual tension in *Rosemary's Baby* doesn't lie in any easily isolatable element. The two explanations of Rosemary's ordeal – innate paranoia or her destined role in a satanic ritual – are not mutually exclusive. Eroticism is the common element. Paranoia or persecution operates through violation of will (through the drugging of Chocolate Mousse, or having her ankles bound with bed sheets) whilst the Devil, part animal, subjugates her to uncontrollable sexual urges. Meanwhile, love, whilst not forgotten, disappears from the picture when Guy prostitutes Rosemary both in terms of her sexuality and in her motherhood. If Carol's madness in *Repulsion* is externalised, Rosemary's is eroticised.

Dionysiac Uprising Polanski emphasises the arrival of the Antichrist as a turning point in the antagonistic struggle between Christianity and the Devil. Rosemary's visions are of formal plastic conceptions of majestic visions, both old (the Sistine Chapel) and contemporary (Kennedy's Yacht). At threat are Apollonian values: static (personal relationships), order (political) and rules (both moral and lawful). Alternatively, it was these very values which underpin American Society that brought them in the Sixties to the brink of Nuclear War (Cuban Missile Crisis) and apathetic remorse (Kennedy's assassination). However, reigned over by a ragbag of affluent geriatrics and a selfish actor, the future promises to be more orgiastic though it seems equally futile. If the Devil was conceived as God's converse, then ultimately there is very little difference between them.

The Devil's Eyes But do we see the Antichrist? Synopses of *Rosemary's Baby* generally refer to Rosemary's demonic baby. However, all that appears in the film is a subliminal superimposition of a cat's eyes which stare down at Rosemary during the nightmare she experiences whilst being raped at the beginning of the film. It's a hackneyed expression that horror films were scarier when they left things to imagination; Polanski's inspiration, however, stemmed from scientific fact. Polanski's approach to film making was not styled on the manuals of Pudovkin or the writings of Eisenstein but rather on the work of an English neuropsychologist Richard Gregory. According to Polanski, Gregory's books, which include *Eye And Brain* and *The Intelligent Eye*, lent scientific confirmation to many of his ideas that he'd instinctively believed in since his film school days, notably about the subjects of perspective, size constancy and optical illusions. Crucial to the climax of *Rosemary's Baby* is Gregory's belief in how our perceptions are shaped by the sum of our visual experiences. "My film-making ideal has always been to involve audiences so deeply in what they see that their visual experience approximates living reality. Anything that enhances this 'wraparound' effect – colour, large screens, stereo sound – is an asset." What keeps the humanist interpretation of events open is that we don't see a demonic child at the end of *Rosemary's Baby*. What keeps the demonic interpretation open is Rosemary's memory of her hallucination.

The Verdict Rosemary's Baby remains Polanski's biggest box-office success. However, Polanski's astute handling of potentially exploitative material (schlockmeister William Castle sold the rights of Ira Levin's book to Robert Evans at Paramount) doesn't betray its genre roots. Though Rosemary lives in a claustrophobic enclosure of Satanists, we empathise with her because she's nice, pretty and rather average. Perhaps if Castle did direct his property (as he originally intended to) it might have been titled *I Married A Satanist*. It's a commercial manoeuvre nonetheless, erring on the side of caution. With the impending collapse of the Renaissance ceilings upholding the Christian era, the forecast for the Satanic era seems equally pessimistic. Rosemary's fantasies of the high-life with the Kennedys and Guy's ultimately materialist aspirations (acting success is equated with property and location) paint a rather venal picture of the average Sixties couple. The risk of such cynicism is that the viewer feels as if they've endured a succession of exhilarating yet facile manipulations by a cold individual who is ultimately unconcerned. But Polanski's risk pays off. 5/5

5: Life Imitating Art (1971-1972)

In 1969 Polanski scripted and produced with Gene Gutowski *A Day At The Beach*, an Angelo-Danish production starring Mark Burns and Peter Sellers. Shot in Denmark, adapted from a Dutch novel by Heere Heresma and directed by a young Moroccan, Simon Hesera. Cadre Films' other production, Jerzy (who now called himself Yurek) Skolimowski's multimillion dollar Italian production *The Adventures Of Gerard* (1969), was an expensive disaster, even by the director's own admission. At this point Polanski decided to dissolve his partnership with Gutowski. That same year Sharon Tate discovered she was pregnant.

Polanski developed two projects for himself to direct. The first was based on the life of the virtuoso violinist Niccolo Paganini, infamous for his scandalous lifestyle not to mention his rumoured pact with the Devil (a film of Paganini's life was eventually realised by Klaus Kinski as *Paganini*, 1989). The second project was a western about cannibalism, *Donner's Pass*. However, both projects were put aside when United Artists offered Polanski the chance to adapt and direct Robert Merle's *The Day Of The Dolphin* with Andrew Braunsberg as producer. While Tate was in Italy working on *Twelve + One* (1970), Polanski did pre-production on *The Day Of The Dolphin* in London. Four months pregnant, Tate flew to Los Angeles intent on buying a larger home for the Polanski family.

Tate and Polanski moved into their house on Cielo Drive on February 15, 1969. Polanski returned to London to complete pre-production, whilst Sharon returned to Rome to complete *Twelve + One*. The house was occupied by Wojtek Frykowski and his partner Abigail Folger. Tate and Polanski decided to have their baby in America. Tate boarded the QE2 in Southampton whilst Polanski planned to fly back. Tate joined Frykowski, Folger and her ex-boyfriend, Jay Sebring in Cielo Drive.

The Manson Murders

The bodies of Tate, Frykowski, Folger and Sebring were discovered on August 9, 1969. Further down Cielo drive, the police found the body of eighteen-year-old Steven Parent. Parent had been shot three times in the chest and once in the head. The bodies of Frykowski and Folger were found outside. Folger had twenty-eight stab wounds whilst Frykowski had fifty-one, two gun shot wounds and a bludgeoned head. Tate, eight and a half months pregnant, had sixteen stab wounds both in the chest and back. Her body was found hanging from a rafter on the ceiling, joined to Jay Sebring whose neck was also tied. Sebring had been shot once and stabbed seven times.

Polanski returned to Los Angeles with Victor Lownes. Sharon Tate was buried on August 13. In the press, Jerzy Kosinski was reported as saying that Frykowski had invited him to Cielo Drive on August 9. According to Kosinski, he narrowly escaped death due to a luggage mix-up. Lownes had recently read Kosinski's *Steps* (1968) and was so disturbed by the novel's sadistic, violent sexual episodes that he sent a letter to the LA Homicide Division suggesting that they question Kosinski. Lownes' speculation was unfounded but, as Barbara Leaming points out, Lownes' letter indicates how easy it is with a writer like Kosinski, who confronts art and life, to assume that the author is fully capable of living out his fictional work. Kosinski, like Polanski, had keyed his work to the audience's consciousness o f his image and has subtly encouraged this confusion.

Press coverage of the crimes implied that Polanski, by making such violent and grotesque films, had in some way brought the tragedy upon himself. The police began to investigate the idea that the murders were connected to the hedonistic lifestyle of Polanski and the victims. However, in December 1969, Susan Atkins, one of Charles Manson's 'Family', in jail for another crime, confessed to a cellmate. Atkins' confession implicated Manson. Manson had ordered his followers to go to the house on Cielo Drive, once rented by Terry Melcher. Manson was aware that Melcher was no longer the resident, though he wanted to kill whoever was there. Atkins, Manson, Charles 'Tex' Watson and Patricia Krenwinkel were prosecuted for the murders. A fifth member of the family, Linda Kasabian, was never prosecuted in return for becoming a witness for the prosecution. The Manson trial is famously documented in Vincent Bugliosi's book *Helter Skelter*.

Unable to concentrate in the aftermath of the murders, Polanski scrapped *The Day of the Dolphin* project. After trying unsuccessfully to develop a film based on *Papillon*, Polanski contacted a friend in London, Kenneth Tynan.

Kenneth Tynan and *Oh! Calcutta!*

When Tynan organised *Oh! Calcutta!* in 1969, he had commissioned Polanski to make two four-minute films, each a single take. However, Polanski insisted that the films were shot using the widescreen format, which was financially unfeasible. Tynan was acting as literary advisor to the National Theatre in London and Polanski suggested that they collaborate on a film of Shakespeare's *Macbeth*.

Macbeth (1971)

Cast Jon Finch (Macbeth), Francesca Annis (Lady Macbeth), Martin Shaw (Banquo), Nicholas Selby (Duncan), John Stride (Ross), Stephen Chase (Malcolm), Vic Abbott (Cawdor), Keith Chegwin (Fleance).

Crew: Director: Roman Polanski; Producers: Andrew Braunsberg, Roman Polanski; Screenplay: Roman Polanski, Kenneth Tynan, based on the play by William Shakespeare; Cinematography: Gilbert Taylor; Editor: Alastair McIntyre; Production Designer: Wilfred Shingleton; Second Unit Director: Hercules Bellville; Associate Producer: Timothy Burrill; Executive Producer: Hugh M Hefner. 140 minutes.

Story Three witches predict that Macbeth will be Thane of Cawdor and King of Scotland, and Banquo will be the father of kings. Almost immediately, Macbeth hears that because of his bravery he is to be proclaimed Thane of Cawdor. He contemplates murdering Duncan, King of Scotland, so as to occupy the throne. Lady Macbeth, hearing of Macbeth's new title and the news that Duncan plans to visit their castle in Inverness, coerces Macbeth into murdering Duncan. Macbeth has a vision of a bloody dagger floating before him, leading him to Duncan's room. Duncan is horrifically murdered with daggers which Lady Macbeth plants on the bodyguards. Macbeth then kills the two bodyguards. When Malcolm, Duncan's son, flees, he is suspected of the murder and

Macbeth is crowned King of Scotland. In order to throw the witches prophecy, Macbeth intends to have Banquo and his son Fleance killed. Whilst Banquo is murdered, Fleance escapes. Banquo appears in an hallucination, driving Macbeth insane. Lady Macbeth tries to cover Macbeth's crisis. Macbeth visits the witches to hear of his future. He's told that he'll only fall when Birnam Wood comes to the castle and no man born of a woman can harm him. Macbeth interprets this riddle as a prophecy that he's infallible. However, Macbeth's Thanes turn away from him. Malcolm and Macduff conspire to topple Macbeth. Lady Macbeth dreams of not being able to wash the blood from her hands whilst sleepwalking naked. Malcolm attacks Macbeth's castle. Macduff challenges Macbeth to a fight, revealing that he wasn't born of a woman, but ripped out of his mother's womb. Macduff decapitates Macbeth and Malcolm is proclaimed the new King of Scotland.

Adapting Shakespeare "...safe in a ditch he bides, with twenty trenched gashes on his head, the least a death to nature..." (III, iv, 25-7). An obliging fidelity to Shakespeare texts poses a number of obstacles for film-makers. The results are either static, overblown and ultimately rather anonymous affairs (e.g. Kenneth Branagh's *Hamlet*, 1996) or replete with hollow irony (e.g. Michael Almereyda's *Hamlet*, 2000). Occasionally, a film-maker will remember film is about showing and not telling (e.g. Kosintsev's *Hamlet*, 1964). Zulawski recalls Wajda and Polanski studying Kurosawa's stunning Macbeth adaptation, *Throne Of Blood* (1957) on an editing deck back in the 1960s. However, Polanski's *Macbeth* is surprisingly literary, lacking any pictorial momentum, despite a large number of deeply unsettling images.

Throne of Blood The Polish literary critic Jan Kott argued that blood in *Macbeth* is not just a metaphor, for it stains the hands and faces of characters as well as their daggers and swords. Therefore, a production of *Macbeth* that doesn't evoke a bloody world would be false. Polanski's *Macbeth* isn't false. Polanski's pre-Medieval Scotland evokes the bloody passions of both Breughel and Bosch. Bodies are knifed, speared, decapitated, mutilated and hanged. Polanski was adamant that these effects were not facile shock effects. Rather, in order to film the story of a man who is beheaded, you have to show how his head is cut off. Polanski compared omitting violence to telling a dirty joke and leaving out the punch line. *Macbeth* is a violent play, and Polanski knew only too well how violent life is. To not show violence is to be insincere, immoral – "If you don't upset people, then that's obscenity." In addition to his adaptation of Shakespeare's text, Polanski stages the Thane of Cawdor's execution, Duncan's murder and the climactic duel between Macbeth and Macduff. With regards to the latter sequence, Shakespeare merely has Macduff return to the stage with Macbeth's head on a pole. However, Polanski films Macbeth's being decapitated and his body collapsing down the staircase before closing with a shot of the decapitated head on a pole.

Female Nudity Female nudity is prominent in Polanski's adaptation, though its presentation isn't voyeuristic. From the outset, Polanski juxtaposes beauty with the grotesque. One witch is young and pretty whilst the other two are old and withered. Polanski associates his legions of witches with old age – the beautiful and grotesque aren't mutually exclusive, rather one becomes the other. Macbeth and his wife age as they become more and more consumed with murderous ambition. The image of the three witches of Cawdor and sleepy grooms is a homage to Salvador Dali's illustrated *Macbeth*. Needless to say, *Macbeth* being a Playboy Production, a fold-out spread of the witches coincided with the filmed release. Polanski also filmed an all-singing and dancing naked hag "Happy Birthday to Hugh" birthday card for Hefner.

Cathartic? The fact that Polanski filmed *Macbeth*, Shakespeare's most nihilistic play, in such a bloody manner, encouraged the idea that the project was a ' film exorcism' in the aftermath of the Manson murders. On the one hand, the murder of Lady Macduff and her children is poignant, and whilst Jon Finch's Macbeth does resemble Manson, it's doubtful Polanski would have filmed the play in a more restrained manner before the horrific events of his personal life.

Verdict Shakespeare's text and Polanski's apocalyptic visuals are ultimately dislocated in *Macbeth*. Tynan may have been the wrong choice to adapt the play for the screen. For Kurosawa, fidelity to the texts of *Macbeth* and *King Lear* is subordinate to capturing the spirit of the plays in *Throne Of Blood* and *Ran* (1985) respectively. Perhaps Polanski may have benefited from adopting a similar approach. The choice of The Third Ear Band to score the film was an inspired one, but the cranked-up climatic combat now seems faintly ridiculous. 3/5

According to Polanski, after *Macbeth* he "wanted to make another film at once, just to prove I still could." After the problems with sets, wigs, costumes and special effects, Polanski reacted completely against the technicalities of film-making and moved towards stark simplicity. Polanski and Tynan started work on an erotic screenplay in Saint-Tropez, employing neither clothes nor sets. Polanski wanted to make a feature using only nine ten-minute shots. The most famous example of this approach is Alfred Hitchcock's *Rope* (1948). As a formal device perfected and parodied by Miklos Jansco with *The Round-Up* (*Szegenyleg-enyek*, 1965; aka *The Hopeless Ones*), *The Red And The White* (*Csillagosok, Katonak*, 1967) and the exceptional *Red Psalm* (1972; aka *The Red Song/People Still Ask*). The Hungarian Bela Tarr, director of the epic *Satantango* (1997), is a contemporary director who uses monstrously long takes. Polanski may have been inspired by Skolimowski's formal, episodic narratives (e.g. *Walkover*, 1965) or interested in developing the form of *Cul-De-Sac*. His original idea was to devote one shot to an individual day of a man's erotic relationships. The man was to be based on the late Zbigniew Cybulski who had recently been killed whilst trying to catch a train. According to Tynan, Polanski "worshiped" Cybulski because of his intense sexuality and extreme lifestyle. The project faltered. According to Richard Gregory, Polanski then tried to interest some London financiers with the idea of a 3D horror film. Using the funds of the young French producer Jean-Pierre Rassam, Polanski made a series of 3D tests with the aim of applying the process to a "really spectacular erotic film."

What? was developed from a project intended for Jack Nicholson entitled *The Magic Finger*. The character of an eccentric millionaire was based on the oil magnate Calouste 'Mr Five Percent' Gulbenkian. Polanski and Brach concocted a Rabelaisian story about a flower child, wandering innocently around a testosterone heavy French Riviera. The character of Nancy had been conceived as a combination of Sade's Justine and *Playboy*'s Annie Fanny. Rassam dropped out, and Carlo Ponti put up the 1.2 million budget.

What?/Che? (1973)

Cast Sydne Rome (Nancy), Marcello Mastroianni (Alex), Hugh Griffith (Noblart), Romolo Valli (Giovanni), Guido Alberti (Priest), Gianfranco Piacentini (Tony), Roger Middleton (Jimmy), Roman Polanski (Mosquito).

Crew Director: Roman Polanski; Producer: Carlo Ponti; Screenplay: Roman Polanski, Gérard Brach; Cinematography: Marcello Gatti, Giuseppe Ruzzolini; Music: Claudio Gizzi; Art Director: Franco Fumagalli; Sound: Piero Fondi; Editor: Alastair McIntyre; Production Design: Aurelio Crugnola. 113 mins.

Story A naïve young American give, Nancy, is hitch-hiking her way around Europe. After narrowly escaping gang-rape by some Italians who have given her a lift, armed only with a diary and some scant-clothing, she finds refuge in a palatial villa by the sea. The villa is inhabited by a bizarre collection of permanent as well as transient guests. The world of those who inhabit the villa and its private beach is far removed from any morality, let alone sanity that there might be in the outside world. Even time seems unimportant – the only clock in the villa is broken. Nancy sees paraded before her the full range of neurosis and sexual obsessions of people. Alex, a retired pimp oscillating between impotence and homosexuality, is inspired by Nancy to sadism and masochism. Dressed in tiger skin he makes her beat him and, dressed as a carabineri, he whips her. Among the strange guests who pass through the villa are homosexuals, art-dealers, some all-American tourists and a confused priest. The inhabitants of the villa are anticipating the death of its eccentric patriarchal owner, Noblart, Alex's uncle. Nancy excites the old-man and he collapses in bed. Granting his dying wish she reveals her nude body to him and he happily passes away. With the old man dead, Nancy decides that she must leave. Completely naked, she hitches a ride in a truckload of pigs to rejoin the outside world.

The Abuse of Sex Superficially a limp sex comedy, *What?* is nonetheless undercut with a profoundly cynical reduction of the abusive component of sexual relationships.

Victim and Victimiser Though Nancy starts whipping Alex, it's Alex who ends up whipping Nancy. As in *The Fat And The Lean*, *Mammals* and *Cul-De-Sac*, Polanski conceives the existence of both victim and victimiser in a vicious circle. The narrative of *What?* is driven not by character, but by the momentum of ascension and submissions in Nancy's relations with the villa's various inhabitants.

Post-Manson Fairy Tale If *Macbeth* goaded allusions to the Manson murders through blood, *What?* is altogether more oblique in its grotesque presentation of Hippie dream turned nightmare. The various playboy and hippie caricatures are cynical, manipulative cranks solely intent on bedding Nancy. In terms of fairy-tale structure and negative post-hippie temperament (though admittedly little else), *What?* makes a curious parallel with *The Texas Chainsaw Massacre* (1974). The preoccupations with S/M as well as the free-association plotting recall the comic strips of Guido Crepax, especially *Bianca*, which in turn draws heavily from *Repulsion*.

Mosquito Polanski makes a curious cameo in *What?* as Mosquito. He had been given the nickname at the Rio de Janeiro Film Festival because of "his size and irritating behaviour." However, the part isn't so much an in-joke as a disarmingly frank riposte to his public image. When Nancy talks of Alex in amateur psychoanalytic terms, alluding to childhood trauma, Mosquito replies that a difficult childhood is no excuse for being a pain in the ass.

Verdict The formlessness of *What?* is not so much Rabelaisian but more akin to the superficial plotting found in sexploitation films. *What?* wound up on the porn circuit, re-cut and with inserts on a double bill with *Eager Beavers*, retitled *Roman Polanski's Forbidden Dreams*. 2/5

6: Two For Paramount (1973-1975)

Chinatown (1974)

Cast Jack Nicholson (Jake J Gittes), Faye Dunaway (Evelyn Mulwray), John Huston (Noah Cross), Perry Lopez (Escobar), John Hillerman (Yelburton), Darrell Zwerling (Hollis Mulwray), Diane Ladd (Ida Sessions), Roy Jenson (Mulvihill), Roman Polanski (Man with Knife).

Crew Director: Roman Polanski; Producer: Robert Evans; Screenplay: Robert Towne; Cinematography: John A Alonzo; Music: Jerry Goldsmith; Sound: Robert Cornett; Editor: Sam O'Steen; Production Design: Richard Sylbert; Art Direction: Ruby Levitt; Costume Design: Anthea Sylbert; Associate Producer: C O Erickson. 131 mins.

Story Los Angeles, the 1930s. Jake Gittes is a private eye specialising in "matrimonial work," someone who will expose marital infidelities for a price. He is approached by Mrs Evelyn Mulwray to tail her husband, Hollis Mulwray, an engineer for the Water Department. Gittes photographs Mulwray in the company of a young blonde and concludes that the case is shut. However, much to his embarrassment Gittes discovers that he has been put up to the job and that the real Mrs Mulwray had nothing to do with hiring Gittes in the first place. When Hollis turns up dead, Gittes is drawn into further investigations, encountering a shady old people's home, corrupt bureaucrats, angry orange farmers whose livelihood is threatened by the plans of the Water Department and an impish thug in a pink suit who slices Gittes' nose for sniffing around. By the time Gittes confronts Cross, Evelyn's father and Mulwray's former business partner, he thinks he knows everything there is to know about the corruption that required Mulwray's silence, but he soon learns an even more unpleasant truth. Gittes had suspected Evelyn of kidnapping the girl he thought Hollis had been seeing only to learn that she is Evelyn's daughter. But when Gittes forces Evelyn to confess, he learns that the father of the girl isn't Hollis, but Evelyn's father. Gittes arranges for Evelyn and her daughter to escape from Cross, only to be stopped on his old beat in Chinatown. Evelyn is accidentally shot trying to escape, Cross ends up with custody of his daughter and Gittes is consoled with the words of an old colleague: "Forget it, Jake. It's Chinatown."

Critical Nostalgia Polanski's casting of John Huston, director of *The Maltese Falcon*, acknowledges the heritage of the film noir of the Thirties and Forties. The hardboiled detective genre had lain dormant since the late Fifties and *Chinatown* is one of several retooled films noirs made during the Seventies: Robert Altman's *Long Goodbye* (1973), Arthur Penn's *Night Moves* (1975) and Bob Raffleson's Mamet-scripted James M Cain revision *The Postman Always Rings Twice* (1979). Whereas Altman dispenses with period fidelity and invests the genre with all the New Wave modernist trappings, Polanski and set designer Richard Sylbert recreated 1930s LA, and Towne's classically constructed script evoked the halcyon days of the studio system (hence the old-fashioned Paramount logo featured in the opening credits). The film reworked downbeat noir themes for the Seventies: a general pessimism and futility that was very much the Zeitgeist in post-JFK, post-Watergate, and post-Viet Nam America (hence the modern Paramount logo closing the film).

The Chinatown Metaphor At the time of its release, Polanski spoke of how he loved the 'clichés' yet *Chinatown* isn't a postmodern parody. Polanski certainly expresses nostalgia for the genre that sprang from the writings of Hammett and Chandler, but Polanski's pessimism and Towne's script result in a critical nostalgia. *Chinatown* thrives on this tension. Towne based his script on an actual scandal that hit Los Angeles in the early decades of the century, when rich men bought cheap farmland and had it incorporated into the city, thus acquiring control over the area's water supply. Towne's elaborate script is profoundly critical – in a Marxist sense – of America's past, using the period in a similar way in which Bertolucci charts the fascist uprising in his film of Alberto Moravia's novel, *The Conformist* (*La Conformista*, 1970). Gittes learns that by solving the mystery of Mulwray's death he's opened a social can of worms. Towne uses the *Chinatown* of the title as a metaphor for grandiose epic corruption and irrationality in American society. As earlier drafts of Towne's script testify, *Chinatown* wasn't intended to be so black, cynical, or defeatist – Evelyn and her daughter were allowed to escape to Mexico, for instance.

Given Polanski's own background in communist Poland, it's unlikely he was particularly interested in the politics implicit in Towne's script. Polanski's unaccredited final draft of *Chinatown* strips away any armchair politicising in favour of a more pessimistic reading concerning the predominance of evil. In *Chinatown*, elected officials are the easily-purchased pawns of corrupt power brokers whose appetites know no check or balance (raging from greed to incest) and the closest thing we have to an honest and moral guide through this is a fallen private detective – a man whose career dictates that his loyalty can be purchased for a fee. Because Evelyn dies, Cross gets his daughter and Gittes is left helpless, that does not make Polanski amoral. Polanski's film *is* moral. It simply doesn't moralise openly as so many Hollywood films do.

Voyeurism Polanski streamlined Towne's script, emphasising the subjective nature of Gittes' work. As in *Blue Velvet* (1986), *Chinatown* correlates detection with voyeurism. Voyeurism is thus related to cinema: we see Hollis through the cross hairs of the camera lens, and others through window frames. Everyone is watching and being watched. In psychological terms, *Chinatown* is a case study of the 'sadistic gaze'. However, one nagging flaw or concession to audience expectation is the reflection of Hollis in Gittes' camera lens – he should appear to the viewer upside down.

Verdict Chinatown is very much a classic of 1970s Hollywood cinema. Robert Towne's Oscar-winning screenplay is generally regarded as the yardstick of traditional Hollywood narrative, thanks in no small part to the schematic teachings of Robert McKee. However, Polanski himself considers *Chinatown* a mere directing job done to reinvigorate his flagging critical reputation and renew his Hollywood credentials after *Macbeth* and *What?* Praise for *Chinatown* generally single out the producer, Robert Evans, for uniting and controlling a number of brilliant but often wayward talents. *Chinatown* deserves its reputation and can only be faulted for being a little too polished, thus losing some of the definition that characterises the sexual violence typical of Polanski's best work. 3/5

Roland Topor

Polanski's next film, *The Tenant*, was based on a novel by Roland Topor, *Le locataire chimérique*. Topor was born in Paris in 1938, the son of Polish Jewish refugees. He came to prominence in 1962 when he formed *Groupe Panique* with the Spanish playwright Fernando Arrabal, Chilean director Alejandro Jodorowsky and Jacques Sternberg. Polanski had known Topor for years, and Topor had suggested the project to him shortly after *Repulsion*. Polanski, however, had felt the subject was too close to that of the earlier film.

In 1975 Paramount had acquired the project and Polanski jumped at the opportunity of filming *Le locataire chimérique*. Polanski strongly identified with the novel's main character, Trelkovski, a paranoid alien in hostile Paris, and wanted to play him even if someone else directed. After coming to the West, Polanski had kept his Polish passport, but the inconvenience of obtaining visas had led him to apply for French citizenship.

Torpor was also a highly original artist. His perversely funny graphics were brought to a wider audience when he collaborated with René Lalou on the feature-length animation, *The Fantastic Planet* (*La planète sauvage*, 1973). Topor also acted in Makavejev's *Sweet Movie* (1974), Herzog's *Nosferatu the Vampyre* (*Nosferatu: Phantom der Nacht*, 1979) and Schlondorff's *Swann In Love* (*Un amour de Swann*, 1984). Like Lenica, Topor also designed theatre and opera, especially productions of the absurd. He died of a brain haemorrhage in 1997.

The Tenant/Le locataire (1976)

Cast Roman Polanski (Trelkovski), Isabelle Adjani (Stella), Shelly Winters (Concierge), Melvyn Douglas (Monsieur Zy), Jo Van Fleet (Madame Dioz), Lila Kedrova (Madame Gaderian).

Crew: Director: Roman Polanski; Producer: Andrew Braunsberg; Screenplay: Roman Polanski, Gérard Brach; Cinematography: Sven Nykvist; Music: Philippe Sarde; Sound: Michele Boehm; Editor: Françoise Bonnot; Production Design: Pierre Guffroy, Eric Simon; Art Direction: Claude Moeshing, Albert Rajau; Costume Design: Jacques Schmidt; Associate Producer: Alain Sarde; Executive Producer: Hercules Bellville. 126 mins.

Story Trelkovski, a Polish émigré, rents an apartment in a dingy Parisian residential building. The previous tenant, Simone Choule, lies in a coma after throwing herself out of the window. Whilst visiting the ex-tenant in hospital, Trelkovski meets Stella, Simone's girlfriend. Trelkovski's new neighbours are an assortment of old recluses and busybodies who generally eye the new tenant with suspicious contempt. Simone dies and Trelkovski obsesses over her belongings left in the apartment. After a panic attack during her funeral, Trelkovski grows increasingly paranoid about his neighbour's obsession with the slightest noise he makes in the apartment. He finds a tooth of Simone's hidden in the wall, notices that other tenants spend a curiously long time just staring out of the bathroom window across the courtyard opposite his flat. Trelkovski finds himself adopting Simone's tastes, clothes and even her girlfriend. Convinced that the other tenants are forcing him to commit suicide, Trelkovski goes out into the street in search of a gun with which to defend himself only to be run over by a car that may or may not have been driven by one of his neighbours. Even Stella turns out to be in on the 'plot'. Having awkwardly assumed the identity of Simone Choule, Trelkovski completes the act by throwing himself out of the window. Unsuccessful at first, he only succeeds in putting himself in a coma – like Simone – after a second attempt.

A Final Piece of Theatre Silvia Plath famously wrote about dying as an art. *The Tenant* begins and ends with a suicide, a very real act but which, nonetheless, is performed theatrically. *The Tenant* climaxes with a crane shot of Trelkovski, played by Polanski, in full drag to resemble Simone Choule, standing on the window ledge of his apartment. A drum roll accompanies a final pan around the courtyard revealing a literal audience composed of Trelkovski's (formerly Simone's) neighbours, lovers, as well as bystanders and strangers, sitting on rooftops and boxes awaiting the final act. This hallucination is one of many that puncture *The Tenant*.

Voyeurism All hallucinations in *The Tenant* involve an element of theatre. In one performance, Trelkovski watches the ghost of Simone Choule standing in the toilet adjacent to his apartment, unwrapping the bandages which cover the injuries incurred from her suicide attempt as if it were a striptease act. Another has a girl with a clubbed foot being taunted with sticks, her persecutors covering her face with a mask

64

resembling Trelkovski's. But most bizarre of all is a scene in which Trelkovski lies in bed suffering from a fever. He reaches out for a bottle of Perrier at his bedside, only to find that the bottle is, in fact, a cardboard cut-out. The staged qualities of the hallucinations consolidate the notion that suicide involves an internal splitting. When Trelkovski himself takes the place of the mummified body of Simone Choule in the toilet, he sees himself staring back across the courtyard. He has divided into a public self that exposes itself at the chosen moment of self-annihilation and a private self that hides (behind the camera?), directing his public act. Trelkovski's final performance demands visibility, though its purpose is to establish the ultimate privacy. Trelkovski is desperate to conceal himself and be left with a silence that has proved so elusive. As James Breslin wrote in his biography of the painter Mark Rothko, suicide is both an angry imposition and an angry withdrawal of the self.

Simone and I Lying drunk in bed with Stella, Trelkovski gets philosophical about his predicament, rambling on about an incident in which a man who had a limb amputated wanted to have it buried rather than cremated as the authorities requested. Trelkovski asks Stella at what precise moment does an individual cease to be the person he, and everyone else, believes himself to be? "I have an arm amputated, all right. I say: myself and my arm. If both of them are gone, I say: myself and my two arms. If it were my legs it would be the same thing...but if they cut off my head, what could I say then? Myself and my body, or myself and my head? By what right does the head, which isn't even a member like an arm or a leg, claim the title of 'myself'?" The most unpleasant hallucination in *The Tenant* involves Trelkovski, sitting in drag, staring out of the window as a ball is being bounced in the courtyard below. Suddenly the ball rises past the window in slow motion and resembles Trelkovski's decapitated head covered in a blonde wig.

Trelkovski into Simone The horror of *The Tenant* stems from an unbridgeable gulf between the elusiveness of the self and the sum of its representations. Trelkovski's identity is composed of his appearance, behaviour, preference and possessions. However, by the end of the film Trelkovski's identity has become that of the late Simone Choule. The staff at the local bar coerce Trelkovski into smoking Simone's Marlboro cigarettes and drinking chocolate instead of coffee. Thieves (or the other tenants?) steal his photographs, clothes and material possessions leaving Trelkovski with only Simone Choule's clothes. He even shares with Simone the same object of desire, a frumpy Isabelle Adjani, and succumbs to the same obsession of Egyptology. The most disturbing aspect of the film is that by the end Trelkovski has vanished. What remains is merely a grotesque drag parody of Simone Choule. Trelkovski is completely alienated by the other tenants. Trelkovski has become Kosinski's proverbial "painted bird." Polanski himself used the term in describing how he felt as a Pole living in Paris despite having French citizenship. He said at the time of the release of *The Tenant* that in Paris he was always reminded of being a foreigner: "If you park your car wrong, it is not the fact that it's on the sidewalk that matters, but the fact that you speak with an accent."

The Verdict The Tenant was viciously attacked at Cannes but the film remains, for me, Polanski's masterpiece. Jerzy Skolimowski thought that despite all the humiliations, disappointments and compromises Polanski had had to endure over the years, *The Tenant* made it all worthwhile. However, Polanski himself is more critical of his achievement, regarding it merely as a flawed but nonetheless interesting experiment: "With hindsight, I realise that Trelkovski's insanity doesn't build gradually enough – that his hallucinations are too startling and unexpected. The picture labours under an unacceptable change of mood halfway through. Even sophisticated film-goers dislike a mixture of genres. A tragedy must remain a tragedy; a comedy that turns into a drama almost fails." However, some of the most interesting films of recent years lie at the intersection of two genres: *Performance* (Nicolas Roeg/ Donald Cammell, 1969), *Possession* (Andrzej Zulawski, 1981), *Brazil* (Terry Gilliam, 1985*), Fight Club* (David Fincher, 1999). All of these films are, interestingly enough, like *The Tenant* in that they are dramas of 'self' and, unlike Polanski's earlier *Repulsion*, the shift from sanity to madness is catastrophic, not gradual. A pressure to stay faithful to genre boundaries reflects both an inability of genre models to adapt/evolve in response to developments in the film world and a lack of imagination on the part of both the film-maker and (more probably) the studio-marketing department. The only possible fault to be found in the film is a technical one (on the English version at least) – the sound mix seems a little flat, perhaps the result of a rushed post-production to meet the Cannes deadline? 5/5

7: In Search Of A Muse (1979-1988)

After the commercial and critical flop of *The Tenant*, Polanski reluctantly signed a deal with Columbia to direct an adaptation of Lawrence Sander's *The First Deadly Sin*. Also, Polanski accepted an assignment from *Vogue Hommes* to shoot a photo spread on beautiful young girls. Polanski had already photographed Nastassja Kinski in a Pirates themed spread for an issue of *Vogue* that he had guest-edited. However, whereas *Vogue* is about fashion, *Vogue Hommes* is about women. Henri Sera recommended the thirteen-year-old daughter of an old girlfriend as an ideal candidate for Polanski's spread. Polanski agreed and organised several photo shoots and on March 10, 1977, on Mullholland Drive, Los Angeles, Polanski became embroiled in another scandal.

The model's mother arranged for Polanski and her daughter to meet at a house Jack Nicholson rented from Marlon Brando, currently occupied by Anjelica Huston, Jack's girlfriend. Huston was absent and only the caretaker, Helena Kallianiotes, was present. Polanski found a case of champagne in the fridge, which he offered to the girl to relax her during the shoot. They both took some Quaaludes that they found in the bathroom and stripped off naked in Nicholson's jacuzzi. Polanski then had sex with the girl. Huston arrived and Polanski and the girl left. The girl called her seventeen-year-old boyfriend and told him about Polanski. Overhearing their conversation was the girl's elder sister, who in turn informed her mother. A medical examination was undertaken to establish whether the girl had had sexual contact, which was confirmed. Since the girl was under the age of consent, under Californian Law she was a victim of rape. Polanski was arrested the following day at the Beverley Wilshire Hotel under the supervision of District Attorneys James Grodin and David Wells. Polanski was found in possession of Quaaludes. On hearing the news, Columbia cancelled their deal with Polanski as director on *The First Deadly Sin*.

Polanski was taken to court on six indictments: i.) furnishing a controlled substance to a minor, ii.) committing a lewd and lascivious act on a child (i.e. oral sex) iii.) unlawful sexual intercourse, iv.) rape by use of drugs v.) perversion vi.) sodomy. If convicted, Polanski faced up to fifty years in jail. Superior Court Judge Laurence Rittenband was assigned to the case. A trial date was set for August 8 - the eighth anniversary of Tate's murder. Now, strapped for cash, Polanski signed a development deal with Dino De Laurentiis to write and direct a remake of John Ford's *Hurricane*, having recently turned down his offer to direct *King Kong*.

Polanski was permitted to travel abroad to scout for locations. Huston agreed to testify for the prosecution. However, on August 8 a plea bargain was arranged, Polanski was prepared to plead guilty to the charge of unlawful sexual intercourse. Before sentencing, Rittenband secured a team of psychiatrists to determine whether or not Polanski was "a mentally disordered sex offender." Irwin Gold compiled the probation report. Gold noted that although Polanski had endured abnormal stress throughout his life, he had not consulted psychiatric care as it could interfere with the creative process. On September 16 Rittenband planned to send Polanski to the State Facility in Chino for ninety days for a more extensive diagnosis but granted a ninety-day stay to allow Polanski to complete *Hurricane*.

Rittenband was vilified in the press when Polanski started courting 16-year-old Kinski and was photographed partying at the Munich Oktoberfest instead of working on *Hurricane*. Furious, Rittenband announced that he was going to send Polanski to jail immediately. On January 27, 1978, Polanski was released from prison after 42 days of psychiatric investigation. As Rittenband prepared to sentence him, on February 1, Polanski drove to Los Angeles airport and booked a flight to London and then to Paris, returning to an apartment he kept on Avenue Montaigne where he was safe from extradition under French law.

London lawyers advised Polanski that he could be extradited under English law, so his next film, *Tess*, was filmed in France.

Tess (1979)

Cast John Collin (John Durbeyfield), Nastassja Kinski (Tess), Peter Firth (Angel Clare), Leigh Lawson (Alec d'Urberville), Tony Church (Parson Tringham), Arielle Dombasle (Mercy Chant).

Crew Director: Roman Polanski; Producer: Claude Berri; Screenplay: Roman Polanski, Gérard Brach, John Brownjohn, from the novel by Thomas Hardy; Cinematographers: Geoffrey Unsworth, Ghislain Cloquet; Music: Philippe Sarde; Editors: Alastair McIntyre, Tom Priestley; Production Design: Pierre Guffroy; Art Direction: Jack Stephens; Costume Design: Anthony Powell; Co-Producer: Timothy Burrill; Associate Producer: Jean-Pierre Rassam; Executive Producer: Pierre Grunstein. 170 mins.

Story Tess is a poor British peasant girl sent to live with her distant and wealthy relatives, the d'Urbervilles. Though Tess' father had hoped that the girl would be permitted a portion of the d'Urberville's riches, he is in for a major disappointment: Tess' new housemates are not the d'Urbervilles at all, but a group of social climbers who have bought the name. The girl is seduced/raped (it's all a little ambiguous due to a prudish fog making a timely descent). Tess becomes pregnant. Alec abandons her. Tess' baby dies in its infancy and Tess struggles to bury the child in the Church as it was never baptised. A humble farmer takes a shine to Tess and proposes to her. Tess accepts. Angel marries Tess only to spurn her when he learns of her past on their wedding night. Pride and bible bashing parents are to blame. Angel leaves to start a new life in a foreign country. Tess returns home, first to her family, then to Alec. Angel returns, searching all over Dorset for Tess. Finally Angel tracks Tess down on the coast where she is living with Alec. Angel begs for Tess' forgiveness but Tess refuses. However, Alec begins to wear Tess down, so she kills him (off screen). Tess is reunited with Angel at the last minute in melodramatic fashion at a train station. She tells Angel of her crime. Realising Tess' crime will result in her being hanged they head North. Angel and Tess soon run out of places to hide. The couple resort to spending the night at Stonehenge. However, the police finally catch up with them in the morning. A closing credit informs us that Tess was hanged for her crime.

Voyeurism Tess is beautiful. It's a pleasure to watch. But voyeurism underpins the formal structure of the film. Polanski composes *Tess* out of two distinct types of shots. Long formal static shots predominate, which are in turn cut with short, occasionally hand-held so-called 'subjective' camera shots using generally wider lenses. Tess herself is repeatedly composed in long static shots. If these long shots epitomise Polanski's obsession with looking, then point-of-view shots draw attention to characters looking. Whereas Alec and Angel have active gazes, Tess is objectified by Polanski's camera. One example is when Tess returns home after Angel's departure. Like Kwiatkowska (*When Angels Fall*) and Tate (*The Fearless Vampire Killers*), Polanski frames Kinski passively gazing at the camera through a window frame.

Rape Like *Rosemary's Baby*, the crux of the film lies in a scene in which we aren't sure what we've seen. When Alec gropes Tess on the field a fog quickly descends, obscuring the spectacle. It's not clear if Alec seduced or raped Tess. In fact, all acts of violence, including Alec's murder and Tess' eventual hanging, occur off screen. Alec's off-screen death is particularly grizzly: t he maid notices the blood dripping through the ceiling and Angel notices the blood stains around Tess' ankles.

Victim and Victimiser The rape/seduction is precipitated by a very explicit act of violence. Tess rebuffs Alec's advances, pushing him from the horse, banging his head on a rock. The scene is not in Hardy's original text, rather it is drawn from Polanski's own experience, first realised in *The Bicycle*. However, by masochistically exaggerating his role as victim, like the student in *Knife In The Water*, Alec coerces Tess to express her sorrow which he then takes advantage of. Once again, Polanski emphasises the reciprocal nature of victim and victimiser. However, like Borowczyk's *Story Of Sin* (*Dzieje Grzechu*, 1975), Christian society – both contemporary and Victorian – refuses to distinguish between the victim and victimiser. Nevertheless, Tess responds to her humiliation with dignity.

Pessimism Tess of the d'Urbervilles was first filmed ten years before Polanski's birth, in 1923. The film was released with a choice of two endings for exhibitors to choose from, one happy the other sad. Polanski's closure is closer to Hardy's original. His *Tess* is utterly devoid of romance, and it's the self-righteous Angel that comes across as more of a monster than the weak-willed Alec. Even when Angel attempts to smuggle Tess out of the country, like Jake in *Chinatown*, his actions seem motivated more out of guilt and pity than love for Tess. Given the melodramatic content of Hardy's novel, Polanski's handling is remarkably restrained, almost austere, despite a rousing score by Philippe Sarde.

A Tragic Production The beauty of *Tess* can be attributed to four people: Polanski for his attention to detail, Pierre Guffroy for exceptional set design, and Geoffrey Unsworth and Ghislain Cloquet's cinematography. Unsworth was one of the greatest British cinematographers, lensing Kubrick's *2001: A Space Odyssey* (1968), Crichton's *The Great Train Robbery* (1977) and Donner's *Superman* (1978). Tragically, Unsworth had a heart attack during the production and died, leaving Cloquet with the unenviable task of completing the principle photography. Cloquet himself was an excellent cinematographer and *Tess* received Oscars® for Cinematography, Costume Design and Art Direction.

At one stage it seemed unlikely whether *Tess* would have a US release at all. The project was originally organised by Claude Berri's Renn Productions. Berri is a director/producer who has, over the last twenty-five years, produced a number of multimillion dollar French productions, including Patrice Chereau's *La Reine Margot* (1994). However, the sheer size of Polanski's film demanded a co-producer to share the costs. This was met by an English producer, Timothy Burrill. When it came to distributing *Tess* in the US, Francis Ford Coppola expressed interest in selling the film through his Zoetrope Studios. However, Coppola imposed a number of conditions: first the film should be completely re-cut making it a third shorter and considerably pacier; secondly, Coppola made the bizarre request that the film ought to start with Hardy's book being opened by hand and have a voice-over narrating the story.

Verdict Tess is not only a brilliant, perverse riposte to a public scandal that would have decimated the career of just about any other filmmaker, it is also an exceptional piece of craftsmanship. Alongside Kubrick's masterpiece, *Barry Lyndon* (1975), Polanski's *Tess* stands out as one of the finest mainstream period dramas of the Seventies. 4/5

Pirates (1986)

Cast Walter Matthau (Captain Red), Damien Thomas (Don Alfonso), Richard Pearson (Padre), Cris Campion (The Frog), Charlotte Lewis (Dolores), Olu Jacobs (Boumako), Roy Kinnear (Dutch), Ferdy Mayne (Captain Linares), Tony Peck (Spanish Officer).

Crew Director: Roman Polanski; Producer: Tarak Ben Ammar; Screenplay: Roman Polanski, Gérard Brach, John Brownjohn; Cinematography: Witold Sobocinski; Music: Philippe Sarde; Editor: Hervé de Luze, William Reynolds; Production Design: Pino Butti; Co-Executive Producers: Mark Lombardo, Umberto Sambuco; Executive Producer: Thom Mount. 124 mins.

Story Having escaped from the island where they'd been stranded since a defeat at the battle of Boco del Toro, Captain Red and loyal Frog are floating in a raft in the middle of the ocean. Red lost a leg in the battle and is assumed to be dead. They spot a Spanish galleon, the Neptune. Red and Frog clamber on board the ship, only to be thrown into the brig. It is there that the duo run into Boumako, the ship's cook, accused of poisoning the captain who was actually killed by the 1st Lieutenant, Don Alfonso. However, what excites Red is the solid gold throne of Capatec Anahuac, the Aztec King, which he discovers while looking through a peephole in the wall. In a plot to get the throne, Red plans to start a m u tiny by putting a rat in the crew's soup. The crew turns against their oppressors. Frog falls in love with Dolores, the niece of the governor of Maracaibo. Red sails the Neptune to an old friend, Dutch. They throw a party, during which Don Alfonso and the officers of the Neptune escape. The Neptune is reclaimed and Red has lost both the ship and his treasure. Red and Frog buy a modest ship and sail to Maracaibo with a plan to steal the throne back. Disguised as a priest, Red forces the governor of Maracaibo to sign over the throne, holding Dolores as hostage. However, Red and Frog are captured by the Spanish whilst collecting the throne. Dolores visits Red and Frog in jail, bearing the bad news that the pair are both to be hanged for crimes against the Spanish government. Red's crew come to their rescue, breaking them out of jail and recapturing both the Neptune and the throne. The battle ends with Dolores choosing between her good life with Don Alfonso or joining Frog as a pirate. The film ends, as it opened, with both Red and Frog adrift on a raft.

Another Genre Spoof Polanski first attempted to get *Pirates* made immediately after *Chinatown*. The high-budget costume film was to star Jack Nicholson but Andrew Braunsberg had difficulty raising money for the film and Nicholson dropped out. Robert Shaw, who also starred in *Macbeth*, temporarily replaced him but also dropped out and the project faltered. When Polanski finally made the film in 1986 with Walter Matthau it was a disappointment, both to himself and the audience. As a genre spoof, *Pirates* is decidedly less successful than *The Fearless Vampire Killers*. The pirate genre has proved to be a remarkably difficult genre to parody, although *Pirates* is funnier than *Yellow Beard* (1983). Polanski can almost be forgiven for indulging in such a mess in the light of Renny Harlin's spectacularly dreadful, not to mention far costlier, *Cutthroat Island* (1996).

The Absurd Opening and closing on Frog and Red adrift on a raft, it seems Polanski intended to expand the playful energy evident in earlier shorts like *The Fat And The Lean* and *Mammals* to feature length.

Cannon A wealthy Tunisian, Tarak Ben Ammar, and the legendary Italian mogul Dino De Laurentiis produced *Pirates*. Originally *Pirates* was to have been distributed by MGM who had invested 10 million dollars in the 30 million dollar production. When they backed out, Ben Ammar negotiated, with the help of Crédit Lyonnais, to buy back the rights from MGM, although MGM retained some of their investment in *Pirates*. De Laurentiis' 15 million dollar stake gave him all foreign rights to the film. Ben Ammar approached Yoram Globus and Menahem Golan of Cannon films to distribute the film in the US and UK.

Unfortunately, Cannon scheduled *Pirates* to open the same day as James Cameron's *Aliens* (1986) and *Pirates'* opening weekend takings rank as one of the worst ever in motion picture history. *Pirates* only managed to recoup 1.5 million dollars in the whole of the US. As one production executive said (with the benefit of hindsight, it must be added): "People were talking bullshit, in telephone numbers, ridiculous images were being created in people's minds – and no one said 'STOP: This is fucking ludicrous.'"

The Verdict Whilst not particularly interesting in any sense, compared to what is generally considered acceptable as big-budget entertainment today, Polanski's *Pirates* is not that bad. Walter Matthau did not have the star power in the 1980s to carry such a large production and opening against *Aliens* did not help. The best thing that can be said about *Pirates* is that it was an obsession brought to the screen at all cost and when it finally arrived, it was a decade too late. 1/5

Emmanuelle Seigner

Emmanuelle Seigner was the granddaughter of Louis Seigner, the legendary Comédie Française actor. Her father was a photographer, and her mother was an interior designer. At seventeen, Seigner started modelling before being cast by Jean-Luc Godard in *Detective* (1985). She met Polanski, thirty-five years her senior, in 1985. Polanski became Seigner's Svengali and developed her acting skills for a supporting role in his next project for Warner Brothers, *Frantic*.

Frantic (1988)

Cast Harrison Ford (Richard Walker), Betty Buckley (Sondra), Emmanuelle Seigner (Michelle), Gérard Klein (Gaillard), Patrice Melennec (Hotel Detective), David Huddleston (Peter), Alexandra Stewart (Edie), Robert Barr (Irwin), Raouf Ben Amor (Dr Metlaoui).

Crew Director: Roman Polanski; Producers: Tim Hampton, Thom Mount; Screenplay: Roman Polanski, Gérard Brach; Cinematography: Witold Sobocinski; Music: Ennio Morricone, Astor Piazzolla; Editor: Sam O'Steen; Production Design: Pierre Guffroy; Costume Design: Anthony Powell. 120 mins.

Story Richard Walker, an American doctor, and his wife Sondra arrive in Paris from San Francisco for a conference. While Walker is taking a shower, his wife leaves and does not return. It becomes apparent that they have picked up the wrong suitcase at the airport. Having looked around the hotel and the surrounding area, Walker finds her necklace in the gutter. It looks like she's been kidnapped. The police are uninterested and the American Embassy offers no help so Walker decides to make his own investigation. He tracks down the young Parisian dope smuggler, Michelle, who mistakenly picked up their suitcase. Things are made worse when they both realise that she is involved with Arab terrorists smuggling parts for a nuclear bomb. In the final showdown Walker gets Sondra back, the Arabs escape and Michelle is inadvertently shot dead.

Hitchcock Homage In terms of its beautifully simple premise and the effortless atmosphere of paranoia conjured up by Polanski, *Frantic* is a very efficient Hitchcock homage. Unfortunately, as the films of Brian DePalma or *What Lies Beneath* (2000) prove, Hitchcock homages aren't in short supply. *Frantic* is essentially a riff on *The Man Who Knew Too Much* (1956) with the protagonist's wife kidnapped instead of his son. There are many general references to Hitchcock's work, for example, Walker's inadvertent coke-snorting ordeal in the bar recalls a drunk Cary Grant in *North By North West* (1959) trying to regain control of a car after his ordeal at Vandamm's residence.

Existential Angst The confusion at the airport is a chance mistake. The absence of Walker's wife taints the Paris locations. There's nothing abstract or intellectual about *Frantic*. Rather, the film is anxious, atmospheric and, frankly, rather depressing. The Eiffel Tower only appears as a tacky tourist gift used to conceal part of a nuclear bomb. Like the Paris depicted in *The Tenant*, the Parisian authorities are presented as indifferent, disinterested and entrenched in bureaucracy.

Verdict A good solid thriller, with a jazzy Morricone score. Harrison Ford does what he usually does, which is to fret in a macho kind of way. Emmanuelle Seigner is sexy, if not much else, whilst the Arabs are just ruthless. An air of anonymity hangs around *Frantic*. Don't expect anything out of the ordinary. Except, that is, for the downbeat ending. 2/5

8: Bitter End? (1992-2002)

Bitter Moon (1992)

Cast Hugh Grant (Nigel), Peter Coyote (Oscar), Emmanuelle Seigner (Mimi), Kristin Scott Thomas (Fiona), Victor Banerjee (Mr Sikh).

Crew Director: Roman Polanski; Producer: Robert Benmussa; Screenplay: Gérard Brach, John Brownjohn, Jeff Gross, Roman Polanski; Cinematographer: Tonino Delli Colli; Music: Vangelis; Editor: Hervé de Luze; Production Design: Willy Holt, Gérard Viard; Set Decoration: Philippe Turlure; Costume Design: Jackie Budin; Co-Producer: Alain Sarde; Executive Producer: Robert Benmussa. 139 mins.

Story Nigel and Fiona are celebrating their wedding anniversary when they encounter a bizarre couple on a cruise ship. Oscar is a gregarious, crippled American writer and his 'minder' is a voluptuous young French girl, Mimi. Nigel, a socially inept London banker, unsuccessfully tries to pick up Mimi. Oscar warns Nigel that she's dangerous. He invites Nigel to his cabin to tell him his story. Flashback to Paris: Oscar is obsessed by a bus ticket-dodging young girl. He finally runs into Mimi whilst on a date. She's a waitress with a passion for dance. Oscar details the increasingly perverse sexual relationship. Nigel tries to dismiss Oscar as a kinky old pervert, but he too is obsessed with Mimi and returns to hear the rest of Oscar's story. Oscar and Mimi unsuccessfully attempt to rejuvenate their relationship with sadomasochistic games, but it is only when Oscar grows tired of Mimi that the real power games begin. Whilst Mimi is still madly in love with Oscar, he can only get his kicks from humiliating her in public. Growing increasingly tired of Mimi, Oscar tricks her into boarding a plane for a tropical island with only a single ticket in her possession. Thinking he is now rid of Mimi, Oscar resumes his hedonistic lifestyle. However, Oscar is cut down when he's run over by a bus. Mimi suddenly appears at Oscar's hospital bedside. She tricks Oscar into overextending his injured back, leaving him paralysed. Mimi becomes Oscar's nurse. Now Oscar is the victim, trapped in his own flat and constantly being humiliated. The games of Oscar and Mimi put the relationship between Nigel and Fiona under increasing stress. Oscar coerces Nigel into seducing Mimi but Fiona pulls the rug from under Nigel's feet by seducing her. Oscar blows his brains out with a pistol before killing Mimi.

Adult Fairy Tale Only the perverse fantasy can still save us, Goethe wrote. *Bitter Moon* certainly saved my interest in Polanski's films. *Bitter Moon* not only rekindles the kinkiness of *What?* but it also exhibits the originality of *Cul-De-Sac*. Loosely based on Pascal Bruckner's novel *Lune de Fiel*, *Bitter Moon*, like Leonard Schrader's *Naked Tango* (1989) and Donald Cammell's *Wild Side* (1995), employs the trappings of soft porn to fashion an excellent perverted black comedy about power. In an interview during his return to Poland in the late Seventies, Polanski assured an audience that normal love isn't interesting in cinema and that, if anything, it's completely boring. True to his words, *Bitter Moon* is a love story that is anything but normal. Featuring a seemingly respectable chap succumbing to latent sexual perversity, *Bitter Moon* is a particularly savage parable about the loss of innocence, a tradition encompassing such diverse films as Jerzy Skolimowski's *Deep End* (1970) and Lynch's *Blue Velvet*.

The Victim as Victimiser Oscar's sadomasochist fantasies are no fun because they are just that – fantasies. Oscar discovers there is no real *frisson* to be found in bondage, let alone pretending to be a pig. However, whilst Oscar plays the victim in the couple's fantasy games, Mimi's masochistic love for Oscar renders her open to cruel abuse. Like Andrzej in *Knife In The Water* and Jake in *Chinatown*, the fox is soon outfoxed and foxed once again. Just as Oscar's disappearing act on an international flight leads him to think that he is now rid of Mimi, Mimi upon her return tricks Oscar into paralysing himself whilst lying in his own hospital bed. And just as Nigel goes about deceiving Fiona, he too gets his come-uppance when Mimi succumbs to Fiona's advances under the passive gaze of a shocked Nigel and a cynical Oscar.

Flashback Structure Interestingly, *Bitter Moon* employs a similar flashback structure to Polanski's student short, *Where Angels Fall*. The form allows a number of structured, reflective and finally pessimistic scenes that permit a wider drama to be recounted from the past whilst retaining the claustrophobic tension of the cruise liner framing the present drama.

Grotesque Humour With *Bitter Moon*, Polanski is at his most vulgar. To the strains of an overwrought Vangelis soundtrack Polanski juxtaposes nauseating romantic cliché s (e.g. holding hands on fairground swings) with near pornographic sex scenes. Highlights include Mimi dribbling a mouthful of full fat milk over her breasts in front of Oscar at the breakfast table whilst George Michael's 'Faith' plays on the radio and Oscar accidentally strangling a call girl's poodle whilst he's having a blow job.

Cruelty Despite its reputation, the most shocking aspects of *Bitter Moon* are not the sex scenes. Real violence occurs in *Bitter Moon* in the abrupt, almost mundane treatment of Oscar being knocked over by a bus. Conversely, the most uncomfortable sequences in *Bitter Moon* involve Mimi allowing Oscar to wet himself in his wheelchair and her deliberately slack use of hypodermics.

Verdict Bitter Moon is very black, utterly vulgar, thoroughly cruel and one of the most undervalued films of the Nineties. 4/5

Death And The Maiden (1994)

Cast Sigourney Weaver (Paulina Escobar), Stuart Wilson II (Gerardo Escobar), Ben Kingsley (Dr Roberto Miranda).

Crew Director: Roman Polanski; Producers: Josh Kramer, Thom Mount; Screenplay: Ariel Dorfman, Rafael Yglesias, based on the play by Ariel Dorfman; Cinematography: Tonino Delli Colli; Music: Wojciech Kilar; Editor: Hervé de Luze; Production Design: Pierre Guffroy; Art Direction: Claude Moesching; Costume Design: Milena Canonero; Co-Producers: Ariel Dorfman, Bonnie Timmermann; Associate Producer: Gladys Nederlander; Executive Producers: Jane Barclay, Sharon Harel. 103 mins.

Story In an anonymous, recently democratised South American country, Gerardo Escobar, a lawyer who has recently landed a job that involves bringing criminals of the old regime to justice, is driving home to a secluded house which he shares with his wife, Paulina. A tyre blows out of Gerardo's car. However, upon replacing the wheel, Gerardo discovers that his spare is flat too. Luckily another driver offers his spare tyre to Gerardo. Gerardo thanks the good Samaritan, a Doctor, and returns home. However, the doctor returns to Gerardo's house under the pretence of retrieving his tyre, though his real motive is to express his gratitude for Gerardo's work in bringing the crimes of the old regime to justice. Meanwhile Paulina, upon hearing the doctor's voice, becomes terrified. She drives off in the doctor's car, confiscates a tape of Schubert's *Death And The Maiden* before toppling the car over a cliff. She returns to the house, gags the doctor and binds him to a chair threatening him at gunpoint. Paulina cannot believe her luck: as a student activist under the old regime, unbeknown to Gerardo, she was blindfolded, electrocuted by her interrogators and subsequently raped repeatedly by a doctor installed to ensure her medical well-being. The doctor violently denies any such involvement in any such crime, protesting to having been in residence at a hospital in Spain during the period of Paulina's ordeal in the late Seventies. Gerardo initially thinks Paulina has gone mad, but starts to believe her when she mentions that the doctor was fond of quoting Nietzsche, something he had experience of whilst conversing with the doctor earlier. Though originally intent on killing t he doctor, Paulina settles for a mock trial, where Gerardo ends up defending the doctor, thus stretching his relationship with Paulina to breaking point. Gerardo is caught in the middle of Paulina and the doctor and right up until the end is still not sure that Paulina has the right man. At a cliff top the doctor confesses to his crimes and each party wanders off in a catatonic state.

Just Another Power Play? For *Death And The Maiden*, Polanski employs a whole range of stylistic and plot devices from his repertoire to the point where the film should be self-parody. However, despite the claustrophobic settings, the isolated drama, a violent power play between a victim of sexual abuse, a monster who has managed to hide himself within reformed society and a largely impotent husband, *Death And The Maiden* feels distinctly unlike any other Polanski film. Polanski's handling of the drama can't be faulted. Technically, set design and photography are efficient, if undistinguished. However, what jars are the roots in Dorfman's stage play.

Polanski's drama is hampered by the preachy, po-faced, overly liberal tone of Dorfman's simplistic play that essentially contrasts instinctive emotion with cerebral democratic beliefs. Maybe because of the knowledge that Dorfman's play was based on real political terror tactics used in South America, what *Death And The Maiden* offers is a crossing-out of the perversities so evident in, for example, *Bitter Moon*.

Ironically, the central image of *Death And The Maiden*, that of the doctor gagged and bound to a chair whilst Paulina threatens him almost sensually with a gun, is remarkably similar to Oscar's sadomasochistic fantasy in *Bitter Moon*. The difference here is that in *Bitter Moon* it was Oscar's fantasy, whereas the implicit rape of Paulina in *Death And The Maiden* is very real, and therefore, instantly condemnable. The disturbing element of Dorfman's piece is how a doctor, someone whose job it is to care for people, succumbs to playing a role in the torture and abuse of political prisoners. However, Dorfman deals with the issue in a simplistic polarised state of good and bad. This is completely at odds with the rest of Polanski's work. Polanski has always explored the relationship between victim and victimiser and the very real issue of how victims are disturbingly associated with the crimes committed against them.

In fact Liliana Caviani's *Night Porter* (the best film Polanski never made?) is not only more disturbing in its exploration of a similar theme but is also much more convincing. Caviani's film involves a Jewish woman checking into a classy hotel after the war only to find her Nazi interrogator working as a night porter. Unlike Dorfman's play, and more typical of a Polanski drama, rather than enact revenge, the pair resume the sadomasochistic relationship they first played out in the camps. Caviani's story does sound exploitative and sensationalist compared to Dorfman's play but was actually developed from a series of interviews with Holocaust captives for an Italian television documentary.

Verdict An efficient, entertaining and atmospheric drama marred by preachy source material and cramped slightly by stagy (though admittedly impressive) performances. 2/5

Polanski's next project was to be based on an original screenplay by Gérard Brach and himself, *The Double*. Early publicity suggested the project was to be a William Wilson style drama of a man haunted by his doppelgänger. John Travolta, fresh from *Pulp Fiction* (1994), was secured for the leading role and Isabelle Adjani was to play a supporting role in the Paris-based production. As *The Double* entered its first week of production in 1996, Travolta and Polanski had an argument that resulting in Travolta walking off the set. The production continued without him until finally Adjani also quit, which led to the production being closed down. Eager to make another film as quickly as possible, Polanski turned to Arturo Pérez-Reverte's *Il Club Dumas*. Johnny Depp, who bears an uncanny resemblance to Pérez-Reverte in the film, was cast in the lead role. Filming took place in Portugal, Spain and France in 1998.

The Ninth Gate/La neuvième porte (1999)

Cast Johnny Depp (Dean Corso), Lena Olin (Liana Telfer), Frank Langella (Boris Balkan), James Russo (Bernie), Jack Taylor (Victor Fargas), Barbara Jefford (Baroness Kessler), Emmanuelle Seigner (The Girl).

Crew Director: Roman Polanski; Producer: Roman Polanski; Screenplay: Enrique Urbizu, John Brownjohn, Roman Polanski, based on the novel *Il Club Dumas* by Arturo Pérez-Reverte; Cinematography: Darius Khondji; Music: Wojciech Kilar; Production Design: Dean Tavoularis; Art Direction: Gérard Viard; Set Decoration : Philippe Turlure; Costume Design: Anthony Powell; Co-Producers: Mark Allan, Antonio Cardenal, Iñaki Núñez, Alain Vannier; Associate Producer: Adam Kempton; Executive Producers: Michel Cheyko, Wolfgang Glattes. 133 mins.

Story Dean Corso, a Manhattan rare book dealer, is hired by Boris Balkan, a wealthy collector with an unhealthy interest in the Devil, to compare his copy of the *Nine Gates To The Kingdom of Shadows* with the only two copies that remain in existence. For this Corso has to travel to Portugal and France. The book, reputedly a transcription of a tome written in part by the Devil himself, contains a set of engravings hiding the key to the kingdom of shadows. Balkan had acquired his copy of the *Nine Gates* from the late Telfer, whose seductive widow, Liana, uses her charms on Corso to try and get the copy back. In Portugal Corso notices some discrepancies in two of the three copies of the *Nine Gates*. Shortly after, Corso finds the owner of the second copy dead and the engravings stolen from his copy of the *Nine Gates*. Corso suspects a mysterious grungy blonde-haired girl who has been following him.

In Paris, Corso encounters Baroness Kessler, a wheelchair bound authority on the Devil. Initially reluctant to co-operate because of Balkan financing Corso's investigations, she reveals that Liana Telfer is the head of a Satanic sect which converge annually to read from the *Nine Gates*, thus explaining why she's so keen to get her copy back. Corso is knocked out cold whilst researching in Kessler's archive, finds his host strangled and her apartment on fire. As before, the engravings have been stolen from her copy of the *Nine Gates*. Soon after, Liana steals Corso's copy from his swanky five-star hotel. Balkan threatens to kill Corso if he doesn't retrieve his copy of the *Nine Gates* immediately. Corso and the mysterious girl trace Liana to a Château on the outskirts of Paris. Having infiltrated Liana's Black Mass, Balkan makes a grand entrance, denouncing Liana's rituals as mumbo-jumbo, before garrotting her and stealing his copy back. The climax takes place in a castle where Balkan accidentally immolates himself whilst attempting to summon the Devil. After making love to Corso, the girl leaves him with a note directing him back to Toledo. Corso discovers that the ninth engraving of Balkan's copy is, in fact, fake. Now with a full set of engravings, Corso enters the Ninth Gate.

Book Fetishism Above all else, *The Ninth Gate* is a thriller involving bibliophiles, fanatical collectors of what seem destined to be relics of the second millennium. *The Ninth Gate* is also a film about books. Polanski takes great pleasure in emphasising the tactile quality of these coveted as well as perishable items. He invests an almost sensual attention to detail: forgeries are detected by the sound of the paper, the bindings of the books are smelled, imperfections of the ink press are noted and recorded. Like Dario Argento's occult book horror story, *Inferno* (1980), Polanski invests an almost fetishistic interest in the three copies of *The Nine Gates*. Eccentric book dealers drop cigarette ash on the covers, pages become progressively stained with scotch whilst readers puzzle over their secrets. Engravings are torn out, hidden on top of bookcases, the missing pages only to be replaced by painstaking forgeries. The ephemeral signifiers of the digital age – mobile phones, television, the internet – are all conspicuously absent.

A Reaction If *The Ninth Gate* is reactionary in spirit, Polanski's execution also harks back to a cinema of the past. Through a disciplined use of steadicam and relatively wide-angle lenses, *The Ninth Gate* unfolds through a procession of simple though judicious takes. As a story of a "book detective," to use Liana's description, *The Ninth Gate* is closest in style to *Chinatown*. Robert Towne recently spoke of how he thought that it would be impossible to produce *Chinatown* today because of its pace, style and the degree of patience it demands from an audience. The lukewarm commercial response to *The Ninth Gate* adds weight to Towne's assumption, which is a little depressing. Although lacking the breakneck editing and wall-to-wall music, there is form, pattern and a definite structure to *The Ninth Gate*. The film feels pleasantly stranded somewhere between the Fifties and Nineties. The casting recalls, consciously or not, genres of the Sixties and Seventies – Hammer veteran Barbara Jefford plays the eccentric Baroness Kessler whilst Jack Taylor summons up an entire legion of Jess Franco films and sundry other Spanish horrors.

Parallels With Kubrick's Eyes Wide Shut A curious parallel can be drawn between *The Ninth Gate* and another film that made no attempt to hide its roots in the past, *Eyes Wide Shut*. Stanley Kubrick's last film was released almost simultaneously with Polanski's in Europe. In what must be a bizarre coincidence, both self-imposed exiles reconstructed sections of Manhattan in their adopted homes of France and England for two films that reached their high point of sorts with cloaked orgies in secluded mansions.

The Devil Again After *Rosemary's Baby*, *The Ninth Gate* is Polanski's second film concerning the Devil. However, unlike *Rosemary's Baby*, *The Ninth Gate* received a rather unsympathetic critical and commercial reception upon its release in 1999. Sadly, this verdict is more indicative of the inability of a marketing department to recognise and champion the qualities of the film. *The Ninth Gate* doesn't fit neatly into any one genre. It reflects badly on a critical community that is becoming more conservative in taste though ultimately less demanding. The most sympathetic British review of *The Ninth Gate* came from an unlikely source, Gilbert Adair.

Verdict The Ninth Gate is an intelligent, exciting and resoundingly unpretentious drama. Beautifully photographed by Darius Khondji and gracefully scored by Wojciech Kilar, *The Ninth Gate* has a sophisticated yet playful menace, reminiscent of Hitchcock, though one only hopes that for this film Polanski put his real demons on hold rather than losing them entirely. 3/5

The Pianist/Der Pianist (2002)

Cast Adrien Brody, Thomas Kretschmann, Ed Stoppard, Emilia Fox, Frank Finlay, Julia Rayner, Jessica Kate Meyer, Maureen Lipman.

Crew Director: Roman Polanski; Screenplay: Ronald Harwood, Roman Polanski, based on the book by Wladyslaw Szpilman; Cinematography: Pawel Edelman; Music: Wojciech Kilar; Production Design: Allan Starski; Set Decoration: Gabriele Wolff; Costume Design: Anna B Sheppard.

Whatever there is to make of Polanski's assertion that *The Pianist* is the most important film of his life, it does constitute his first film to deal explicitly with the Polish experience of the Second World War. Polanski had already turned down Steven Spielberg's offer to direct *Schindler's List* in 1993. This is all the more remarkable given Polanski's tendency to both recreate, control and ultimately theatricalise events in his own personal life. As Barbara Leaming suggests in her biography of Polanski, his films are keyed into the viewer's consciousness of the Polanski persona: a life inflected by sex and violence. During the 1970s, especially around the time of *Tess*, Polanski mastered his own image in the press, in turn using it as material for his films. However, given the erratic critical and commercial success of Polanski's films during the last two decades, the question is just how much a presence is Polanski in the viewer's consciousness? Will the fact that he himself endured years in the Cracow ghetto have any bearing on how we perceive *The Pianist*?

Polanski has been reluctant to make a film based on his own experiences, suggesting that he probably would not be capable of producing such a work. However, by filming Wladyslaw Szpilman's novel, Polanski has found a model that, whilst detached from his own experience, nonetheless exhibits parallels with his own life. According to Ronald Harwood, who adapted the book with Polanski, the director's emotional experiences in the Cracow ghetto during his formative years appear in every scene, guaranteeing the film's authenticity and realism.

Wladyslaw Szpilman's Memoirs Szpilman's book was first published in Poland in 1946 under the title *Death Of A City*. It was also published in German under the title *Das wunderbare überleben [The Miraculous Survival]* and was reissued two years ago, just one year before the noted pianist died. Szpilman was the only one of his family to survive the Holocaust. However, back in 1946 *The Pianist* was almost immediately withdrawn from circulation by the Polish authorities now under the puppet rule of Stalin. Wolf Biermann argues that Szpilman's book contained too many truths about the collaboration of defeated Russian, Poles, Ukrainians, Latvians and Jews with the German Nazis. Even in Israel people did not want to hear about such things. The subject was intolerable to all concerned, victims and perpetrators alike, although for opposite reasons.

As Polanski must know only too well, Anti-Semitism was flourishing in Poland long before the German invasion. However, three to four hundred thousand Poles risked their lives to save Jews. If you hid a Jew in France, the penalty was prison or a concentration camp, in Germany it cost you your life – but in Poland it cost the lives of your entire family.

Szpilman's story tells of his part in the Jewish resistance. Szpilman was among those who were taken out daily in labour columns to the Aryan side of the city, smuggling food and ammunition for the Jewish resistance, similar to Polanski's experiences in the Cracow ghetto.

Szpilman would probably have not survived if it were not for a Wehrmacht officer, Wilm Hosenfeld. Hosenfeld was a teacher who had already served in the First World War and was considered too old for service in the front line. Hosenfeld found the half-dead pianist in the ashes of Warsaw. Instead of killing Szpilman, Hosenfeld brought him food, found him a coat to wear and a quilt. There is something perverse about Polanski making a film of the Shoah that has the form of a Hollywood fairy tale, yet it is nonetheless a true story. Knowing the Germans had now lost the War, Szpilman gave Hosenfeld some information in return. "If anything happens to you, if I can help you in any way, remember my name: Szpilman, Polish Radio." Szpilman tried unsuccessfully to locate his saviour after the war but Hosenfeld had been taken prisoner by the Soviet army and died in captivity at Stalingrad seven years later. In a cruel twist, for having the nerve to claim that he'd saved a Jew, Hosenfeld was tortured by Soviet officers.

Szpilman resumed his work for Radio Warsaw as a pianist. He opened the broadcasting service after the war with Chopin's *Nocturne In C Minor* that he had been playing live on radio during the invasion.

Polanski heard Szpilman play a concert in Warsaw a decade ago without being aware of the musician's past.

Back to Poland Originally Polanski had planned to shoot *The Pianist* entirely in Poland, making it the first film he had shot in his native country since *Knife In The Water* almost forty years earlier. However, Polanski was unable to find suitable locations and sufficient studio capacity for the large production. *The Pianist* was the third big-budget production to be shot at Berlin's Studio Babelsberg (the others were Jean-Jacques Annaud's Leningrad epic *Enemy At The Gates* (2000) and István Szabó's own Shoah epic *Taking Sides* (2000)). The film was shot over five weeks in the spring of 2001, followed by eleven weeks of location shooting in Warsaw.

The Production Ronald Harwood adapted Szpilman's book for the screen with Polanski. It was not unfamiliar ground for Harwood, who had written the screenplay for Szabó's *Taking Sides*, which was based on Berlin Philharmonic director Kurt Furtwaengler's relations with the Nazis and his efforts to save the lives of his Jewish musicians. Polanski's technical crew was a mixture of Polish and international talents, including cinematographer Pawel Edelman (whose photography for Andrzej Wajda's turgid *Pan Tadeusz* was probably the film's strongest asset), a score by Wojciech Kilar, set design by Allan Starski and costume design by Anna Sheppard. Both Starski and Sheppard were highly acclaimed for creating the look of Spielberg's Holocaust epic, *Schindler's List*. Thirty years after the demise of Cadre Films, Gene Gutowski returned to work with Polanski, this time acting as co-producer, backed up by Robert Benmussa and A lain Sarde who had collaborated with Polanski on *Bitter Moon*.

Polanski originally intended to cast an unknown actor for the part of Szpilman, though despite selecting thirty hopefuls for screen tests out of the thousands who had responded to an advert in the *Guardian*, he finally decided on a professional actor, Adrien Brody, who had starred in Terrence Malick's *The Thin Red Line* (1999). Brody had taken piano lessons as a child from his mother and practised diligently in preparation for his role. Thomas Kretschmann (*Il Sindrome di Stendhal*, 1996) plays Hosenfeld.

The success or failure of *The Pianist* will be crucial to Polanski's place in film history. While Polanski has demonstrated a remarkable versatility when it comes to working in foreign countries and different genres, this may lead to the neglecting of his films since film histories tend to be organised around either nationality or genre. Polanski's idiosyncratic vision may endure, though it could equally be neglected as a product of its time. Either way, Polanski's films will continue to act as bitter antidotes to the usual saccharine fare of conventional Hollywood cinema.

9: Bibliography And Resources

Biographies

Kiernan, Thomas, *The Roman Polanski Story*. New York, Delilah/Grove Press, 1980; reprinted in 1981 as *Roman Polanski: A Biography* (Black Cat) and as *Repulsion: The Life And Times Of Roman Polanski*, London, New English Library, 1981. Contrived tripe churned out in haste by A Polanski hanger-on. Whole films are omitted, not to mention suspect tales quoted from dubious interviews with anonymous 'friends'. However, as an exercise in sheer sensationalism, the book succeeds admirably.

Leaming, Barbara, *Polanski: The Film-maker As Voyeur: A Biography*. New York, Simon & Schuster, and as *Polanski: His Life And Films*, London, Hamish Hamilton, 1982. Leaming pursues a thesis that the impact of Polanski's films hinges on the audience being aware of Polanski and how the director uses personal tragedies and catastrophes to sculpt his public persona. Whether or not you buy Leaming's idea, the rest of the book stands admirably on its own. It is both well researched and offers a number of delicate insights, especially with regard to often ignored films like *What?* Leaming's book is the best Polanski biography by a wide margin.

Parker, John, *Polanski*. London, Victor Gollancz, 1993. By-the -numbers cut and paste biography that is only interesting for the information squeezed out of Basia Kwiatkowska. It's now twenty years since Polanski had a decent biography in English, and this effort clearly won't do.

Polanski, Roman, *Roman By Polanski*. New York, Morrow, and London, William Heinemann, 1984. Leaming's biography was used by Polanski and his editors as a template for this autobiography, though Polanski's own contributions and revisions make for a highly entertaining read.

Critical Studies

Bisplinghoff, Gretchen & Virginia Wright Wexman, *Roman Polanski: A Guide To References And Resources*. Boston, G K Hall, 1979.

Butler, Ivan, *The Cinema Of Roman Polanski*. New York, A S Barnes, and London, Zwemmer, 1970. Butler's small book is a useful source of information on Polanski's British films, containing interview material with Polanski, Alastair McIntyre and Douglas Slocombe.

Durgnat, Raymond, *Sexual Alienation In The Cinema*. London, Studio Vista, 1972. Durgnat is quite simply one the best writers on film, full stop. If 'serious' film criticism has degenerated into a ragbag of third-rate rehashed psychoanalysis and hackneyed linguistics, then Durgnat's brilliant essays remind us of what film criticism was and, more importantly, what it could be.

Goulding, Daniel J, *Five Film-makers: Tarkovsky, Forman, Polanski, Szabó, Makavejev*. Bloomington, Indiana University Press, 1994.

Polanski, Roman & Gérard Brach, *Roman Polanski's What?*. New York, Third Press, and London, Lorrimer Publishing, 1973. Screenplay to Polanski's movie.

Polanski, Roman, *Cul-De-Sac/Repulsion/Knife In The Water*. New York, Harper & Row, and London, Lorrimer Publishing, 1975. Having all three scripts of Polanski's first films in one volume is an opportunity to see how similar each drama works as a chamber piece. Also included are the corresponding *Monthly Film Bulletin* Reviews. Much more interesting is a translation of an extensive *Cahiers du Cinéma* interview.

Wexman, Virginia Wright, *Roman Polanski*. Boston, Twayne, 1985, and London, Columbus, 1987.

Polish Cinema

Beylie, Claude, *L'avant-scène cinéma Spécial Wajda* 239/240.

Beylie, Claude, *L'avant-scène cinéma Spécial Cinéma Polonais* 317/318.
Contains an interview with Polanski as well as an interesting article
that draws a contrast between the films of Andrzej Wajda, the
"king of Polish cinema" and those of his (then) exiled protégé, Andrzej
Zulawski, the " cursed king of Polish cinema" (in French).

Cameron, Ian, *et al*, *Second Wave: Newer Than New Wave Names In World
Cinema*. Lon don, Studio Vista, 1970. A good compendium of articles on
film-makers who are generally ignored or forgotten these days, including
Jerzy Skolimowski.

Fuksiewicz, Jacek, *Polish Cinema*, translated by Ewa Gromek-Guzinska.
Warszawa, Interpress Publishers, 1973. As with all Interpress titles,
whilst useful as a source of facts and figures about Polish film production, there's no critical insight whatsoever.

Furdal, Malgorzata, *et al*, *Krzysztof Komeda*. Milano, Kind of Blue Jazz
Film Festival, 1999. Contains interviews with Polanski and Skolimowski
on Komeda (in Italian).

Furdal, Malgorzata & Roberto Turigliatto, *Jerzy Skolimowski*. Torino,
Lindau (XIV Festival Internazionale Cinema Giovani), 1996 (in Italian).

Janicki, Stanislaw, *The Polish Film*. Warszawa, Interpress Publishers, 1985.
Like Fuksiewicz, but heavily illustrated.

McArthur. Colin, *Andrzej Wajda: Polish Cinema*. London, A BFI Education Department Dossier, December 1970.

Michalek, Boleslaw, *et al*, *Le Cinéma Polonais*. Paris, Centre Georges Pompidou, 1992. The text was originally published in a separate volume in
English (*The Modern Cinema Of Poland* by Michalek Boleslaw & Frank
Turaj, Bloomington, Indiana University Press, 1988) and whilst it contains a number of glaring factual errors the French translation is accom-
panied by a number of other texts, all of which have an element of
interest in their own right. However, the real bonus of the Centre
Georges Pompidou books is their exhaustive and beautifully reproduced
illustrations.

Plazewsky, J., *Andrzej Munk*. Paris, Anthologie du Cinéma, 1967 (in
French).

Vogel, Amos, *Film As A Subversive Art*. New York, Random House, and
London, Weidenfeld & Nicolson, 1974. Contains an excellent chapter on
subversive form and content in films produced by socialist countries during the 1960s. Whilst generally dismissive of Polanski's non-Polish

films, Vogel's book is nonetheless a fascinating source of information on a dazzling array of films and trends.

Miscellaneous

Borowski, Tadeusz, *This Way For The Gas, Ladies And Gentlemen, and other stories*, translated by Barbara Vedder. London, Cape, 1967. Reissued by Penguin in 1976 with an introduction by Jan Kott.

Bugliosi, Vincent, with Curt Gentry, *Helter Skelter*. New York, Norton, 1974; as *The Manson Murders. An investigation into motive*, London, Bodley Head, 1975. An abridged version was published by Penguin (as *Helter Skelter*) in 1977. The full text was reprinted by Arrow in 1992.

Bulgakov, Mikhail, *The Master And Margarita* (translated and with notes by Richard Pevear and Larissa Volokhonsky). London, Penguin, 1997. A number of other translations exist but this one is the most readily available.

Caro Baroja, Julio, *The World Of Witches (Las Brujas y su mundo*, translated by Nigel Glendinning). London, Weidenfield & Nicolson, 1964.

Cook, Richard and Brian Morton, *The Penguin Guide To Jazz On CD. Fourth Edition*. London, Penguin, 1998. First published in 1992.

Gregory, Richard, *Eye And Brain: The Psychology of Seeing*. London, Weidenfeld & Nicolson, 1966. Put aside the rants of Deleuze or Zizek, anyone with a real interest in cinema should get hold of a copy of Gregory's physiology/perceptual psychology primer.

King, Greg, *Sharon Tate And The Manson Murders*. Edinburgh, Mainstream, 2000.

Kosinski, Jerzy, *The Painted Bird*. Boston, Houghton Mifflin Co., 1965, and London, W H Allen, 1966. Kosinski's campus favourite has long since fallen from grace. These days it's more likely to be found propping up other paperbacks in charity shops around the country but is well worth seeking out.

Pérez-Reverte, Arturo, *The Dumas Club (El club Dumas*, 1993, translated by Sonia Soto). London, Harvill Press, 1996. Anyone who enjoyed the playfulness of Polanski's *The Ninth Gate* should definitely read the source novel, which is considerably more complexly plotted and compulsively crafted.

Milosz, Czeslaw, *The Captive Mind* (translated from the Polish by Jane Zielonko). London, Secker & Warburg, 1953. Also published in paperback by Penguin.

Pirie, David, *The Vampire Cinema*. London, Hamlyn, 1977. Written in the days when critics could write about vampire films seriously without feeling obliged to mention menstruation.

Powaga, Wiesiek, *The Dedalus Book Of Polish Fantasy* (translated from the Polish by Wiesiek Powaga). Sawtry, Cambridgshire, Dedalus, and New York, Hippocrene, 1996. Dedalus have published a number of translations from Polish fantastic literature, though this compendium offers a broad sample with a good introduction.

Sloan, James Parker, *Jerzy Kosinski*. New York, Dutton Press, and London, Penguin, 1996. Exhaustively researched and sympathetically written, Sloan offers a mixture of biography and critical analysis of Kosinski and his bizarre novels. He also ventures into the contentious issue of evaluating just how much a role Kosinski's team of editors (usually doctorate students at various Universities where Kosinski taught) played in the writing of his later novels.

Szasz, Thomas S, *The Manufacture Of Madness*. New York, Harper & Row, 1970, and London, Routledge & Kegan Paul, 1971. Probably redundant in terms of contemporary psychiatry, but nevertheless an interesting book that is both excessive in the ideas it entertains and thorough in its exploration of them.

Topor, Roland, *The Tenant* (*Le locataire chimérique*, translated by Francis K Price). London, W H Allen, 1966. Delicately written in the third person, Topor's finest novel is a frightening read. It's fascinating to see just how much of the original novel Polanski and Brach preserved in the screenplay.

Tynan, Kenneth, *The Diaries of Kenneth Tynan*, edited by John Lahr. London, Bloomsbury, 2001.

Yule, Andrew, *Hollywood A Go-Go: The True Story Of The Cannon Film Empire*. London, Sphere, 1987. Although pathetic in its attempt, to my knowledge this is the only book that charts the rise and fall of Menaham Golan and Yoram Globus film empire. Given the miserable efforts churned out in Hollywood these days, I've become particularly nostalgic about such Cannon productions as *Life Force* (1985) and *The Texas Chainsaw Massacre Part 2* (1986), not to mention *Ruiz's Treasure Island*, Cassavettes' *Love Streams*, Konchalovsky's *Runaway Train* and Godard's *Detective*. Move over Alan Parker, Israel's finest ought to take their place at the head of the Film Council.

Websites Of Interest

Walerian Borowczyk – www.vidmarc.demon.co.uk/mondo-erotico/
  index_boro.html
Krzysztof Komeda – www.komeda.vernet.pl/
Roman Polanski – www.cafeinternet.co.uk/polanski/
Andrzej Wajda – www.wajda.pl
Andrzej Zulawski – home.att.net/~zulawski/
Central European Cinema – www.kinoeye.org

Videos

This is a list of English language Polanski videos in the VHS/PAL format
  which are currently available or have been recently deleted. The titles
  marked with an asterisk (*) have also been released on DVD.

Knife In The Water (1962), Connoisseur Video
Repulsion (1964), Odyssey Video
Cul-De-Sac (1965), Odyssey Video
The Fearless Vampire Killers (1967), Warner Home Video (deleted).
Rosemary's Baby (1968), Paramount Home Entertainment
Macbeth (1971), Cinema Club
Chinatown (1973), Paramount Home Entertainment
The Tenant (1975), Paramount Home Entertainment (deleted).
Tess (1979), Pathé Distribution
Pirates (1986), Cinema Club (deleted).
Frantic (1987), Warner Home Video
Bitter Moon (1992), Columbia Tri-Star Home Video
Death And The Maiden (1994), 4 Front Video
The Ninth Gate (1999), Vision Entertainment

The Essential Library: Best-Sellers

Build up your library with new titles every month

Alfred Hitchcock (Revised & Updated Edition) by Paul Duncan, £3.99

More than 20 years after his death, Alfred Hitchcock is still a household name, most people in the Western world have seen at least one of his films, and he popularised the action movie format we see every week on the cinema screen. He was both a great artist and dynamite at the box office. This book examines the genius and enduring popularity of one of the most influential figures in the history of the cinema!

Orson Welles (Revised & Updated Edition) by Martin Fitzgerald, £3.99

The popular myth is that after the artistic success of *Citizen Kane* it all went downhill for Orson Welles, that he was some kind of fallen genius. Yet, despite overwhelming odds, he went on to make great Films Noirs like *The Lady From Shanghai* and *Touch Of Evil*. He translated Shakespeare's work into films with heart and soul (*Othello*, *Chimes At Midnight*, *Macbeth*), and he gave voice to bitterness, regret and desperation in *The Magnificent Ambersons* and *The Trial*. Far from being down and out, Welles became one of the first cutting-edge independent film-makers.

Woody Allen (Revised & Updated Edition) by Martin Fitzgerald, £3.99

Woody Allen: Neurotic. Jewish. Funny. Inept. Loser. A man with problems. Or so you would think from the characters he plays in his movies. But hold on. Allen has written and directed 30 films. He may be a funny man, but he is also one of the most serious American film-makers of his generation. This revised and updated edition includes *Sweet And Lowdown* and *Small Time Crooks*.

Film Noir by Paul Duncan, £3.99

The laconic private eye, the corrupt cop, the heist that goes wrong, the femme fatale with the rich husband and the dim lover - these are the trademark characters of Film Noir. This book charts the progression of the Noir style as a vehicle for film-makers who wanted to record the darkness at the heart of American society as it emerged from World War to the Cold War. As well as an introduction explaining the origins of Film Noir, seven films are examined in detail and an exhaustive list of over 500 Films Noirs are listed.

Noir Fiction by Paul Duncan, £2.99

For every light that shines, there must always fall a shadow, a dark side - Noir. Noir has infiltrated our world, like some insidious disease, and we cannot get rid of it. The threads of its growth and development have been hinted at but no-one has yet tried to bind them together, to weave the whole picture. This book takes you down the dark highways of the Noir experience, and examines the history of Noir in literature, art, film, and pulps. Sensitive readers are warned - you may find the Noir world disturbing, terrifying and ultimately pessimistic. Features: Jim Thompson, Cornell Woolrich, David Goodis, James Ellroy, Derek Raymond, Charles Willeford and more.

The Essential Library: Recent Releases

Build up your library with new titles every month

Stanley Kubrick (Revised & Updated Edition) by Paul Duncan, £3.99

Kubrick's work, like all masterpieces, has a timeless quality. His vision is so complete, the detail so meticulous, that you believe you are in a three-dimensional space displayed on a two-dimensional screen. He was commercially successful because he embraced traditional genres like War (*Paths Of Glory, Full Metal Jacket*), Crime (*The Killing*), Science Fiction (*2001*), Horror (*The Shining*) and Love (*Barry Lyndon*). At the same time, he stretched the boundaries of film with controversial themes: underage sex (*Lolita*); ultra violence (*A Clockwork Orange*); and erotica (*Eyes Wide Shut*).

Tim Burton by Colin Odell & Michelle Le Blanc, £3.99

Tim Burton makes films about outsiders on the periphery of society. His heroes are psychologically scarred, perpetually naive and childlike, misunderstood or unintentionally disruptive. They upset convential society and morality. Even his villains are rarely without merit - circumstance blurs the divide between moral fortitude and personal action. But most of all, his films have an aura of the fairytale, the fantastical and the magical.

French New Wave by Chris Wiegand, £3.99

The directors of the French New Wave were the original film geeks - a collection of celluloid-crazed cinéphiles with a background in film criticism and a love for American auteurs. Having spent countless hours slumped in Parisian cinémathèques, they armed themselves with handheld cameras, rejected conventions, and successfully moved movies out of the studios and on to the streets at the end of the 1950s.

Borrowing liberally from the varied traditions of film noir, musicals and science fiction, they released a string of innovative and influential pictures, including the classics *Jules Et Jim* and *A Bout De Souffle*. By the mid-1960s, the likes of Jean-Luc Godard, François Truffaut, Claude Chabrol, Louis Malle, Eric Rohmer and Alain Resnais had changed the rules of film-making forever.

Mike Hodges by Mark Adams, £3.99

Features an extensive interview with Mike Hodges. His first film, *Get Carter*, has achieved cult status (recently voted the best British film ever in *Hotdog* magazine) and continues to be the benchmark by which every British crime film is measured. His latest film, *Croupier*, was such a hit in the US that is was re-issued in the UK. His work includes crime drama (*Pulp*), science-fiction (*Flash Gordon* and *The Terminal Man*), comedy (*Morons From Outer Space*) and watchable oddities such as *A Prayer For The Dying* and *Black Rainbow*. Mike Hodges is one of the great maverick British filmmakers.

The Essential Library: Currently Available

Film Directors:

Woody Allen (Revised)	Tim Burton	Ang Lee
Jane Campion*	John Carpenter	Steve Soderbergh
Jackie Chan	Joel & Ethan Coen	Clint Eastwood
David Cronenberg	Terry Gilliam*	Michael Mann
Alfred Hitchcock	Krzysztof Kieslowski*	Roman Polanski
Stanley Kubrick	Sergio Leone	
David Lynch	Brian De Palma*	
Sam Peckinpah*	Ridley Scott	
Orson Welles	Billy Wilder	
Steven Spielberg	Mike Hodges	

Film Genres:

Blaxploitation Films	Bollywood	French New Wave
Horror Films	Slasher Movies	Spaghetti Westerns
Vampire Films*	Film Noir	Heroic Bloodshed*

Film Subjects:

Laurel & Hardy	Marx Brothers	Animation
Steve McQueen*	Marilyn Monroe	The Oscars®
Filming On A Microbudget	Bruce Lee	Film Music

TV:

Doctor Who

Literature:

Cyberpunk	Philip K Dick	The Beat Generation
Agatha Christie	Sherlock Holmes	Noir Fiction*
Terry Pratchett	Hitchhiker's Guide	Alan Moore

Ideas:

Conspiracy Theories	Nietzsche	UFOs
Feminism	Freud & Psychoanalysis	

History:

Alchemy & Alchemists	The Crusades	The Black Death
Jack The Ripper	The Rise Of New Labour	Ancient Greece
American Civil War	American Indian Wars	

Miscellaneous:

The Madchester Scene	Stock Market Essentials
How To Succeed As A Sports Agent	

Available at all good bookstores or send a cheque (payable to 'Oldcastle Books') to: **Pocket Essentials (Dept RP), 18 Coleswood Rd, Harpenden, Herts, AL5 1EQ, UK**. £3.99 each (£2.99 if marked with an *) . For each book add 50p postage & packing in the UK and £1 elsewhere.